ENDLESS

"Oh death, where is thy victory?"

by

S. B. Niccum

Endless

"O death, where is thy victory?

O grave, where is thy sting?"

1 Corinthians 15:15

"The works of God continue,

And worlds and lives abound;

Improvement and progression

Have one eternal round.

There is no end to matter;

There is no end to space;

There is no end to spirit;

There is no end to race."

[1]William W. Phelps

1. If You Could Hie To Kolob. p.284, verse 3. Hymns Of The Church Of Jesus Christ Of Latter Day Saints.

A note to the reader:

Once again, I want to remind all those who might be reading this book, that this story is a work of fiction and not doctrine. I use my imagination to illustrate biblical concepts, but my interpretation of them is purely speculative. That said, please feel free to open your mind and have fun speculating with me. I always welcome comments and ideas through my web site www.sbniccum.com or my Facebook page www.facebook.com/silvina.niccum

Sincerely,

S.B.

Acknowledgements:

I'd like to give a very warm and special thanks to Liliana Riboldi, Larry Sidwell, Naomi DeLaTorre, and Jody Jarvis for spending count-less hours going over my manuscript and polishing it. They are won-derful, dedicated, and talented. They are selfless and kind. Thank you so very much, from the bottom of my heart. I'd also like to thank my husband and my family for their continued support while I pursue my dreams.

Contents

Prologue

When you run away from the light, you are left in total darkness. Not just darkness, but an unnatural black void, vast and still, that has left me with a distinct feeling of foreboding. It's also deathly silent here. It feels like a warning, and it permeates the air, amplifying my unease. This feeling, of being left this desolate, and this isolated, is a rude awakening from the last peaceful moments of my death.

Celeste, my dead grandmother, who I could hear while I still lived, had once explained to me that spirits don't really go to Hell, but rather exist in a state of being called Spirit Prison. Immediately after death, the spirits of the guilty are engulfed by the darkness they have created, and imprison themselves in a self-imposed cage of sorts, a purgatory-like state, where they are forced to reevaluate their lives; and their guilty consciences force them to relive all their misdeeds. What happens after this? I don't know. She never said. I guess I'll soon find out.

Chapter 1

Celeste's screams have faded some time ago. I completely disregarded her pleas—no—shouts that I go toward the light, and defiantly, I flew straight into this darkness. I walked away from the warmth and the peace that the light offered me, and deliberately came here, so that I could find Alex, my soul mate, and my father, Leo.

I feel no physical chill, but my soul feels cold, and the emptiness of this space is pervasive. The blackness is unlike anything that I have ever experienced. It's not like a moonless, starless night, nor is it like a room without a light; it's more like a storm, inky black, with a heavy dark fog, that clings close to the ground, giving you the distinct feeling that you are in the wrong place at the wrong time.

All my instincts tell me to get out, and quickly. I'm almost tempted to, except—I feel him. Barely, but I feel him. Alex is here. I know he is. He's weeping for me, crying inwardly, with a soul wrenching groan and howl that immediately robs me of my calm.

"Alex?" I call to him, hoping to reach him through the nothingness. But there's no response, and his cry fades away into the emptiness. Like a feather blown by the wind, the feeling that Alex is near, starts to feel just out of my reach. It moves aimlessly in the darkness and I try to grasp it, thinking that I feel it pass by me again, but I can't quite hold it—it's too elusive. Determinedly, I keep floating aimlessly in this bottomless darkness, and something like desperation creeps up into my essence—or whatever I am—for I'm no longer corporeal. But I'm still alive, living, present, existing, or whatever you call it. One thing I know for sure: I'm frustrated, for this is not going as planned.

Having no body makes me feel oddly detached from reality. All I feel is what my mind tells me to feel, and instinctively I keep waiting for a signal from my body, so I can react to the sensation of fear accordingly, but no signal ever comes. No hair ever stands up on the back of my neck, no goose bumps raise my skin, no shallow breathing, nor quickened heartbeat—nothing—and somehow this is worse.

I never doubted that I would still exist after death. I've had too many encounters with the realm of the dead while I was mortal. In life,

I had a gift—a sixth sense—that allowed me to hear voices from other realms of existence. I was able to hear my dead grandmother, Celeste, who had been assigned as my guardian angel. I could also hear other voices, vicious ones that Celeste taught me to tune out, to block completely, because they were destructive. Then there was Alex's voice. I heard him in my dreams when he was alive, and when he died, I heard him as a spirit. At first I loved it, but soon the bane of being separated by the gulf of death wore on me, and his presence almost drove me crazy. His guilt over having almost ruined my life trapped him in this place, and that's why I have come to rescue him. However, something seems wrong about the whole thing. What made perfect sense to me the moment I died, has now become disjointed and blurred by the darkness.

I had a plan: Find Alex, and my father, who has also inadvertently locked himself here, and get out. But now I see that the finding will prove to be a lot harder than what I first anticipated.

Something stirs in the distance. I'm not sure if I see it, or feel it. I don't even know if my eyes are open. I try blinking, but it makes no difference. There! Something! I definitely see something this time. It's moving! Toward me! I stay put, telling myself that I'm already dead. What harm could come to me now?

Whatever it is that is coming toward me looks like it has something inside of it. After further inspection, I can see what looks to be a crystal ball filled with a scene of sorts. I'm too focused on this particular sphere to notice the others. Not just two or three, but millions and millions of spheres, just like the first one. They're all clustered together like a giant beehive filled with cells, and as they move closer they seem to grow in size. Each of these balls encapsulates what looks to be someone's reality, apparently projecting whatever the inhabitant wants it to project. Whole scenarios change, as the person moves and interacts with its little environment.

I stand and stare, dumbfounded, wondering what it all means—when suddenly they start moving toward me a lot faster. They are coming at me from all angles—top, bottom, and all sides—there's no escaping them. I'm not sure if this is good or bad. I just hover here and watch them come toward me. I brace for the worst by closing my eyes and shielding my face, but nothing seems to happen. I feel no impact, or any type of change at all.

"You don't understand!" an emaciated looking girl with gaunt, hollow eyes and a shabby prom dress says, grabbing me by my clothes, and shaking me as if I were a rag doll. As soon as she sees that she could grab hold of me, she lets go, startled. Then she looks around, stunned, looking wildly around as if she smelled foul play. "Who are you? Are you a doctor? I won't go back to that hospital. I'm fine! I'm fine!" she shouts viciously.

I stare back at her with dumb amazement. Her dress is in complete ruins; her puffy pink sleeves are covered in dust and cobwebs. Her hair, that at one point had been skillfully done up, is now disheveled, yet most strands still hold its original intended form, thanks to some serious hairspray action.

"I—I'm not a doctor." I look around and notice that all the other spheres have disappeared. All I can see is what looks to be a high school gym that was decorated for a dance a long time ago, but now is cob-webby and looks more like Miss Havisham's house, complete with rot-ting refreshments, and blanketed by dust and mold. A part of a song from the eighties plays in the background like a broken record, and scat-tered groups of teenagers cluster together around the dirty bleachers, while some others dance maladroitly in one spot. Only one girl looks radiant, clean, and beautiful. She has a crown on her head and is holding hands with a boy who also has a crown on his head.

"No!!!" the ghoulish girl that attacked me shouts when she sees them together, heading to the dance floor like two wooden puppets. She charges toward them like a mad bull, and knocks the pretty queen to the floor, like she would a chess piece. "I'm the queen! Me!" Then, the ghoulish girl, turns her attention back to me, "I worked hard for this you know!" she accuses with one finger. "I starved myself so I could fit into this dress! I'm the pretty one, not her! He's mine!"

"But, you're dead," I point out the obvious.

"I most certainly am not!" she shouts, distorted and grotesque, and I think her jaw dislocates in the process. "I'm not dead! Why does every-one keep telling me this?"

"This—is not real." I point to her dance, and she charges toward me again, shoving me hard.

"I didn't go through with it! I didn't jump!" she shouts, and gives me one more push. All of a sudden, I'm somewhere else. This new place is horrible, not at all like the harmless goblin girl's dance. Here there are bodies strewn all over the place. There's no blood, just bodies lying inert, some are bent over chairs or sofas, others are leaning up against the wall barely holding themselves up, some are sort of stacked on each other, like they just fell over and never bothered to move. Their eyes are open and glazed over, staring at nothing. Seeing me, a heavily tattooed guy starts coming toward me with shock and curiosity carved on his features.

"Do you have some?" he asks hopefully.

I frown, confused. "No," I say, not sure of what he's asking.

"You! I need more, you hear!" he shouts, bringing his hands up to his face and scratching himself compulsively. Then he shakes his head violently from side to side, and starts screaming at the top of his lungs. I start to back away, trying to avoid the bodies. "W—what's wrong with them?" I stammer, not knowing what this psycho can do to me.

"They? They're in nirvana." He looks down at them enviously, "but I can't get there." He looks up at me with a wild look in his eyes, "I beg you," his voice trembles and the scenery changes. We are now in a hospital of sorts, a deserted dark hospital that gives me the creeps.

He extends one arm toward me, and I can see needle marks in his veins. "I can't endure this. You understand? I c—c—can't quit cold turkey." He sweeps his hands over his face and starts shaking uncontrollably once again. The lights in the desolate hallway start to flicker on and off, and I'm running out room to back into. The hallway seems to end right behind me, and I feel like I'm trapped in a horror movie.

"This is not real, you know," I say tentatively, echoing the words I just got done saying to the ghoulish girl. "You—you can move on." I assure him, not really knowing if this is true or not.

"Move on?" he yells, and looks up again. "I need a fix! I can't move on until I get my next fix! I'm dying here!" His features contort and twitch, he tries to control them, but can't.

"You're already dead, you no longer need a fix." This last comment somehow angers him and he too, starts coming toward me.

"Don't tell me what I am or am not! Don't tell me what I need or don't need! Don't you come here pretending like you know what it's like to feel the way I feel, and tell me I'm not really feeling it!"

"It's all in your head! All of this!" I inform him.

"Get out! GET OUT!" he shouts. I back away further and further from him, then trip over something, and suddenly find myself in the backseat of a car. The driver is a young boy, sixteen maybe, his eyes are puffy and red as if he's been crying.

He mutters something angry and spiteful that I can't quite make out. I turn and look forward and realize he's at the edge of a cliff. He puts the car in gear and steps on the gas. "This will show her!" he declares, like a child throwing a tantrum.

I can't believe it! He's driving us off the cliff! When I sense that the front wheels are no longer touching the ground I start to scream, and the car plunges forward in a nosedive. It's not until now that the full realization of what he's doing hits him. His eyes grow big and he starts screaming too.

"Oh no!" he yells, panic stricken. "No, no, no! I didn't mean it! I'm sorry! Go back! Go back! I don't want to diiieee…" Those are the last words he utters before we hit the ground with a splat.

I get out of the smashed vehicle unharmed, but seriously freaked out. He's still inside the car, lying there, broken, his eyes open—perfectly still—with fear and regret registered in them.

I walk around to the driver's side and tap him on the shoulder. He doesn't stir. He just sits there crushed, staring at nothing. I want to say something, but I'm not sure what. I have no advice to give him, I feel so inadequate. I can't tell him everything will be okay because…it's not. I can't tell him that it's not too late, because it is. He's dead. I can tell him to stop reliving his death, to move on, but how? I don't know.

"Leave…" the boy groans, still unmoving. "There's nothing you can do, leave."

So I do. I walk right out of there, feeling incompetent and discouraged, and a nagging thought creeps in. What is my plan here? Even if I did find Alex or my dad in this sea of anguish, self-deprecation, and torture, I wouldn't know how to escape. This aspect of my plan never crossed my mind.

The next reality looks like a Civil War re-enactment. So I take to my heels and start running, or flying rather, unwilling to see what sort of nightmare this is. I don't stop until I cross over into several realities. The scenes change, and change, and change, and there is no end to these self-imposed prisons.

I used to think that Hell was more of a communal place, where a fire was constantly burning and it stank of brimstone. I imagined a place where all the tortured souls felt a constant burning over their guilt, gnashed their teeth, and complained about their regret to each other, but I was wrong. This lonely, solitary place is far worse than a big bonfire and a group of angry people. Here you're alone, completely alone, lost in your own head—the worse place of all—because how do you escape yourself?

The scenes that I pass through range from the brutally violent—people who relished their evil acts and recall them over and over again for their own sick pleasure—to the ones who are literally imprisoned by their guilt, and relive their mistakes in order to punish themselves.

Other souls look like they are in complete denial. Knowingly or unknowingly they have created a virtual life where they simply escape, and bide their time by going through the every day motions of living. But like in a dream where you're aware you're dreaming, and willingly change the outcome, this virtual life feels hollow and fabricated, and yields no satisfaction. Even so, these people who are biding their time seem less harmful to me. They seem to be working through their own mistakes and appear to feel actual guilt for what they've done.

The realities also range in time periods, encompassing scenes from the dawn of man to modern times. I think I might run into Cain soon, and this thought sobers me. How am I going to find Alex and my father, just two souls among so many?

It feels wrong here, as it should, I guess. It doesn't help that I'm an Empath, and I can sense their guilt, sadness, and pain. I can even feel the thrill they get over their disgusting deeds. These thoughts and feelings are all mine too now, thanks to my gift. Having the gift of discernment feels more like a curse here. It's torturous, and it makes my old perception of Hell, with the never quenching fire and the stinky brimstone, seem like a party. Perhaps the never-ending-fire rages inside of them, and the brimstone is the bad taste that I have in my mouth, or the memory of having a bad taste. Either way, I hate it here! Whatever *here* is, Purgatory or Hell, it doesn't matter.

I stop at a reality that looks less hideous to me. It's just a forest, and thankfully no dead bodies. It must be an old place because it's too pristine to be from more modern times. I know it's not a good place, because I feel the lust in the air like a thick cloud that permeates this bubble. But as I sit here and rest my mind, I let the full realization of my own predicament work through me. *I will have to sift through all of these realities in order to find Alex*—and discouragement hits me like a ton of bricks.

When I first entered the darkness, I saw billions of these bubbles. If I'm inside them right now, it will take forever to find them! If only I could just get to that darkness again, just the plain emptiness that I initially encountered! That, at least, would be an improvement over this. What would happen to me if I stayed trapped in here for a long time? What would that do to me? But I have no time to muse over that now—someone is coming.

I'm sitting on a rock, in the middle of some mossy forest when a man, dressed like he has just come out of a Shakespearean festival, steps out from behind a tree. His look of sheer evil makes me sick. It is an interesting feeling since I have no actual stomach, but the memory of that feeling remains with me and it feels as real as if I were about to throw up.

From behind me a young girl appears. She's about fourteen or fifteen, and as she looks at him, her face registers terror. The man is holding a rope in his hand. He wraps it around his hands, pulling it taut, and beckons us to come nearer.

"Hold my hand," I tell the girl, not sure whether I am in the man's reality or the girl's. "I'll get you out of here!" But she doesn't seem to hear me. She is petrified with horror.

I stretch my hand and lean in to grab her, but my hand goes right through her. As I do this, the man cocks his head to the right and the girl evaporates into thin air. "Darn, it's his reality," I mutter.

"So, you really are here?" he licks his lips. "All the other ones..." he laughs, "they were not real. But *you* are!" His eyes grow large and hungry.

This revolts me, and an anger I didn't even know I had in me surfaces. "You disgusting medieval pig!" I shout and charge toward him with such force, that I knock us both into another place. He looks disoriented and surprised by my reaction. His eyes dart around, and he looks confused by this new environment—doubly so, because we are back in the twenty-first century, a place he knows nothing about.

We're in the middle of a populated city and loud distorted rap music plays in the background. There's no melody to it, just jarring noises, recreated from memory. A gang of about ten guys starts to surround us, and I'm not sure which one of them is the owner of this reality. At this point, frankly, I don't care. It will be fun to leave this feudal freak with the gang and let them sort out their differences. Already, they're cat calling to me and shouting profanities at the guy in tights.

With a sneer I turn and run for it, hoping that somehow the next reality will be more pleasant. But it isn't. My heart sinks even further, and I start to wonder if I'll ever find a way out of this place. Was it like this for Alex? Did he start just like me and then finally give up? I feel like giving up. I don't know how many more gruesome and disgusting places I can endure. It is affecting me and not in a good way. I can feel myself changing. I'm becoming cynical, hardened, callused, past-feeling—if that makes sense.

I realize that the only thing to do now is to survive at all costs in this hostile environment. I've got to toughen up, become an avenging angel of sorts, and start kicking some spiritual butts. I could dress up in a black leather jumpsuit with high-heeled, black boots, and a pair of matching black wings. Now that would be cool! ...Either that or give in—let my mind create its own environment. At least there, I would be able to control my surroundings; I could make it safe and familiar. I could have Alex with me! Sure, *he* would be a figment of my imagination—the real Alex would be out here somewhere—probably doing the same thing. How sad for us, both lost here, dreaming of each other. This was definitely not what I had in mind when I made my vows to him—that death would not do us apart.

I drift in and out of bubbles. Some spirits acknowledge me, and want me to come to them, but others tell me to get out, and others either ignore me or don't even notice me. One particular bubble attracts my attention. It looks like a living room of an old Tudor mansion. There's a roaring fire in the ornate hearth. Two red velvet high-backed chairs sit side by side in front of the fire, each has its own footstool, and a full-length mirror has been placed off to one side. A man is standing there, perfectly still, looking at himself in the mirror.

I intrude and make myself comfortable in one of the chairs, propping my feet, one on top of the other on the virtual footstool. Since it's not really there, I have to pretend like my feet are resting, but it's not hard. I'm ready for a harmless illusion of comfort. The man has a long, shaggy salt and pepper beard, and unkempt long hair tied up in a ponytail. He's wearing a long red satin robe, and he looks oddly familiar; in spite of the fact that I know I've never, ever seen him in my life.

"Did you just get here?" he asks, not moving from in front of the mirror.

"Yes," I say wearily.

"I would say welcome, but..." he shrugs.

We say nothing for a long time. I sit here, looking at the fire; and he stands there, looking at himself in the mirror. Then, annoyed either with me or with himself, he breaks his reverie and swings his hand through the mirror, making it disappear. He then slumps on the other chair next to mine and with another wave of the hand, makes two glasses of wine appear. "I have magic here," he says dryly. "Too bad we can't taste it."

I turn and look at the glass, and ignore it. What's the point in pretending?

"So, you're a realist," he says conversationally, and I notice the trace of an accent—Irish maybe.

"I guess," I sigh, tired.

"I did that for a while."

"Then you gave up?"

"Yes. We all give up eventually."

"Why did you come here?"

"I was a selfish bastard," he says without guile.

I nod, as if I understand perfectly well what he's talking about.

"And you?"

"I came here to find someone."

He laughs, a roaring, loud laughter that makes me turn away from the fire and look at him. "So you're telling me that you could have escaped all of this, but you chose to come here?" he asks.

"I am. I did."

"Why?"

"My husband and my father," I say, as if that explained it all. "They shouldn't be here, either," I add. "Well...my father might have inadvertently done something bad. But he didn't mean it. He was filled with anger." The stranger nods, understandingly. I don't know why, but I feel comfortable here, in this bubble.

"How noble of you. Unfortunately, I alienated my wife to the point that she would never risk her eternal salvation to rescue me."

We fall into a long silence again, both staring at the flames.

"How can I find them?" I finally ask, not shifting my eyes from the flames.

He shrugs. "Beats me, I've never tried to find anyone. When I first got here I found one of my old acquaintances, quite by accident I might add." He shakes his head. "It was such an unpleasant experience that I created my own bubble just to get away from him."

"Why the mirror?"

He turns and looks where it had been standing and it suddenly appears again and *he* stares at it longingly for a long while. "It's complicated."

Suddenly, I get impatient and abruptly stand up. "I can't stay," I say. "I have to go find them! I'm wasting time."

"I see no white rabbit," he says, craning his neck in all directions as if looking for something. "Time no longer exists, not anymore." The more he talks the more I hear his accent; as it's definitely Irish.

"Well, there is something." I say. "Time must be passing somewhere."

"You're a go-getter, aren't ya'?"

"I hate standing still. Drives me nuts."

"Then go," he counsels, glumly. He wants company, he wants me to stay and make his eternal doom less painful. But as he said so himself, he had been a jerk in life, and the last thing I want to do is spend my afterlife with a jerk.

I glide away from his reality, and he lets me go without so much as a good-bye. I immediately enter another reality, one that is oddly familiar. I hadn't seen this place in ages, but it's exactly as I remember it—my High School hallway—complete with my classmates and everything.

Chapter 2

I rub my face, hoping to clear away some of the haze I feel. "You're looking for Alex!" I scold myself. "You can't make your own bubble! Find Alex and get out of here!"

"I'm sure you'd like to," a mocking voice says from behind.

In turning I find myself face to face with Eugenia. She's dressed in her cheering outfit, but she doesn't look beautiful as she did back in high school. Deep lines on her face distort her, making her look like an old hag. Her hair is charred in places, and she tries to hide those by way of an intricate comb-over hairdo. Scabby grayish scars now mar her once flawless skin, and her eyes look wild and deranged.

"Eugenia?"

"It's over, Tess. You've lost," she says smugly and starts walking around me in circles like she's inspecting my appearance. "Mm…you still fail to impress. It's no wonder he's settled here, with me."

I laugh. "O—kay." Not only does she look like a crazy old bat, she is one!

My reaction seems to trigger some insecurity in her, so she quickly looks inside her locker, where there's a mirror. She checks herself in it, and relaxes once she sees, *apparently*, whatever she wants to see. She dabs at her lips and moves a strand of half scorched hair away from her face, and pats it tenderly into the desired spot. "I've always been so much more beautiful than you. That's why I don't understand why…" she frowns and her nostrils flare, "never mind that. I've forgiven him. What's important is that he is now mine and has no interest in you."

"You're deranged," I note.

"No!" she screams, "you are!"

Down the hall I see the rest of the cheering squad making their entrance as if down a runway, not differently I suppose than from how it used to be in real life. They smile at Eugenia, seeing nothing of what I see, and together they start closing in on me.

Instinctively, I start to back away, but I feel movement behind me, so I turn. It's Alex! Behind him are his old high school friends. My heart skips a beat at the sight of him; he looks exactly as he did back in High School.

"Alex!" I exclaim breathlessly and reach for him.

The look of disgust on his face, when I call his name, hurts. "Don't touch me," he says derisively.

I stare dumbly at him. "Alex?" Then it dawns on me. He couldn't possibly be *my* Alex. Of course this would be Eugenia's own imaginary Alex who is filled with spite, just like her. So to prove my point, and to teach her a lesson, I lunge at him, making the mirage vanish into thin air. Then to really drive it home I wave my arms wildly about me, and make all his friends vanish as well. I feel a cynical smile forming— I've just crushed her world—and I relish the waves of disappointment that emanate from her.

"Noooo!" Eugenia screams with rage, and throws herself at me. Futilely, she tries to scratch me, bite me, hit me, and pull my hair. But none of those things hurt in the least, so I just stand there triumphantly and smirk.

"I see you've found your way to familiar grounds," a well-known voice says from the shadows. "I knew I'd find you here. Eventually we all find our way back to those who make us miserable. Just like the saying goes, misery does love company."

Surprised by the sound of the voice, Eugenia stops dead in her tracks and looks into the shadows from where the acid voice is coming. Slowly, a black hooded figure glides out of the darkness. The cloak covers the face completely.

"Great!" I think, "It's the family reunion from Hell!" I'm tired of all this, I want to find the real Alex and get out! Now I realize that they were right; all their warnings about coming here unprepared were spot on. I'm different here, and the longer I stay, the worse it gets. All I can feel now is spite, anger, and rage. I find that I hate, truly hate, like I've never hated before. I'm not me anymore. *I* am lost.

"What you two ever saw in that most average boy is beyond me." Agatha says, from under her cloak.

Eugenia straightens out and smoothens the pleats of her cheerleader mini-skirt. "Better than that bloated purple pig you married," she states sourly and I laugh. It appears Eugenia and I agree on at least one thing. On hearing me laugh, Eugenia looks at me with a mixture of surprise and annoyance on her face.

With slow determined movements, Agatha pulls down her hood and reveals a gruesome sight. Her face is completely disfigured by fire and it literally looks like it has melted right off. One of her eyelids is gone leaving the eye socket exposed. Her nose looks like it has been smeared off to one side and part of her upper lip is gone as well. It's not so much the burn scars that make her look monstrous, it's her—*she* is monstrous. She finally reflects who she truly is inside, and all her foulness is finally expressed on her face.

"It's fitting that all three of us would find our way here, after all we've been through." Agatha says as she moves closer to me. "How do you like it here, Tess?" she asks, then smiles with what is left of her face. "Not very well I take it."

My lack of response encourages her to come closer, and she touches my undamaged hair. "Mmm, interesting, you were the only one to escape from that fire unscathed."

"That fire was not intended to burn the—"

"The what? The good people?" she laughs. "Little good it did you in the end! We all ended up in the same place, just like I predicted." Memories of her saying that she would see me in Hell flash before my memory, and my mind gives me an accurate recall of how it felt to shudder.

"I didn't end up here. I came here on purpose." I state.

"Oh? And what would that purpose be, huh?" She smirks, then laughs, and her laugh crescendos. "Maybe this is it, Tess. Maybe the spirits who talked to you in life, lied and there is no other afterlife. Have you thought about that? We are *all* here. Alex, your father..." She lets go of my hair and starts gliding around me in circles again, making me dizzy. "I found him, you know. It didn't take me long to find out what this place was all about. Not like some people," she looks at Eugenia with derision, and the latter turns away contemptuously.

"I prefer reality, don't you Tess? Yes, I know you do. Or you would have formed a bubble of your own to escape already. But you're stuck now, and you know it. You've come to realize, too late I'm afraid, that no one leaves here."

"That's not true," I say on a whim. "Anyone can leave, you just have to—to—"

"To nothing. Tess, you know as well as I do that we are here for good! There is no other afterlife!" she barks, then regains her composure. "Let me cut to the chase. I can help you," she adds, in a more subdued tone.

"Ha!"

She starts making a tsking noise with her mouth and moves a skeletal finger back and forth. "Don't be so hasty Tess, I know where he is. The real one!" she directs her last remark at Eugenia with a sharp look.

"You're lying."

"No. I'm not. I found him while out on one of my roams—I call them walks in the park!" She chuckles, then shakes her head with a pleasant smile, as if these memories of roaming through these awful realities were enjoyable to her. "As I was saying, Alex is stuck in a bad place. Not as bad, mind you, as some others. But he is stuck. He did it, no doubt, to survive here. He got tired of trying to escape. It's always better to devise a reality of your own, rather than inhabiting someone else's reality. You, of all people, know this by now."

"I don't believe you," I say stubbornly. If I know anything about Agatha, it is that she always knows what to say in order to get you to do something that would serve her purposes somehow.

"I watched him for a while. His reality varies from two main themes. Once I found out what he had come here to do, I went ahead and finished the job for him. So you see…I also know where your father is." She smiles venomously, and her face looks grotesque in the process.

"If you know where they are, show me," I say defiantly.

"To show you that I'm not lying, I'll give you a peek, but I will not let you free until you agree to do something for me first."

"What could I possibly do for you here? Don't you see? It's over! We're dead."

"That's where you're wrong, my dear Tess. It's not over. There're lots of things we can do while dead, things that don't include an extended stay in a virtual reality show." Her eyes dart over to Eugenia and she smiles that horrid half-smile of hers. I can tell that she'll never tire of pestering Eugenia; it's like a new hobby for her. "I'm talking about a *real* out of body existence." Agatha says and opens the one eye wide, looking more horrid than ever.

"I have it as a personal rule not to ever listen to you."

"Then go ahead, go find him! Let's see how long you can survive out here before you too succumb to your own delusions."

She's right about that. Already, I've been enjoying Agatha and Eugenia's company to that of the other residents here—and that thought alone is scary. When, in my wildest dreams or nightmares, would I have willingly chosen the company of these two over that of anyone else?

The fact is that I don't want to go back out there and start sifting though all those millions of hells again. I would lose myself entirely, either to a delusion or to this pervasive demoralization. Either way I wouldn't be able to endure it. How did *she* ever deal with it?

As if guessing my thoughts, Agatha smiles, showing sinews and bones in the process. "I find this place...amusing. To see what people think about when they think that no one is looking, it gives me great satisfaction and an advantage I've never had over others before. I've already made some interesting friends."

Now I understand. She's been establishing a network of her own, but to what end? "Always the schemer, aren't you? What are you planning? Why do you need me?" I say, coming to the point.

"I am who I am. I can't help it, I suppose. But don't you worry too much about me, or my plans yet. All you need to know is that I require your special abilities."

"I won't do anything until I see them."

"Fine," she turns to leave, then casts one last pitiful look at Eugenia. "Come," she commands as she would a dog, while lowering her hood over her face.

Eugenia obeys, but as she turns, she takes one last look at her pretend world. Her eyes sweep past the mirror that—for once—shows her as she really looks. Wordlessly, she gives me a hateful look as her bubble, quite literally, bursts.

We follow Agatha through a series of realities, where she's apparently known and respected. This is her network. Those whom she has coerced or befriended and have agreed to help her. In exchange for what, I wonder?

"There's your father."

I start to move toward his bubble, but she stops me with a tsk of her tongue and a waving finger. "No, no, no. You can't talk to either one of them until you help me."

Behind my father's bubble, I see several rough looking characters who are perched on top of my father's reality, waiting for Agatha's signal, and ready to submerge themselves inside my father's already self-tormented existence.

My dad's bubble is erratic. It seems to display whatever his mind is thinking at the moment. One minute he's reliving a pleasant memory of himself and my mother, and another they are hastily packing, bundling a small child, and leaving town in a hurry. The next moment he's yelling at a young Eros, telling him exactly what he thinks of him. Then he's in prison talking to the guards, then again with my mom. It's dizzying to see how quickly he jumps from scene to scene, each one only lasting a few seconds.

"I've been able to piece together quite the timeline, just by watching him," Agatha comments, and this angers me to no end. How dare she intrude on my father's privacy! Seeing my anger, Agatha brightens. "If my Hellhounds get their wish and pounce on him, they'll torture him for centuries. I'm afraid that no spirit could recover from that."

"Show me Alex," I growl. I want to take her away and let my poor tormented father be. Agatha lets out a short cynical laugh, then turns and leads us through another long string of realities. I feel like a mole, burrowing through some infernal underground tunnel. The scenes we pass vary from bizarre to extremely grotesque, and to plain disgusting. A couple of them in particular look slightly familiar. As I pass them, I let my eyes linger on them, trying to place them. Who are they, and why do I feel like I've seen them before? Their infernal faces seem to come from the pages of history maybe.

As we float by, the inhabitants of the various realities stop in the middle of what they are doing and watch us glide by as if we were an underworld royal procession. They simply freeze their actions, with all their imaginary people, while we pass. Some of them nod to Agatha or simply stare with ghoulish interest, and once we've passed, they go back to whatever they were doing. The two I seem to recognize leave their bubbles and silently join our procession.

"There he is," she points to a bubble far away. I can barely see him. I tell her this, but with a sneer she tells me that she will not risk bringing me any closer. The two that had followed us fly toward him and take their places on either side of his bubble with their gaze trained on me, like a warning. Three more appear out of nowhere, completely surrounding Alex's bubble.

"It was you who were meant to die that night, not *him*," Eugenia leans over, and whispers hoarsely in my ear. I'm not sure if she's gloating, or apologizing—either way I don't care—so I ignore her and focus all my energy on Alex. I might not be able to get closer, but I might be able to reach him. "*Alex I'm here! I've come to get you out!*"

Alex is in the middle of reliving the night that he had to say goodbye to me. After his untimely death, he had refused to leave my side. And even though I wanted him with me, the result of his ghostly com-

"Mind over matter, Tess, mind over matter," she says pointing to her temple. "It takes a lot of concentration and a lot of self control, I haven't seen too many spirits do it successfully for too long. You have to be able to multitask and not let any of the things you're juggling fall." She smiles broadly, stretching full glossy lips across her face. "Let's get back to business though, I didn't bring you here to exchange eternal beauty tips, I want to tell you my plan, Tess. As you know, I always have a plan. In that sense, you and I are the same. We both work best when we have a clear plot in motion. We are both driven achievers, unlike some others who are content to let things fall into their lap." She casts a guarded, gentle look toward Eugenia, who understands every word, but seems to not mind them coming from such a divine looking creature. At this, Agatha titters playfully, like a child delighted with a furry gerbil. I cringe at her giggle, and shake my head.

"In fact," Agatha continues coquettishly, flipping a shimmery strand of rich, buttery, blond hair out of her neckline and letting it bounce playfully behind her. "I've always felt like we've had a special connection, much more than just being raised in the same home. It's weird, I can't explain it, but I've always felt that you could understand me better than anyone else. We've even shared the same ability of hearing voices from other realms of existence. You can't tell me that that is not a coincidence. If we didn't look so physically different, I would have ventured to say that we were related."

Enthralled by her friendly manner and her spellbinding beauty, I watch her in silence. I also want to see where she's going with all this. I'm aware of the fact that she's acting a part and that she wants something from me. There's a scheme of sorts at play here, and I want to see what it is. No doubt it's something that in her mind would elevate her status among the ones who run this place, maybe even something that would put her at the very top of the bad guys—but what could that be? What can possibly be done in a place such as this? Everyone's dead, and there is no place to go, nothing to do. She had mentioned earlier that she needed *my* special abilities. I'm not aware of anything special that I can do here.

"I know you've thought about this before. I know you've made this connection," she continues. "There have been times when we have understood each other so well."

"It's true that I know you well, but I can't relate with you at all."

She smiles a disarmingly beautiful smile, yet there is no comforting warmth in it. "It's true. It's like we are different sides of the same

21

coin. We understand each other, but we can't relate. However, I think I might be able to change that now. Our life is over, we are dead, and... here!" she says, sticking her arms out displaying the darkness that saturates everything in this void. "We are here and we're stuck. Even if you could approach your beloved Alex, or your father, how would you get them out? Do you know how? Or did you come straight here like I did?" A knowing, malicious smile spreads across her face, marring her beauty for a split second. Swishing one of her arms in front of her, erasing that last nasty look, she continues. "I have had some time to dwell on this matter, unlike you, who just showed up, and are still in shock from all of this."

"I can't imagine any plan of yours ever amounting to anything good. Besides, as you so well put it, we are dead! What can we possibly do? Where could we go? It's over. And if I ever figure out how to get out of here and back to Heaven, I would never take you, or you, with me," I say, pointing to each of them in turn.

"That's just it!" She gets close to me and her flawless milky skin sparkles with a soft shimmery glow. "I'm not looking to get into Heaven." She beams a radiant smile.

"Then where?"

"Earth."

"Earth?" Both Eugenia and I inquire in shocked unison.

"Earth." Agatha asserts genially. "Back to the mortal realm."

"Whatever for?" I ask.

"Whatever we want," she states. "Wouldn't it be wonderful to be back among the living?"

I shake my head, remembering what Celeste had told me once about being a spirit among mortals. She said it was torturous, almost too hard for even a trained angel to endure. Memories of having a body, and the constant reminder that your own life was over, was a lot harder than one would imagine. My own memories of having Alex perpetually by my side were not the fondest memories I have of him. I didn't see it at the time. I wasn't ready to let him go, but having him always with me day and night was too much. It almost cost me my sanity and Robyn's guardianship.

I open my mouth to start giving her all the reasons why I think this would be a bad idea, when the thought that perhaps Agatha would deserve a stint at such a hellish existence stops me. Maybe being among mortals and feeling miserable would not be such a bad thing for her. Roguish thoughts of her being wracked and tormented by the constant reminder of her current state start to fill my mind, and give me slight pleasure.

"I know you can do it. I know you have the unique ability of opening a rift into the mortal realm. I've tried, but sadly, I don't seem to possess such a helpful gift." She pouts with her pretend full, rosy, lips.

"What makes you think I have this ability?"

"Your father did it," she says matter-of-factly. "I've seen it in his bubble. I saw him re-enact in his mind—the whole thing. How Alex found himself dead, and angry at his early demise—"

"That you two caused!" I accuse the two of them.

"Yes," she says kindly and thankfully, as if I had just reminded her to water her plants. "He was going to die sooner or later, dear. But you see, your father suggested they go back to the mortal realm and was able to create a rift."

"That doesn't mean I can."

"I think it does. You have been able to connect with the realm of the dead at will. I think you can open a rift."

"Why me? Why don't you ask my father to open the rift if you're so sure he can do it."

"Because, my dear, your father is teetering on the verge of a very dangerous cliff, and I'm thinking of his well being, really. You see, opening rifts is frowned upon, even here. If he opens another rift for me, he will be adding further condemnation on his head. He hasn't just opened this rift one time," she whispers, as if telling a secret. "He has opened it several times, and on the last trip into the mortal realm, he haunted Eros, his own step-brother, and caused his death. I wouldn't want him to have any more marks against him."

With awe I watch as she skillfully puts forward a good point. How cleverly she speaks, and how dexterous she is at punching you right where it would cause the most damage. She knows too well that I would never let my dad suffer unnecessarily, and she also knows that I'm feeling disgruntled and tired. She knows that I'm at my wit's end, and that I want to get out of here at all costs. But does she know what crossing over would do to her?

"Why?" I bark abruptly.

"Why what?"

"Why do you want to open this rift?"

"Because, like you, I'm sick of this place."

"No. That's a lie, you're not sick of this place. You want to be here! Or rather, you want to be *noticed* here. You feel right at home, and you want to be revered by all the slime that have a say in this realm. Am I right?"

Hatred flares up in her eyes. She's been unmasked and she knows it. Her façade falls right before my eyes and she shows me her true self— the horrid, half-melted face—with exposed sinew and one eye barely hanging inside its socket. Eugenia starts in disgust. The spell that she has been under is broken and she recoils from Agatha, as you would from any disgusting creature.

"I can torture them, and I will! Not just me, dearie, but all those Hellhounds I have at my beck and call! Until you decide to be cooperative, I can assign a few of those to torture your father and Alex indefinitely!" she snarls, dropping all pretense of being beautiful and gentle. "Like you said, we are not going anywhere! We've got nothing but time! So either you start working on a rift, or they get it!"

"I *hate* you!" I yell.

A crooked smile spreads across her disfigured face. "The feeling is mutual."

Chapter 3

I see no point in prolonging it. I either do it, or watch them suffer. As a precaution, she leaves those nasty looking Hellhounds, as she called them, around my father's and Alex's bubbles. If I let them suffer, she would eventually go to my father and ask him to open the rift, and if he does it would be as she said—eternally detrimental to him. If I do it, it will be eternally detrimental to me, but at least I have a pretty good record, and maybe, just maybe, I might be able to get forgiven for it. But I try not to think too much about the consequences. Right now, it would seem, I have no other choice—let the consequences of my actions follow as they may. *"I'm sorry Alex,"* I groan inwardly. *"I'm so sorry for what I'm about to do."* And without further ado, I close my eyes and think of the mortal realm—but nothing happens.

"What are you waiting for? Do it now! Open the rift!"

In the distance I can see the bubbles all clustered together. I can safely assume that those hideous spirits are still hovering over Alex and my father, ready to strike and torture them for as long as Agatha wills it.

"They don't have much time, Tess. My Hellhounds want to play."

I close my eyes and try to focus again, but nothing happens. "I don't know how," I protest.

"Focus!"

I try again, but to no avail. "Why do you want to go to the other side?" I ask again, trying to buy myself some time—time to think, time to come up with some other options, because I feel like I'm making the biggest mistake of my life—or afterlife.

"That is my business. Now you do what I ask, and I'll have Eugenia here lead you back to your precious Alex and your father; she knows the way." I look back at Eugenia and she looks back at me with a smirk, like she's finally proud of having one up on me.

"You'll never find them alone, Tess, you need my help. You're done for. I can see it in your eyes, you're ready for your own mental break, and once you form a bubble of your own, you'll always prefer it to reality. See?" She points to one of the spirits who was following us in the procession. He had already gone back into his bubble.

"When your mind wanders, it reverts back in there by default. It's like a drug."

I hate to admit it, but Agatha is right. I'm done, and I don't want to live a lie. So I close my eyes and try again. This time, I focus on the only thing that still ties me to mortality—Robyn.

My weary mind has a hard time of it, but I try to think of her and our last moments together. I think about what she might be doing right now, but it's hard. I have no idea how much time has elapsed on earth since my death. For all I know, years could have gone by. When I left her she had just gotten married. I didn't get to know her husband well, for I was ill. The fire had hurt my lungs and I always suffered from it. I was relatively young when I passed, but old enough I suppose. I was ready to go. I had done my duty. I raised Robyn and left her financially and emotionally well off, I thought. So when I think of her, I think of her doing what she loved to do—designing clothes. In my mind, I see her sitting there, next to me in our house in Mexico, sketchbook in hand, sticking her tongue out, just like Dorian used to do. When suddenly, I hear something. Screaming! Loud, ear piercing shrieks that make me wince! I open my eyes and a flash of light rips through the darkness like a lightning strike. Then another scream cuts through the fabric of our realm, and with alarm for Robyn's safety I try to widen the gap, but it closes up like a clam.

"Try again!" Agatha insists with wild excitement in her hideous face.

With renewed focus, I try again, and another gash appears, rending the stillness with yet another ear splitting scream. The gap is bigger this time, and I'm pretty sure that if I try one more time I will be able to make it big enough for me to squeeze through.

"Look at you," Agatha says approvingly. "See? I knew you could do it! You've always been an impressive little thing. Always playing by the rules. Too bad it was all for nothing. You and your little boy toy over there tried so hard, and now…. Well at least you'll always be together— in *Hell*!" She laughs maliciously.

"I came here to get him, and then get out!" I say in protest, when panic over what I've just done starts to seize me.

"And he came here because…?"

"To rescue my father," I snap.

She laughs loudly. "What good did it do you all to try so hard? Your whole family is here!" She taunts. Her face loses all the laughter and she looks at me with her large deranged eyes. She always looked freaky when she did this in life; now she looks like something out of a horror movie. "Since you died," she asks with a more serious tone, "have you experienced any other form of existence other than what you see here?"

"No, but—"

"But—but—" she stutters mockingly. "Look at me, Tess. I'm taking charge, and I suggest you do too."

"It's wrong," I say, now sorry for opening the rift, and confused by the whole messed up situation. "If you cross this rift, you'll regret it, Agatha. You'll—you'll be miserable," I finally admit, because a terrible, uneasy feeling fills my frame, and I feel compelled to warn her, earnestly now, of the dangers of what she's about to encounter. "Celeste always told me that the spirits of the dead have to train and—"

A dark shadow zooms past on the mortal side of the realm, I turn, distracted, to see what it is, but it's gone. "I'm afraid that you'll do things you shouldn't, things that you won't be able to take back," I continue, stammering my way through a speech that sounds hollow, even to me. I want to sound convincing, but my thoughts are disjointed. I feel dizzy, like I don't know what is going on too well, and my mind is foggy, like when you're about to go under anesthesia. Then another shadow zooms past, and another, and another, until it can no longer be disputed. "Something evil this way comes..." is all I can think of to say in my despondent state.

"It's you!" Agatha exclaims with both apprehension and elation, and looks past me at something on the mortal realm behind me. Turning, I try to focus my attention on what or who she's talking about, and all I can see is a man, an average looking man. Nothing about him makes him stand out, or seem particularly important or impressive—except—his aura. It's a black hole. It sucks, and sucks like a vacuum, from everything and everyone that surrounds him, myself included. He only seems interested in extracting, or feeding on my aura and anything else that might possibly have goodness in it. He doesn't seem much interested in Agatha's own dark and murky one.

This ordinary looking wraith is swallowing whatever reserve I have of hope, and is leaving me completely and utterly helpless, cold, and discarded, like an empty shell. Death has never felt nearer or more real than it does now. Not even while running through those networks of hellish bubbles did I feel this desolate and afraid.

"Don't, Agatha," I plead hoarsely with one last desperate attempt. "Don't go with him. There's nothing good for you there."

"That's also where you're wrong, Tessy," she sounds both excited and anxious.

"You're dead Agatha, you don't belong in the realm of the living." I remind her, as if she doesn't know this already, but I'm out of ideas, and my reasoning is not working properly.

"That's where you're wrong, Tess. The mortal realm is exactly where I'll finally live up to my true potential."

"Tess!" The husky groan comes from somewhere behind me, and I recognize it at once.

"Alex?" I turn, perplexed, feeling even more disoriented than before. Alex is out of his bubble, hovering some distance away. He is far enough that I can barely make him out, but I know it's him. Behind him, I see the four Hellhounds, but Alex doesn't seem to know they're there, only I see them. As they get closer to Alex, I can make out one of them clearly shaking his head, "No." He's warning me not to do anything silly, or Alex might get it.

"You left me?" Alex asks through our link. I can hear accusation and disappointment in his voice. He doesn't know, he doesn't understand! I want to explain it all to him, but my mind is processing things slowly and all I can think in reply is how he shouldn't be here.

"Stay as far from me and this soul-sucking wraith as possible," I start to warn him through the link. However, in the middle of formulating this admonition, he disappears from my view, and suddenly, I find myself surrounded by light.

Brightness floods my eyes and I'm totally blinded. Like a bat, I instinctively I cover my face with my arm, and slowly my new surroundings start to take shape. Voices start becoming distinct, and my eyes adjust to the glare. I'm hovering in the middle of an operating room. Nurses are cleaning up blood-soaked rags and other gory stuff. On a table lies a woman. She's out, but the monitors say she's alive. Nurses and aids bustle around the room, and in one corner, a baby's wail assaults my hearing.

The numbness I felt seconds ago starts to disappear and it's replaced with a wave of horror, as I realize where I am, and what I've done. Alex, the accusation in his mind and his eyes, the shadowy, soul sucking man, the numbness, Agatha, everything starts to fall into place, and make sense. I've opened a rift. I've let Agatha through and somehow got sucked in myself! I've abandoned Alex, and now...now I'm stuck here!

Cradling my face with my hands, I scream, and scream, and scream, both in anger and frustration. *"If I hadn't done it, those spirits would have tortured you, Alex!"* I yell inside my head, using all my strength, hoping that he can hear me. *"I didn't leave you, I swear!"* I sob, then wait and listen, hoping to get some response from him. But all I can hear are the baby's wails and all I can see is that last look on Alex's face. It was a look of shock at my betrayal. All he had heard through the link before I disappeared was, *"stay as away from me..."*

Ignoring the baby's relentless cries, I try to focus on Alex instead. "I've opened this rift once, I can do it again," I tell myself. So I try to imagine that if I can reach through the veil that separates these worlds, I will find him on the other side. But no—nothing happens. I scream again, this time I don't muffle my voice. I scream as loud as I can like a hysterical ghost, but all I accomplish is to upset the baby, who cries even harder in response.

Darting frantically around the room like a possessed ball in a pin-ball machine, I notice something odd. The woman that lies on the bed is no stranger. I know her! Slowing down, I float above her, like a mirror image on the ceiling. "Robyn," I breathe out. I then look back and forth between her and the baby and everything starts to make sense— her screams—she was in labor! An emergency C-section by the looks of it. The wrinkly baby boy is beautiful, and I'm filled with emotion over the fact that my little Robyn is now a mother, yet something seems to be off. Where's her husband, and why is she passed out? Nurses wheel the baby out of the room, no doubt to the nursery. I feel torn between following the baby or staying with Robyn. If I were alive, she would want me to follow the baby, so I do.

At the nursery, a couple dressed in loaned hospital gowns and masks jump for joy at the sight of him and to my complete shock, they take Robyn's baby from the basinet and hold him tenderly.

"Duncan?" the woman says with a high-pitched voice. "Hello Duncan, nice to meet you. I'm your mommy," she coos. The man beams at the baby as well, and gently brushes his cheek with the back of one finger.

"No," I shake my head, as I look around, looking for clues as to this terrible misunderstanding. "This can't be!"

I fly through the hospital, checking every room, trying to avoid other spirits who are watching their loved ones. They look at me oddly, like they know that I'm not supposed to be here. But I ignore their displeased stares and their mumbled objections to my presence. I just keep moving like the disembodied soul that I am, until I find Robyn again.

She's still totally out, and her face doesn't have that glow of happiness that should be there. She looks tired and careworn. That empty feeling that I've been carrying around for a while, gets even emptier now. Am I really here or did I make a bubble? Part of me hopes that I made a bubble; that I'm still in Spirit Prison, that none of this is true, that I'm close to Alex. Yet my instincts tell me that I'm on earth, that I've opened the rift, that I got pulled in, and that Alex is probably being tortured by those dark spirits this very minute.

Alex…The thought of him brings on another wave of agony. I want to leave here so badly and go straight to him and explain myself. He saw me leave when Agatha showed me his bubble. His made-up world had gone blank, and he saw me. Then when he came to find me, all he heard me say was to stay away from him! "Oh," I groan. "What are you thinking right now, Alex?" If I'm really in the mortal realm, and not trapped in some nightmarish bubble back in prison, then Alex must think that I've turned my back on him and abandoned him there to rot! The thought brings on a stabbing pain in my middle. It's not a physical pain, but a soul-wrenching ache that's even worse than any bodily sensation, because physical pain eventually fades, and this does not. This stays rooted to the spot and festers.

"Tess, what are you doing here?"

"Jase?" I turn and see Robyn's father hovering in the doorway. He and Katie had been watching over their daughter since they died in a plane crash when she was a little girl. They had begged me to take care and raise Robyn as my own child while I was still alive, and I've always felt like we shared custody of her with them. I did raise her as my own, and I did love her as my own, so his implication that I wasn't welcome at her bedside was offensive. "What do you think?" I bark back, suddenly on guard and ready to strike.

Jase tilts his head to one side and looks at me like I'm off my rocker. "You…are dead."

"Thanks, I hadn't noticed."

"But," he pauses, trying to put together a thought. "You are not where you're supposed to be."

I stare at him blankly. Yes, it's true, but beside the point right now. "She gave up her own child, why?" I demand.

"It doesn't concern you, Tess," he says delicately, not wanting to offend me, but stating the obvious.

"It sure does. I'm her godmother. I raised her! I—I love her!" Suddenly my own words bring something else to mind, the vague memory of hearing those same stubborn words coming from Alex, after he had passed. He had come back to be with me, and we had quickly developed a very unhealthy relationship. So my own previous words stick to my throat like stale bread.

"You know better than anyone what happens when spirits from the other side come here unassigned," Jase edges.

I stare at him for a minute, then nod and glide away from her bedside. "I'll leave, but please tell me what happened to her."

He hesitates, then looks around to see if there are any other angels checking on him. "She got married, but her husband was a total jerk. He finally left her for another woman, and took all her money to boot. Her business too."

"What? Where—?"

"That's why I didn't want to tell you!" he says cutting me short, and holding me by the shoulders. "You can't go after him! You can't! Promise me you won't! If you do anything to him you'll be responsible and you, of all people, know too well what happens when spirits go around the mortal realm with a vendetta."

Right again. I do know all about this, and only now do I understand fully what Alex and my father must have felt like. They had this power, this ability to move about unrestrained in the mortal realm, and right at the height of their ire, they were told not to do anything about it. They were told to let things go and let events unfold on their own. But the temptation to get involved was—and is—too great.

"Okay, I promise," I say, still fuming. But my promise to not involve myself was mostly done for Robyn's sake, not my own. I had messed up big time already, what would one little haunt do to me now?

Once Jase looks satisfied with my promise that I won't just fly off to torture that man, he resumes the story. "Soon after he left her, Robyn found out that she was pregnant. She told him, but he didn't believe her. He said that it was a ploy to get him back." He shook his head, obviously irate himself at the man. "He told her that he would never want anything to do with her or her child." Jase paced the length of the room, pressing his lips into a thin, tight line of displeasure. "He took everything from her! Even her self-esteem," Jase accuses, looking at me with that same look of barely restrained anger that I mirrored in my face. "She sank into a deep depression, as you could imagine. It was hard to see her suffer like that. She wanted a family so badly, but not like this. She had taken a back seat in her company to start a family with this guy, and she gave him most of the reins as he suggested and then..." He sighs, and shakes his head. "Adoption seemed like a good option to her. She really is in no state to raise a child. That jerk has messed her up, big time. I swear, Tess, when I'm given the okay, that man will pay!"

"You may be spared the trouble," I say dryly. "When he dies, he'll be in his own special Hell. Trust me, that place is punishment enough."

Jase looks at me with those big blue eyes that Katie had found irresistible, I can see why. They are deep like an ocean and peaceful like the sky. "Are you going to tell me what happened to you?"

I shake my head. I'm too ashamed. "I still don't understand," I say, changing the subject. "She could have raised him all on her own."

He shakes his head, no. "Robyn's broken. She's not well."

"Like, crazy or something?"

"More like depressed, angry, and damaged. She's not acting like herself."

"But the child!"

"I too wish that she would keep him. But at the same time, if she's not fit to be a parent..." He presses his lips into a thin line. "She found a good family for him. I think that in her mind she believes that they will give him what she can't—the ideal family."

I look back at Robyn, lying there on her bed, and my essence weeps for her. There are no actual tears, just waves of sadness. She looks like she's in her late thirties. She has plenty of time to pull herself together, and she has to! If she waits until after death, it will be so much harder. "Tell her..." I say to Jase, while looking at Robyn's resting form. "Tell her that she has to get better in this life. Tell her that she can't die with guilt and remorse. Tell her it's worse on the other side if you don't take care of your issues now."

Chapter 4

I feel so hopeless and so aimless. I want to help with Robyn, but I can't. I want to help Alex and my father, but I'm stuck in the mortal realm—again—only this time, I'm dead! And all my attempts at getting back to the other side are proving unsuccessful. So I wander. I float about with no particular destination, noticing nothing, trying hard not to interfere with anyone's life and avoiding those dark shadows that zoom by me now and then with what looks like a clear purpose.

From a distance I check on Robyn, making sure I stay far enough away to not alert her of my presence, and also far away from Jase's and Katie's accusatory eye. I don't want them to see me, stuck as I am. I've already asked them for help in getting back, and they simply said that I needed to find my own way back. I have done as they suggested, but have failed. I have even followed after several spirits who had just died, and tried to sneak in after them, as they went toward the light or the darkness—at this point I didn't care too much where I went—but none of those tricks worked; the rift admits only one.

At first, Robyn's life spirals out of control. Then I watch as her guardian angel parents patiently help her put her life back on track. As the years fly by, I witness her recovery and how she slowly gets back on her feet, and starts doing productive things again. Her son grows into a teenager and finds her. This relationship seems to change Robyn's life for the better, and she finds the strength to fix her life for good. At some point though, I lose track of her, and I start to feel like I've lost all my tethers to this realm. Maybe Robyn has passed too.

I'm not sure why, but I find myself roaming familiar places that are now being inhabited by strangers. As I make my rounds of these old haunts, I find myself back at the cemetery. I see a grown man with a small child. He looks somber and sad, and as I float to them, I realize that they are standing around an old grave. The headstone reads, Robyn Mallory-Preston. I look around to see if by any chance I might see her spirit, but no, she's gone, and with her, Katie and Jase, the last of my family. This man might be family, but I don't know him.

If I had been feeling cold and empty before, I'm more so now. I feel like death itself has settled in on me. I feel so lost. I have nothing to anchor me to this realm anymore; all my ties to this realm are gone. Who is left that I know or have a bond with? No one. All my attempts at trying to make a connection with someone in the spirit realm fail. Is there no one looking for me, or wondering where I am and what I'm doing? Is my case really this hopeless? Have I committed some unpardonable sin that is keeping me here?

Suddenly I'm seized with the desire to push some sort of rewind button, to go back to my body and reenter it. I want to do my death all over again and do things differently. I close my eyes and try to go back, back, back. When I open them, all is dark. Maybe my eyes are not open, I can't tell. So I will my eyes open again, but the darkness is pervasive. Slowly my sight adjusts, and when it does, right away I wish it hadn't. I'm staring straight into a hollow eye socket—my eye socket—putrid and decaying, along with the rest of my skeletal remains. I'm trapped in my own casket with my carcass. That is me! Screeching and screaming like a banshee, I try to scratch and claw my way out of my own tomb, but it's all to no avail. I'm in here, trapped it seems.

"Please," I plead to whoever might hear me. "Please! I want out." As if I were Lazarus, as soon as that plea is uttered, I'm released from my prison and let out into the fresh turf of the cemetery. Next to my grave is Alex's grave. I throw myself on top of it and give in to my misery.

I'm not sure when, or for how long I stay there, wailing, whimpering, and bemoaning my wretched state—but I see people come and go, I see day dawn and set—and at some point I start to wander again. I try my best not to interfere with the natural course of things. But a new stupor has settled over me, that last outpouring of misery has purged my soul of all feeling. I'm empty.

I glide and see, but I don't seem to feel or really register anything. I can tell that the world is different, things are changing, and something is amiss. Dazed as I am, I can't quite put my finger on the problem, but things are definitely different.

"Hello," a friendly voice addresses me directly, for the first time in what seems like ages. "We meet again."

I stare at him for a while, trying to bring him into focus. After some time a vague recollection strikes me. "John!" I say with awe. He looks exactly as he did the first time I saw him when I was a teenager and he was investigating Agatha's disappearance. His timeless appearance hits me anew. Here he is—decades, or centuries, later—still here on Earth, still young and vibrant, still performing his duties as an Aeonian. John the Revelator had chosen to stay on Earth until the end of the world, as he saw it in his visions and recorded in the book of Revelations. He's no longer a mortal, but is not yet an immortal being. He's an Aeonian, and walks the world, helping out in whatever way he can, until the world ends.

"Hi, Tess." He grins. His hands are tucked in his pockets and he looks casually around, to see if anyone is watching him talk to thin air. "So...of all spirits to find here," he says with disapproval in his voice. "What are you doing here?"

"I—I—was pulled in," I frown. "Or out. I don't know exactly. I was—I was..." Have I really forgotten why I'm here? What's wrong with me? "I was looking for Alex," I say, happy to have gotten that much right. But the truth is, I feel slightly disoriented, like I'm sleep-walking through an endless dream.

Sensing my confusion, John's mouth turns into a sympathetic smile. "Why don't you follow me to my place, where we can talk without blowing my cover?" he suggests reasonably.

His place was a small run-down apartment with scant, old-fashioned furniture, which had seen better days a few decades ago. His small kitchenette only has one plate, one cup, one glass, and a single set of utensils. "You don't entertain much, do you?"

John smiles over his shoulder, as he works on boiling some water on a kettle. "No, never really have. Not part of the job."

"I didn't know you liked tea?" I say, as John pulls a tea bag from the cupboard.

"A habit left over from my days in England while I worked with William Tyndale on the translation of the Bible."

"Really?"

"Yep. You, in fact, assisted me one time while on one of my many stays in that country. That was much later of course, the eighteenth century if I recall. I've come and gone quite a bit," he admits.

"I helped you?"

John nods. "You were an unborn spirit then. Your mind has been veiled from that life. That's why you can't remember it." He waves his hand in front of his face signifying a veil.

"Mm..." Something does ring true about that. "I do remember a creature telling me that I had made some promises, and then she gave me that fire that didn't burn me, but burned Agatha's house down."

John nods again, and once his water is ready he sits down in a very uncomfortable looking chair and sips his tea daintily. "What else do you remember about that part of your existence?" he asks, sounding like Dane did when he was in "shrink" mode.

"Not much," I say evasively.

"Why don't you try? Tell me anything that you remember about any part of your existence."

I think about it for a while. I mention remembering him, and his first visit when Agatha had run away. And a few other inconsequential details about that time, but the harder I try to remember, the less I do. Something is keeping my mind perfectly blank.

John is insistent though, and probes and prods until he has me retelling him my whole life story, all the way up to my death.

"Oh…" is all I can say once I realize, again, what I have just done. "I—I let Agatha come over here." I say, as if it were news to me. "How could I forget?" I say perplexed.

"Yes, you did." He looks at me like a parent who is displeased with his misbehaving child. "I think you've been trying to block your own reality."

"I'm sorry," I say childishly. Honestly, I am. But the whole situation is so overwhelming that I have no idea what else to say or do.

"Do you know what Agatha's been up to?"

"No," I admit.

"She has joined forces with the cast-outs, and they have been letting the worst of the imprisoned spirits out by way of your rift, and together they have seized control of all the mortals who rule the nations of Earth. They are in the process of making a new world order, one where, if you don't join willingly, you'll be made to join by force. There are a few groups of people who are resisting here and there, but communications are being monitored and these rebels—as they are called—are completely isolated from each other. If any of them are caught, they are put to death."

"My rift?" My brain struggles to quantify the scope of this deed, but it all sounds so bad, that I can't even feel guilt. "My rift?" I ask again, now feeling a little bit of hope. "Can I go through my rift?"

"Haven't you tried already?"

I think back to that day in the hospital. I did try, and couldn't. I nod in response, ashamed for being more concerned about leaving, than the actual problem that I have caused. "I've caused this?" I finally ask, remorsefully.

"Well, no. You didn't personally cause Agatha and the Second One to organize, but you opened the rift that allowed them to join forces."

Seeing the stunned look on my face, John sighs. "But it was bound to happen. If you hadn't opened the rift, someone else would have; you father maybe, or your mother, and there are others too." He sighs. "Agatha was determined enough, even if none of you had done it—who she knew for sure could do this thing—she would have searched and searched until she found someone else who could."

"But it was me…"

"Yes, it was."

"What will happen to me now?"

"Well, that I don't know. I do have to add though, that this was bound to happen. I mean, I did foresee this. This is the start of Armageddon."

"And I've caused Armageddon?" I mutter incredulously.

John doesn't answer. He remains quiet and somber, looking down into his empty cup.

I opened the rift, I let Agatha join the Second One, and I have brought about the end of the world! I know that panic should start to set in any minute now, but it doesn't. It doesn't set in while John finishes another cup of tea, or when he washes his cup, or even after he excuses himself and goes to bed. It still doesn't set in when he wakes up and finds me still hovering in that same spot. Not after he assures me that the timing for this awful event is right on schedule, and that the end is supposed to come now. Nothing he says adds or detracts from my complete lack of feeling. I know that I should feel something, guilt, sadness, shame, anger—but no—I feel nothing.

"You're welcome to stay," John says at some point. I'm not entirely sure how many days have gone by for him, but I think I remember him coming and going a few times, and sitting in that chair, drinking something, or eating something, then going to his room, then coming out again. How many times has he done this? I can't remember. But when I see him walk in again, I know that I have to go. He doesn't look mad, or annoyed at all. He looks…disappointed. Is it possible to haunt an Aeonian? "I—I—will go now."

"Where?" he asks, suddenly worried.

"Don't know," I admit.

"You have to get back to where you belong."

"I wish I could, but I don't know how. And—and," frankly, I dreaded going back to Prison. I know now that that's where I belong, due to my colossal mistake. But the thought of going back there roots me to my current spot.

"Don't you want to find Alex?" John asks, curiously.

"Alex?" I murmur, distractedly. Then a mild guilt over forgetting him, and leaving him alone in Prison this whole time, envelops me. But it isn't nearly enough to ignite any sort of spark of action in me.

Ashamed and despondent, I glide out of John's apartment, and resume my wandering. I no longer recognize any of my surroundings. Everything looks colorless, gray, dirty, and run-down. The dark figures that zoom past me now and then no longer bother me. The spirits who roam free regard me only long enough to make up their minds about something, and then pass by me, like I'm a pariah. I guess I'm of no consequence to anyone.

Spirits—there seems to be a lot more of those around here lately. One in particular catches my attention. He's tall, has dark hair gathered at the base of his neck in a ponytail, and is following a mortal dressed in uniform. When the spirit sees me, he turns to me with interest, leaving his mortal to follow me. At first I think nothing of it, but then, his trailing me starts to get annoying.

"Leave me alone," I say dispassionately, suddenly stopping, and turning to face him.

"I'm not bothering you," he says, lifting his hands up like he's surrendering. "I'm just curious to see what you're doing."

"Nothing. I'm doing nothing," I say defensively. Perhaps too defensively, because he smiles broadly and gives me wry, unconvinced, look. "Who are you?" I finally ask, after several unsuccessful attempts at shaking him off my trail.

He regards me for a moment. "That's right, we never did meet in life. I'm Eros, your uncle." He bows graciously and extends one arm. Instinctively, I give him my hand, and instead of shaking it, he kisses it. "It is so nice to finally meet you. Though, I must say I expected...." He takes a minute to come up with the right words, while looking theatrically thoughtful. "I guess I just expected more," he finally declares with a mocking grin.

"Sorry to disappoint you, Uncle," I say dryly. I'm not in the mood for games; I'm not in the mood for anything actually. I just want to be left alone. I want to bide my time, and do as little damage as possible until I find a way to leave. So turning sharply, I fly off, hoping that—as disappointed as he is in me—he will leave me be. But I guess I'm not so lucky.

"What do you want with me?" I ask him exasperated, after a few more attempts at ditching him.

"Since you're here, you might as well come with us," he suggests sensibly.

"No."

This seems humorous to him and he laughs. "Agatha always made it sound like you were such a go-getter, so active, so involved. Why are you going against your nature?"

"I'm not where I should be," I respond simply, not really knowing where the right place for me is anymore, but clearly knowing that Earth is not it.

"Cut a hole in the veil, and you can go anywhere you'd like to go. Why, with your ability, I would certainly take advantage of that. I would explore pre-mortal earth! I would sneak into Paradise! I would..." He thinks about it for a second, closing his eyes, and picturing the joys of moving from realm to realm freely. "I would turn all the realms into a great big colander." He smiles, obviously pleased with the image he painted for me.

A group of mortals dressed in military attire pass through us, and they each in turn shiver. I find it odd that soldiers would be roaming in this manner. They look so official, yet their uniform doesn't have the American flag on it. John must be right. Armageddon is starting. The thought should spark something in me, a desire to help, the need to be useful, or at the very least, the wish to be forgiven for what I had unleashed on Earth. But no, I feel nothing. I'm perfectly despondent. I simply stand there like a statue, mute, inert, empty. Even Eros gets tired of my inactivity and leaves me, shaking his head and laughing to himself. As he glides away, he mutters something about me having been a complete disappointment, so easily broken.

I suppose he's right, I am finally broken. At some point I drift away from that spot and move somewhere else, a room I think. People move about me—in and out, in and out—mortals move so quickly, they remind me of squirrels. Then, for a long time...nothing. People stop coming and absolutely no one, and not a single thing stirs.

"This is enough, Tess, you've got to stop it." A bright, blinding light shines in front of me. It's so sudden and so bright that I have to shield my eyes. "Come on! Snap out of it!" the voice demands, but it means nothing to me. It does sound vaguely familiar, but there's something wrong with it. So I stare on, ignoring his pleas. This, however, does not seem to deter him from his discourse, and he keeps on talking as if I were an avid listener.

"Interesting," he rambles on. "That you chose to shut yourself up in this old place. Of all the places that we've lived in, you decided to come here. Consciously or unconsciously, you must miss me." He smiles a bright, toothy smile that warms me. "Somewhere in that troubled head of yours, you made a silent plea—for me!" He sighs and looks distractedly around. "But now you're ignoring me, so…"

"Who are you?" I finally ask, perplexed by the incessant chatterer before me. His dark skin is only made more startling by the whiteness of his clothes and the light that radiates from him. There's something that is very familiar about him, yet something is very different too.

Startled by my sudden question, he turns, and a smile spreads widely over his face, changing his features again, from familiar to foreign. "Dorian," he says.

"Dorian?"

"Yeah, in the—well not flesh—but in spirit anyway."

"But, you're…different."

"I'm me." He nods reassuringly.

Curious and puzzled, I find myself at his side, inspecting him from all angles. "Yes, yes, it is you," I remark as I look him over. "You're Dorian!"

"You're funny!" he laughs, then grabs me by the hand and sits me on his lap like a child. Instantly, some of the coldness I feel inside starts to melt. Looking deep into his eyes, I see it. That glint that I used to see buried deep inside his eyes, that memory of someone forgotten or someone trapped. That person is now free and whole.

"Dorian, it really is you!" I waste no time in wrapping my arms around his neck and hug him tightly. We stay like this for a long time; I don't want to let go of him for fear of losing myself again.

"I'm afraid," I confess. "I've done something terrible."

"I know," he says as he pats me on the head. "But you're back, right?" He pulls me away, taking his turn at inspecting me. "You do remember who you are, and where you are, and that you're not in the right place, right?"

I have to think about this for a while. Who was I? The answer does not come readily, yet slowly, flashes of memory start coming back to me. Dorian and I clinging to each other, on this very spot, and me promising him that I would look after him like a sister. Another flash, not a happy one, of Agatha as a child chasing Dorian all over the house, scaring him, and me kicking her in the chest, then locking Dorian and me in this room. Suddenly, all the memories start pouring out from my

unconscious into my conscious mind. I stare mutely at him with amazement, as I relive all these moments, and I'm astonished at how I could
have possibly forgotten them to begin with.

"I do know who I am, and we're..." I look around and see that we
were in our old foster home. The place looks dilapidated by time and
disuse. This particular room seems to have been shut up for a long time.
There's no furniture and a thick layer of dust covers the wooden floor-
boards. Large cobwebs hang heavy with dust; nothing has been living
here for a long time, not even the spiders that spun those webs. Dorian
is sitting in mid-air, as if he were resting comfortably on an easy chair,
while I still hover on the spot where he found me. "We're at Charlotte's
house," I tell him.

"Yes," he says approvingly. "We're in our old room. And I'd never
thought I'd say this, but it looked better when we lived here."

I nod in reply, then slowly glide toward the little window. I try to
open it, but my essence does not match the solid mortal realm, so I fly
through it instead, and float over the little rooftop where we used to do
our homework. Dorian follows me and we sit on the same spots where
we used to sit long, long ago. "How long has it been?" I ask.

"We've been dead for a long time, Tess. I'm afraid that a few
decades have gone by just with you sitting here, staring at the walls. You
might have spooked a few mortals in the process."

"I've—I've haunted people?" I gasp, horrified. That's exactly what I
wanted to avoid.

"Well, not intentionally. While you were here, some people went
through you and felt the chills. Others, the more sensitive ones, could
feel a presence. But you never reacted, or encouraged them, so...all in
all I think you did okay. Only one little girl might remember you, and I
think she likes you."

"A little girl?"

"Yes, she used to live here as a child. I think she might have
seen you, and talked to you. But you never talked back." He shrugs
dismissively.

"How do you know all this?"

"I've been tracking you. I was assigned as your...err...guardian of
sorts."

I look at him suspiciously. "What do you mean?"

"Well, all unauthorized spirits from Prison or otherwise," he says
significantly, "have to be caught and sent back. I volunteered to come
get you."

"Like a criminal?"

He nods with a goofy look on his face. Somehow it feels like I should be angry, hurt, or mad, at this, but the fact that I'm talking—TALKING—to Dorian, a whole two-sided conversation with him, makes me so happy that I can't get mad. While we were alive, Dorian was autistic. He hardly ever talked and didn't like to be touched. He was also savant, and drew inexplicable and detailed pictures of things and people he couldn't have known or seen. He was handicapped enough that he needed to live with someone, yet aware enough that without his help I could not have made it through my own mortal life. We had an understanding of sorts; he would let me be near him on occasions, and somehow I could always tell what he needed. No words were ever necessary. It was as if I could read his mind, just by looking at him.

"It's so good to *see* you. I mean, it's really *you*, the way you were supposed to be." I say in awe.

"I was who I was supposed to be," he says, shaking his head. "If I hadn't been autistic, nothing would have worked out the way it was supposed to. I knew about it too, you know. Coming in, I mean. I agreed to be born with a disability."

"You knew this while you were alive?"

"No, of course not. I didn't know then. But I remember it all now. Before our mortal life, I knew that I would be born with a disability of sorts. I didn't know which one, but I knew I would have one. I also knew that once I crossed the Veil, I would forget all about that previous life. That's where you come in. You and I were great friends and we made a pact that we would help each other in mortality. I trusted you, and you came through for me!"

"How do you know all this?"

"I'm Open!" he says as if that explained it all.

"What's that?"

"Oh, that's right," he nods, berating himself for not seeing something obvious. "You haven't been to Paradise yet. Well, basically Opening unlocks your mind, so you can remember not just your whole mind, but your whole existence."

"Why?"

"So you can repent, and fix any unresolved issues. I was an "innocent" in life because of my disability, so I had nothing to fix from my mortal life—innocents are automatically redeemed. When I died, I automatically Opened and got *all* my memories back. I clearly remember you and me making a pact that we would be there for each other, just like as you and Alex made a pact to find each other and be soul mates."

"Alex," I groan, pulling my hands over my face. Alex's face before I was pulled into the rift will forever be etched in my mind. Remembering that look brings an onslaught of anxiety, regret, and pain so intense that I feel like screaming. I tell Dorian this and he nods solemnly.

"I haven't been to see him, but—"

"But what?" I demand.

"I don't know, I think—" he bites his lip and makes a funny gesture. "I think he might have made the wrong assumption."

"What do you mean?"

"Luz has been keeping me in the loop. She stops by when she has a free moment."

"Luz? My aunt Luz?"

"Yeah," he grins and his whole face brightens.

"Are you and she…"

"Yeah," he smirks that cocky smirk again, such a foreign gesture for him. Maybe foreign is not the right word—new gesture, perhaps describes it better. New to me, who only remembers the mortal Dorian, the "innocent" boy who lived trapped inside an imperfect body. "We are engaged. We'll get married as soon as we get our bodies back," he says brightly.

"Oh," I say, trying to reconcile the image of Luz and Dorian as a couple. In mortality, my aunt Luz was also an "innocent." When we first met her, she was a fifty year old with the mind of a ten year old, who liked to wear tutus and pigtails. She and Dorian became fast friends, and they were really cute together, but she was about thirty years older!

"Anyway, Luz keeps in touch with Celeste, who keeps in touch with Valerie, who has been trying to get Alex out of Prison. But apparently, he doesn't want to. It seems he's lost his willpower or something."

"That was my job!" I jump up to my feet and inadvertently fly up a little higher than I first intended.

"I know," Doran admits. "But you didn't follow the light, and then you opened the rift…"

Ignoring his words, I'm seized with impatience and anxiety. I have to get back there, and fast. "Can you take me back, Dorian? I want to go to him right now."

He shakes his head. "Sorry, it doesn't work like that. You are on probation now. You have to follow all the rules if you *both* want to come out of this one."

"What rules?" I ask suspiciously.

"You come with me. You face the High Council, you confess, you beg for forgiveness, you work on Opening, and once you do Open, you can go back in there."

"How long does it take to Open?"

"Now we're talking," he smiles, and as suddenly as turning on a light switch, we're no longer hovering over that rooftop.

Chapter 5

I try blinking, but it is no use. All I can make out are little white and golden dots. I can only hear muted voices that seem to come from all around me. Fear that I have inadvertently created a bubble grips me again. Having no physical sensation always leaves me with the nagging doubt of what *real* really is. What if I've been in a bubble this whole time? What if nothing has been real and it's all been an elaborate mental game of my own design?

"Give her time, give her time," someone whispers.

"Wake up Tess! Wake up! Wake up!" I order my brain, but how am I supposed to distinguish a dream from a reality when nothing is tangible? Everything is mental now that I'm dead. Frustration holds me tightly from within, but I make an effort, and I open my eyes again. Here and there I can now see shapes, human shapes. Everything is still very bright, but the shapes in front of me start coming into focus a little better.

"Dorian?" I ask tentatively.

"Still here. Never left you," he reassures.

"So...it's all real?"

"Yep, all is real. You're back where you belong now."

He waves one hand and someone comes to his side. It's a beautiful silver blond girl, about twenty, with large gray eyes, who happens to bear an uncanny resemblance to—"Luz?" I marvel. My mentally retarded aunt is not only perfectly normal now, but also young again, and beautiful beyond description.

She smiles broadly and embraces me. "Tess, I'm so happy to see you!" Tiny silvery white flowers are attached to several strands of her hair—no more pigtails for her! She's wearing a white tutu, and butterfly wings poke out behind her shoulders. I look at the wings, puzzled, and she twirls around playfully, making them flutter.

"You can wear whatever you can imagine here, so I thought this up. What do you think?"

"It suits you."

"Ahem!"

I turn, and to my great surprise I see them—all of them! Celeste is in front, with a look of annoyance on her face and waving an accusatory finger in front of her. However, she quickly gives up on her silent rebuke and throws herself onto my ghostly form, hugging me tightly. "You had us so worried," she whispers.

Behind her come my two other aunts, who also heap themselves onto me, joining Celeste in a bear hug. I should be feeling short of breath, because of how tightly they're holding on to me, but I feel absolutely nothing.

Once they release me, the rest of my family and Alex's family greets me, including Robyn, who kisses my cheek tenderly. Irene, my mother, stands apart looking nervous and anxious, as though she's worried about coming any closer. Once everyone else has had a chance to greet me, a path is opened for her, and she glides forward. Her simple white dress seems to glow against her dark skin, making her look divine. She's as beautiful as the few pictures I saw of her depicted. I realize I look a lot like her and a strange feeling that I can't identify goes through me. It's a good feeling, like a memory wrapped up in an emotion. I guess it's only natural to feel this way, when you meet your own mother for the first time.

"I couldn't bear the thought of losing you too," she says. Then she too throws her arms around me. It's like she's melting onto me; her essence and mine mesh together strangely well. We are both discerners too, so our mutual feelings merge and pool together.

This overwhelms me, so I pull her at arms length. Not because I'm upset, but because it's just too much right now. I still feel like I'm teetering on some dangerous ledge, and I can barely deal with my own emotions, much less my mother's.

She backs away looking disappointed, but smiles in spite of it. "We have plenty of time to catch up and—and get to know each other," she says, trying to hide the fact that she's disheartened by my cool reaction to her.

I stare at everyone, not sure of what to say or do. Dane, Alex's father, takes quick command of the situation and makes small talk. "Now that you're here, we have plenty to show you. There are parts of Paradise that I know for sure you'll have an interest in."

"Yes!" Celeste jumps in brightly. "There's so much to see, and do. You're home now, you know. There are whole sections of Paradise that are sectioned off to the arts, literature, fashion even!"

I nod and make a feeble attempt at smiling, but I feel unfit to be here and unworthy of their love and kindness. I want to get out of here and hide somewhere again. I wonder how much they know and how they feel about it. I suspect that they're disappointed in me, maybe even appalled by my actions. No one says anything, though. However, I know that deep inside they must all be thinking the same thing: "She failed us."

"They weren't there." I tell myself. *"They don't know what happened; they don't know that my back was up against a wall!"* my mind argues against their unspoken reproach. I suppose that none of this would have occurred if I had listened to Celeste to begin with, and had come toward the light. Perhaps, if I had done this, I would have already been to Prison and back—safely—with Alex and my father among us.

Seeing my unresponsiveness, my welcoming committee excuse themselves one by one, and fly off in different directions—all but Celeste, my mother, and Dorian—who stand by mutely and look at me like they're about to perform an intervention.

"What's wrong with her?" Celeste tilts her head to one side and asks Dorian in a whisper that I pretend I can't hear.

"She was shut down for so long..." he explains.

"Tess?" my mother ventures to ask directly. She can discern me, so she knows that I'm still here. Broken, but here. "I won't pretend to know what you've been through, but I can assure you that we only want to help."

On hearing her voice, I turn to look at her, and her dark beauty suddenly takes me back again. She has high cheekbones that glow, even in her ghostly form, slightly pink under her olive skin. Her eyes are the color of rich dark soil, and her hair is shiny as a raven's wing.

"Okay," I reply somewhat despondently. She smiles in return and keeps looking at me, as if she's never seen me before.

Awkwardly, I move my eyes away from her intense scrutiny and take a moment to take in my surroundings. Behind me there's a thick wall of what looks like a cloud, and tendrils of whiteness ripple on out from the top and the bottom, filling the space in front of it with a hazy fog. In front of me, there's a massive gate that emanates an ethereal pink and yellow glow. There are clusters of people standing around; some stand in front of the fog, waiting it seems, for someone to emerge from the mortal realm. Others are greeting and rejoicing over the arrival of a new family member. Some spirits arrive and have no one but a single angel waiting for them. I see that those are led to the gate and after some discussion, are given the choice, like I had been given long ago, to go back to life or stay here. Most go back, some stay.

"Those are the Gate Keepers. They are angels that get assigned to guard the gate. You've met one before, do you remember?" my mother asks, sounding like an elementary school teacher.

"Yes," I respond. "I do."

I move toward the gate with Dorian, Celeste, and my mother in tow. This time the gate automatically swings open for me, and we pass through it without much fanfare. Celeste and Dorian are talking animatedly about something that I can't understand. My mother glides mutely by them with something on her mind, something that I can't seem to discern. Slowly, once I cross the threshold of the gate, the fog from the veil dissipates and a whole other world, busy and bustling with people and animals appears before me. It looks like earth, but like no part of earth that I've ever been to. Buildings of all kinds are mixed together—tall, short, stores, homes, skyscrapers, and huts—all from different time periods, cultures, and architectural design. The streets are paved in golden cobblestones and there are trees, bushes, potted plants, and flowers with rich, bright colors all around. On one side of the street there's a huge park with a pond, framed by luscious green grass and dotted with massive lily pads that lazily float on its surface. There are spirits all over the place. Some fly above, some lie on the grass, others stand around chatting, while others read from scrolls, books, or electronic pads. Time periods and cultures are meshed perfectly here. Everyone is dressed in white, but the styles vary according to their personal taste, culture, and era. Some are wearing a simple attire—standard issued, I suppose—while others are dressed to the nines, with what looks like lavish dresses that came straight out of Marie Antoinette's court at Versailles. You can pretty much tell when spirits lived by what they are wearing. This to me is of particular interest, and I find myself paying close attention to everyone's attire.

"I thought you'd like the dresses," my mother says quietly.

I turn and look at her dress. It's a simple Mexican dress with a scoop neck and short puffy sleeves. Every edge is embroidered with flowers, all white and long enough to cover her ankles. I loved those dresses while I was alive. I bought myself one every time I went to Mexico. It was my thing; each trip I would make a point to get a new Mexican homemade dress. It didn't take long to have a colorful collection of them, and I wore them often with other accessories like belts, and scarfs.

Looking down at my own dress, I see that I'm wearing a simple white tunic—the standard issued kind. "How do I change it?" I ask my mother.

"It's a combination of thinking about who you are, and how you want others to see you."

Luz had looked like a fairy. In life she had wore a tutu every day and she often reminded me of a grown garden fairy. So it wasn't a shock to see her with wings. They did actually look rather natural on her. Celeste's dress is strapless, long and gauzy, with a bunched up empire waist that wraps around her chest horizontally, flowing vertically down from there in massive amounts of thin, fluid, material, that ripples around her like an angelic Greek goddess. Dorian is wearing a simple linen shirt with a round neck and a slit down the middle that goes down to his chest. His pants are simple too, like something he would wear when he was alive.

I think hard about what I'd like to wear—a combination of who I am and what I'd like others to see—but this ends up being tougher than I first imagined. Nothing really comes to mind, though I try and try to think of who I am. Why am I drawing a blank? I know who I was, but I guess I don't know who I am now. Things have changed for me, I'm not even sure that I belong here anymore. Perhaps once I did, but now? I can still feel the weight of what I've done hanging over me like a huge anvil. I'm still carrying the anger and the insidious hate that I picked up back in Spirit Prison. I'm also carrying the worry over what Alex must be thinking of me right now, and the fact that he might hate me now. All of this churns inside of me, leaving an uneasy feeling in the pit of what used to be my stomach. While I roamed the mortal realm, I tried to ignore all of this—I pushed it down and buried it. If I look inwardly at all, I can see that it's all still there, and part of me now.

Noticing that I'm having a hard time, Irene, my mother, wraps one arm around my shoulder and tells me to give myself some time.

"I don't have time," I tell her with unusual bitterness, moving away from her. This hurts her feelings, I can tell. She wants to have a relationship with me, she wants to be closer to me, but senses my apprehension.

"This is where you always go wrong, Tess," Celeste pipes in, giving me a stern look in the process. "You are always in a hurry. You want to do it all right now, you expect things to happen the moment you want them to happen and are unwilling to wait for the right time."

"But I've wasted decades," I complain.

"Yes, you have, all because you didn't want to wait and do things the way they should have been done!" There, she said it. What I knew everyone was thinking, but not saying.

"Okay, okay," my mother says, trying to defuse the situation. "We are who we are, and we *all* make mistakes, don't we Celeste?"

Dorian is looking from one to another with an untroubled look on his face. He almost looks like he's enjoying our little tiff, but Celeste quickly wipes the grin off his face with a sharp look.

"Why? What have *you* done?" I ask Celeste with suspicious interest.

She shakes her head like she's bothered and glides away from us, then sits on a park bench. I follow her and sit next to her, feeling remorseful for my snippy behavior.

Neither one of us says anything for a long time. Then finally she sighs. "She's right. I've been keeping a secret for a long time," she confesses.

"What?"

"How much do you remember about my life?"

"I remember that you eloped with a priest, Max, and had triplets—Amor, Luz, and Paz. I remember that when he died, you remarried some guy named Ricardo that you knew from before and had my father."

"Yes," she nods. "That's about how it happened, except—" she bites her lips and sighs again. "I don't know why this is so hard to admit, but okay, here it goes." She exhales and her shoulders droop. "When Max died, I was devastated and scared. We weren't rich and he worked two jobs just to keep us going. He tried so hard to provide for me, but he always felt bad that he couldn't give me the standard of living that I had grown up with.

"When my father found out that I had eloped, he disowned me and gave my inheritance to Ricardo, my cousin, who I was supposed to marry in the first place."

"You were supposed to marry your cousin?"

"Yes, disgusting, I know. But my father was old school and very prideful. Anyway, being disowned never bothered me. I didn't care about that money, but Max always felt bad that he was the cause for me losing my inheritance. When he passed, I finally panicked. I didn't know how I was supposed to provide for myself, the girls, and...and...I had just found out that morning that I was pregnant."

"What? Are you saying that my dad is Max's son?"

"Yes."

"So this whole time...this whole mess..."

"Yes. It's all my fault," she admits with a heavy heart.

"Eros was the actual heir, not my father?"

Celeste nods.

"You—you made Ricardo believe that he was the father?"

She nods again, and hangs her head with shame.

"Why didn't you tell him? When you saw Eros, why didn't you come clean then? He would have gotten what he wanted and he would have left my father alone. It could have all been different!"

"I know. I couldn't! I hated him! I hated Ricardo for being who he always had been, a lousy husband, and a poor excuse for a man. Eros reminded me so much of Ricardo, that I couldn't stand the sight of him. That money, that house, that inheritance was supposed to be mine to begin with! Leo should have had it, and I intended for him to have it." Celeste sighs again and her shoulders fall. "If I had known though what was to happen, I would have made a different choice."

I'm speechless. Celeste's choices changed so many lives, ruined them even! Infuriated, I want to lash out, but Dorian places one hand on my shoulder, silently reminding me of my own colossal mistakes. So I try to calm myself and think logically. Like me, Celeste hadn't foreseen what her choices would do. I guess we are all guilty of something. I guess we all have major problems to deal with.

"You have to understand!" she pleads. "The love of my life had died! I was pregnant and had three little girls, one with special needs! I needed that money! That's what I thought then, anyway."

I sigh. "So what now?" I say, at last composed. "What can we do? It's all over, it's done."

"We deal with it," Celeste says, venturing a look in my direction.

My mother kneels next to Celeste and gently puts one hand over hers and wraps it tightly. "I'm sorry, I didn't mean to accuse you," she pleads remorsefully. Here she was, a direct casualty from Celeste's mistakes. Irene lost her life because of a chain of events that was set off by Celeste herself.

"I know," Celeste says, placing her other hand over Irene's. "You're right though, I still have a long way to go."

"How do we deal with it? What does that even mean? We can't undo any of the things we've done, we can't take it back," I say.

"It's called, Opening," Dorian says and stands in front of me. "See? I'm Open and so is Luz. You can see right through us, right?"

"I can see right through everyone," I say matter-of-factly, and Dorian laughs.

"Yes, yes, but I'm easy to read. You can see my intentions. My thoughts are out in the open for everyone to see and hear, if they want to."

51

"Yes..." I say, noticing this for the first time. But it had always been like this with Dorian. Even when we were alive I could always tell what he was thinking. His intentions were always transparent to me.

"That's because they were both innocents," Celeste says defensively. "Innocents Open right away, because they have nothing to work out. They're blameless."

"She's right," Dorian confirms. "It was all part of the deal. All the pre-mortal spirits who agreed to a special mission through mortality knew that a special mission on earth would be hard. We knew we would forget that we agreed to having a disability, so to compensate, we would Open right away so as to understand why we had to endure such difficulties. We'll also be among the first to resurrect and get our bodies back."

"And that's fair," my mother says. "All innocents deserve these privileges. The first are last, and the last are first."

"I still don't know how to Open."

"You have to go before the High Council and plead your case first. Then you can go to the Opening district and request a Spirit Guide," Dorian says sagely. It's still a bit odd to see him like this and I can't help but smile whenever he speaks.

"Are you Opening, Celeste?" I ask because I see how dejected she looks—a lot like me—actually.

"Yes. Being up front with others and admitting your mistakes to those whom you've hurt is part of the process," she says miserably.

"Oh mother," Luz skids to a full stop right in front of Celeste. I'm not even sure where she comes from, or how fast she was just traveling, but not a hair is out of place, every single little strand of her silver-blond locks looks perfect, with all the tiny little silver flowers fastened to the different strands, and her wings fluttering happily behind her. She's unearthly—like a creature out of *A Midsummer Night's Dream*—part human, part angel, and part fairy. She hovers before us, looking earnestly into Celeste's eyes. "You know no one cares. Every single person here is dealing with something."

"You're not," Celeste's mouth curves into a half smile, as she tucks a flower-laden strand of hair behind Luz's ear.

Luz responds by making a tsking sound with her tongue. "No one judges you here."

I look back at Dorian and I can see the love in his eyes. He's not just smitten, he's is totally and helplessly in love with her. And *I* love it! The happiness I feel for them warms a little spot inside of me, like the beginning of a thawing in my soul.

"She's right, Celeste, no one is judging you," my mother adds softly. Celeste looks at me to make sure that I wasn't the exception. She finds that I look so miserable myself that neither one of us is in any position to be judgmental.

"So to Open, you have to go around confessing your sins to everyone?" I sum up in response to Celeste's pleading eyes.

"No, not necessarily," Luz says, looking at me now. "You work with your Spirit Guide at remembering all the parts of your life that need to be dealt with. Once you remember, you can deal with it in whatever way is appropriate. It may be that you'll have to go to all the people that you've offended and ask them for forgiveness, other times you'll have to earn their trust back. Since it's too late to fix the harm, it can be difficult, but everyone can eventually Open up completely to the point where all thoughts and actions are discernable to everyone—like with Dorian and me."

"What?" I ask, still not understanding fully what she means.

"It means you make all your thoughts available for all to see," my mother says, and as she says it, I can feel waves of sadness rippling off of her like heat waves. "It means that you have nothing to hide, that your confidence in the Eternals is absolute and that your desires are one with theirs."

"You mean ..."

"Yes, all your thoughts," she assures me.

No wonder it's hard. I can't imagine making every single one of my thoughts available for anyone to read.

"It's really not that odd or hard," Luz says and reaches her hand toward Dorian. As she does this I can sample what she means. Her thoughts were clear and simple, pure, and undiluted, she loves him and wants nothing more than to resurrect so she can marry him and experience love the way it was meant to be experienced. Her Open thoughts also reveal that she wishes to spend more time alone with him, but they can't because they are both very busy with their angelic duties. Neither one is upset about this lack of private time, but they very much look forward to the day when they'll have nothing to do but be together. Simple. Their thoughts are right there in the open, for everyone to see. They are pure thoughts too. Nothing they think is inappropriate or shameful.

In frustration, I sweep one hand over my face as I try to assimilate all of this. It seems so hard and unattainable to me. Opening sounds like being around a bunch of expert discerners—such as myself—all the time. Why? What is the point in going around with all your thoughts out there in the open? Here's Celeste, working hard to attain some higher plane of living, but looking miserable and ashamed. She can't change anything, yet she has to go around confessing to everyone! And my mother, she too is carrying around some heavy load that I can see is making her sad. I wonder what it is? What is she working on? What's keeping her from Opening?

My mother's dark, piercing eyes are on me, trying to discern, no doubt, what I'm thinking. "You know," she says. "In life, while growing up, I always thought I was…strange, crazy even. I was always getting startled by feelings that were not my own, and things that weren't there. In my mind I used to call them the shadows." She looks at me significantly. "My grandmother was Indian, she would say that I had a rare gift. It never felt like a gift to me though. Then I met your father." She smiles, relishing the memory. "He was always so full of life, always up to something mischievous. I don't know what he saw in me, we had little in common, until," she sighs, "I had one of those episodes. We were at a party, and something dark, something evil, totally paralyzed me with fear. To my amazement, Leo saw what I had felt. There was no denying it.

"We both looked at each other, and that's when we knew that we had a lot more in common than mere attraction. Leo, with his usual frankness, confessed to the fact that sometimes he saw things that no one else saw. He described what he saw and I told him about the shadows, and the feelings I got now and then.

"I told him of all the instances when I had been sure of feeling different shadows. Good ones, like those of dead relatives, and bad ones like the one we felt at that party. He said that growing up, he had seen things too. He'd seen blurry shadows—some dark and some filled with light. Some zoomed by, while others were still, but flickering like a light bulb that's about to go out.

"After we confessed this to each other, we became inseparable. We got married a few months later. Ten months after that, you were born." She smiles tenderly. A shadow passes over her face and the waves of sadness start rippling out again like heat waves.

"I could hear them," I confess. "The cast-outs and the disembodied spirits. It was like listening to a radio with bad reception." I look back at Celeste whose attention is riveted on our conversation.

Irene, my mother, nods in agreement. "I know. We often wondered if you would inherit any of our…gifts. The only consolation we had was that we—we," she chokes up and looks away.

"That you'd be there to help me with it?"

She turns back and looks at me with anxiety on her face. "When I was killed, I—" She shakes her head, indicating how helpless she felt. "I didn't know what to do. You were five and you could already hear Celeste, your grandmother. We knew because you talked to her all the time and it would always coincide with when I felt her presence. When Leo was around, well...he could see her!" Irene turns toward Celeste and they exchange glances.

"I was told that I could be sent down to be with one or the other. Leo was in prison, wrongly accused for *my* murder, and you in foster care. Tess you have to believe me," she pleads. "The decision was impossible! I drove myself half mad trying to figure out what to do and who to be with!

"Then Celeste came up with the idea. We knew that you would be able to hear me, but you no longer remembered us! The shock of that evening had been so great that you shut down completely."

I look back at Celeste, who was intent on watching my mother. Then I look back at Irene, who looks as if she's confessing a major sin. "The night you died, I was so scared," I explain. "I must have blocked it out with all the rest of my memories of you."

"Yes," my mother affirms, her face shows all the pain from that hellish night—the night that my father kept reliving in his bubble—the night that took his freedom and changed all our lives forever. "We talked it over, trust me, Tess. I gave it serious consideration and I knew that perhaps one day you would blame me for the decision, but I didn't know what else to do."

Celeste stands up and comes to stand next to my mother as a sign of support.

"Celeste suggested that we let things be as they were. She would continue to watch over you, while I went to watch over Leo in prison. We also decided that it would be better if no one spoke to you at all, and that we would let you grow up not knowing of your abilities. Celeste assured me that she would keep a watchful eye over you, as she always had, and that she would keep me informed on your life." Irene's eyes turn to me with anxiety. "I hope you didn't think that I didn't care about you, or that I didn't want to be part of your life. Please forgive me if you did." She looks so worried about this that her whole face shows the pain she feels over it. Now I know the source of her pain. Now I see what is keeping my mother from moving forward and Opening.

"I never felt that way, and I never blamed you," I say truthfully.

"Deep inside, I always felt that I had been loved. That was one thing I always knew for certain, it seemed to have been ingrained in me somehow."

"Really? You mean it?"

I nod. She peers into my eyes, trying to discern my truthfulness. She finds it and believes me. Unexpectedly, her face changes right before my eyes, from worry and doubt, to relief. I can literally see as this feeling makes its way through her, distilling the negativity out of her. A transformation starts to take place right before my eyes as gratefulness, peace, and finally joy begins to fill her. Surprisingly, I can see her! All of her life is exposed right before me. I can see her past fears and how she conquered them, I can see her past mistakes and how she fixed them. I can see her completely!

Suddenly, she starts to shine majestically, illuminating from within in a beautiful soft pink hue that almost blinds me. It's like watching a flower bloom.

"What is happening?" I ask with awe, shielding my eyes in the process.

"She's Opening!" Celeste gasps. "Thanks to you, she's finally Opening."

Chapter 6

My mother is engulfed in what looks like fire. Flames dance around her, sweeping her hair up into a whirlwind. Her face is turned upward and her mouth is curved into a smile that reflects joy, peace, love, and confidence all at once.

"Thanks to me? How did I do this?" I marvel.

"You were the catalyst. She's been waiting for your true forgiveness for a long time. In fact, that was the only thing holding her back from Opening and going back in there after your father."

"But, she's had it. I mean, I don't think I ever blamed her. Maybe when I was little..."

"...And said that you would never be the kind of parent who would let her child be raised in foster care?" Dorian clarifies.

"But I didn't know that she was dead."

"It still hurt her," Celeste says.

I'm dumbfounded. To think that all this time I was keeping my mother from progressing because of my lack of forgiveness. "But once I found out what happened, I didn't blame her."

"No, in your mind perhaps you didn't, but your heart never quite opened up to her. You never really called to her, nor put yourself in her shoes, nor wondered what she must have suffered," Dorian says sagely. And he's right. I never really did wonder about her feelings... until now that she told me. And to be perfectly honest, I always did feel a bit resentful over the fact that it was Celeste who I always heard— never her. It never occurred to me that she had to make an impossible choice—like I had to. Is Alex blaming me now in the same way? He saw me watching him, he saw me turn away from him and leave him there stranded. Every time I dredge up this memory, that last look in his eyes flashes in my mind, twisting knots somewhere in my middle. Apparently you don't need a body to feel this, or maybe it's a memory of the awful feeling, but whatever it is, it's real, and I feel sick to my stomach.

Irene is still wrapped in this fiery blanket and looks more and more beautiful and pure as the flames melt away any darkness that she might have had. When she's done, the flames ascend and leave her shining, but with her own inner light.

She looks at me and smiles radiantly. In her eyes, I see the depths of her soul. She rushes to my side and embraces me, and through the embrace, she conveys all her feelings and thoughts to me. Her unspoken words come complete with their exact feelings and meanings attached. I understand her perfectly. I now comprehend what she has endured, what she has suffered, and the joy and hope she now feels. I see her past, her memories of taking care of me as a child, her feelings as she died, her anguish over my predicament, the many times she sneaked out of her angelic post to check on me while I was growing up at Charlotte's.

Reading—that's her favorite pastime! We have that in common; *Les Miserables* is her favorite book. I get to know her through this Link of sorts. I see her falling in love with my dad. I see what she saw in him, and it makes me love him too! I see his love for me through her eyes, and I understand why he kept silent all those years while in prison. I see his strength, his determination, and his easy smile. I see him pleading with John to look after me. I feel full. Full to the brim with their love for me, and now, I can't help but love them back!

She lets go of me and I *know* her. "Mom," I whisper hoarsely, "I'm—I'm—I love you. I'm sorry for—"

"Don't be," she beams, "we will be a family yet. I know that now. Time...there's no such thing as time anymore. We have the eternities to make up for lost time on Earth." She grabs my hands, brings them up to her lips, and kisses them. "I know now how to find your father, I know what to do! I will get him back for us and we'll be the family we have always wanted to be!"

I shake my head, "It's too hard. You won't find him. Those bubbles...there's no end to them! You'll get lost like I did. The only reason why I saw him was because Agatha has some sort of agreement that allows her to pass through them. She has also roamed enough to know her way around that inferno."

My mom shakes her head. "I see the way now! I feel him, I see him!" Her eyes focus on some distant point, she looks as if she is having a vision of sorts. When she snaps out of it, she looks back at me with earnestness. "You have to Open, Tessie. That's the only way you'll find Alex," her eyes are filled with pity. "You're the only one who can do it. Anyone who loves him can find him, but I'm afraid that you're uniquely qualified to get him to leave, since much of the reason why he's stuck there is because of you."

I nod numbly. "I know that."

"Te quiero mi amor, but I have to go." She places one hand tenderly on my cheek and this brings back a memory from my childhood. I've heard those words from her lips before...many, many times before. I recall them at her touch; even though I don't physically feel it—I do feel the spark of the memories flickering around the edges of my conscious mind—and they come forward now.

"Go Mom, go find him."

She smiles. This is the first time I've called her Mom. She kisses my forehead and takes off flying like a shooting star. I feel a tinge of jealousy as I watch her go. I want to feel that confident about heading back in there. But the mere thought of reliving those nightmarish situations hold me back. I feel guilty and cowardly, but how can I let Alex stay in there while I'm out here—free?

"You could do as your mother suggested," Dorian suggests.

"Where do I even start?"

Dorian points to the huge, gleaming, white building behind me, and out of habit, I take in a big breath.

The mansion assigned for spiritual progression is vast. Architecturally, it's Greek, like the Parthenon, but bigger, at least ten times bigger. It has two rows of columns, one set in the outer part of an outdoor corridor and an inner set, framing the indoor structure. This pattern repeats five times over, as there are five stories to this mansion. Each level is identical to the first. There are two massive double doors that are open on the first level, freely inviting anyone who wishes to come in.

When I pass through the front doors I take an involuntary deep breath. Dorian shows me where the High Council meets, and I look at the spot with a little trepidation. But I take another deep breath and face the music. Well...there's technically no music at all, just a huge courtroom that is very intimidating, full of men dressed in white togas like judges in a courtroom. They are the High Council, and they hold my fate in their hands. They hear me out, ask some questions, nod sagely, murmur amongst themselves, and seem to come to some sort of agreement. While they deliberate I can't help wondering how it is that I'm here in the first place. Me? I've never been in trouble before. Not in school, not with my foster parents, not with the law while still alive— never! Now I'm before a Heavenly Council that holds the fate of my eternal soul in their hands.

They all stop their hushed murmurs and face me. One of them, the one who sits in the center of the bar, stands up. "Agatha did put you in a tough situation, one that you would have never been in, had you followed the light to begin with."

"I understand," I say meekly, feeling their eyes on me. All twelve of them are scrutinizing me, judging me. Thankfully, I feel no antagonism coming from them. On the contrary, they emanate a feeling of impartiality and if anything, pity, and a true desire to help me out, and that puts me somewhat at ease.

I don't say anything else so they begin another round of deliberation, this time through a mute telepathic link. After a great deal of what looks to be a mental back and forth, they all finally start nodding in obvious agreement.

"We are pleased that you have expressed a desire to confess and make amends. This you will do: You will be assigned a Spirit Guide, a special Spirit Guide. Him, you will listen to and obey. Him, you will comply with and never leave his side until he deems you ready. Understood?" one of the High Councilors says solemnly. I nod and look to Dorian, with a smile.

"Not him," the High Councilor who was the spokesperson says solemnly.

"Not him? Then who?"

"Me." What looks to be a huge winged statue adorning the wall, emerges from its stillness and moves forward, startling me in the process.

I look in all directions to see if any more of the statues that adorn this room are going to come to life as well. These creatures, that look as solid and immovable as stone, are in fact, not stone at all, but rather shallowly breathing beings that have been here all along—standing perfectly still—like Sentinels. This unnerves me, and I shift uncomfortably in my spot, feeling exposed and a bit deceived.

The reanimated statue is completely white and somewhat shimmery, just like marble. He's dressed like a Native American Indian, with lace-up moccasins and a white fur loincloth. He's bare chested, with straight, long, white hair, and is at least twelve feet tall. Instead of arrows, he has a sheath strapped across his chest, with the hilt of a sword sticking out from behind his back, conveniently placed between his colossal, snowy, white wings, that reach all the way to the ground.

"You sure know how to blend in," I say as I look around me, trying to hide my nervousness. None of the other creatures that line the walls move or even acknowledge my comment, but the one that stepped forward, tries to hide a smirk. He's enjoying this—immensely. I'm willing to bet that seeing the reaction of humans as they step forward gives them a kick every time.

As I look at him, a sudden feeling of familiarity sweeps over me, and for a second I'm sure that I know him. Maybe it's the fact that I have seen this type of creature before. I saw several of them, in fact, protecting Dorian while Agatha was trying to torture us. For some reason though, I wasn't as shocked to see them then as I am now. Perhaps back then I thought they were a figment of my imagination. Maybe at that time, I needed them to be larger than life in order to protect Dorian. Or maybe I was already so freaked out that nothing could have stunned me that night.

"Drymus has been assigned as your Spirit Guide. He is particularly well suited for the job. You must abide by his rules from now on. You must not leave his side. When he deems you ready, you will report back to us. Are you willing to comply?" The speaker for the High Councilors asks.

I turn and look at Drymus. He folds his arms across his chest, puffing it out in the process, intimating that I'm in for a singular experience in his expert, massive hands. The words "cruel and unusual punishment" cross my mind, and these last thoughts seem to escape my mind and reach his, making him bite his lower lip in an attempt at stifling a self-satisfied smile.

"Y—yes," I stammer, and the High Councilor taps the mallet once, making my sentence sound dismal and final.

We leave the High Council room, followed by an eerily mute Drymus, who reminds me of a devoted executioner looking forward to his task.

"So...I guess this is good-bye for now," Celeste says, eyeing the creature with apprehension.

"I guess," I respond hollowly.

"Don't worry, Tess. Drymus will take good care of you, won't you Dry?" Luz flutters to his side and wraps her arms affectionately around the creature's neck. He smiles with half his face and winks at her, while she plants a kiss on his cheek. With the other half of his face he's still eyeing me, like he's afraid to let me out of his sight. "Drymus and I got to work together on a mission sometime back. He'll be great!" Luz flitters back down to Dorian's side and snuggles next to him.

"She's right Tess, you have nothing to worry about. Really!" Dorian pats me on the back. "I've seen it. Trust me. He will help you." He looks intently into my eyes and in them I see the certainty of his words in his eyes. It reminded me of when in life, he would hand me one of his finished drawings; he had that same certainty, and that same surety then. It was his way of saying, "trust me".

"We'll see you soon, okay?" Dorian starts to leave, then turns back. "And I'm really proud of you for going before the High Council and all. It can be a daunting experience, but you'll see…it's better this way, face the issues head on and deal with them quickly." He winks at me, nods to Drymus, then flies off with Luz and Celeste.

Drymus and I are left standing here in the middle of this imposing white mansion, where the walls can literally see and hear. We are both completely speechless for a while, and he's so good at standing still that if I didn't know better I would think he turned back into a statue.

"Well then," he starts conversationally after a long uncomfortable moment passes. "Let's begin by making something very clear. I am NOT a creature, as your mind has been surmising. I am a Cherub."

"O—kay."

"Oh, give her a break, will you? You're not supposed to torment her." From an opening at the very top of the building, a blazing fire comes straight down on us. I shield my eyes with my arm and try to protect myself from the oncoming flames that are about to land right on top of me.

"Do you know what she's done? After all you've taught her! Aren't you the least bit upset?" Drymus speaks to the fireball as if it were an old friend. But the moment that the fire touches down on the ground, the flames extinguish, and a golden humanoid form appears. She looks like freshly polished gold, and is slightly smaller than the Cherub by a few inches. From the waist up, she looks human, with long golden dreadlocks and slightly feline features. From the waist down, she's a lioness—complete with furry hind legs and a long tufty tail. Her chest is covered by a golden fur halter-top, and she too has wings, but they are leathery like a bat's. She's so mesmerizing that my jaw drops, and I stare shamelessly at her.

"I've seen you before too," I finally manage to say, spellbound by her appearance.

"Yes, you have," she asserts, turning her attention back to me. "Many times before, actually." This last comment holds a little bit of bite in it. "I'm Dayspring. I gave you the tools to accomplish your life's mission. I also trained you before mortality."

I nod numbly. I remember bits and pieces of what she's talking about. I remember passing out and having a dream. I remember seeing her in that dream and then she gave me...fire!"

She chuckles. "Boy, you sure are a mess, aren't you Tess? Don't worry, Drymus here will straighten you out in no time. But first, the wedding!"

"You've got to be kidding me!" Drymus protests.

"Not at all," the lioness affirms boldly.

"She has to start right away, I don't know if you're aware of this, but she—"

"I am well aware of what *she's* done," she barks back, and I'm not too sure, but I think she growls a little too. "And *we* know, all too well, what it's like to do stupid things, don't we Drymus!" She enunciates his name slowly and with an edge of warning in her voice. Something in her growl or her voice sobers him right away and he stops protesting. Right then, another Cherub lands right next to Drymus and pats him chummily on the back.

"Hey," they both in turn say in greeting.

"Is she ready?" the newcomer says casually. "We've got to get this show on the road, as you humans say," he directs this last comment to me, with a pleasant smile.

"Kerubiel, she doesn't know what's going on yet. She doesn't remember," the golden creature says.

"Well, remind her, come on!" Kerubiel says impatiently.

The golden lioness turns to me and with a smile she purrs, "Tess, you made me a promise before you were born."

"I did?" I say incredulously.

"Yes, you did." She comes close to me and extends one hand. "May I?" she asks as the palm of her hand reaches for my cheek. I nod and she places her hand on the side of my face. The moment that her hand makes contact with my essence, a flurry of memories flash forward to my conscious mind.

I see a great white span of snowy terrain. I'm standing up above, and looking down on some movement of sorts...a game, a fight. A smile crosses my face when I realize it's a snowball fight! Next to me sits Dayspring, the golden lioness. I know her well, we are friends. She looks sad. Her vision is drawn to one person below—Kerubiel. He senses her and turns to look up at her, he loves her! He has always loved her, ever since they were mortals thousands of year's prior.

Another image flashes in my head: *I'm now surrounded by spirits. Dayspring is right in front of me; she looks annoyed, but happy. "I wanted you to be my Issa'ahot at my wedding,"* she informs me.

"What's an Issa'ahot?"

"Well, our wedding will be a mix between the two worlds—so you'll have to help me find a dress, then walk in front of me at the wedding ceremony while throwing white feathers into the air—so that I will be thoroughly covered in them before I get to the altar—there are more duties too, but I'll tell you about it later."

"That's beautiful, Dayspring, I would love to do it! But..." I look thoughtful for a moment, then crestfallen.

"Don't worry about it, Tess, I wasn't planning on getting married so soon. I mean, I want to...." She smiles at Kerubiel. *"But we have waited this long...and I want to have a big wedding. We want all our loved ones to be there, and it will take a while to get them used to the idea of us being together. Besides, your life won't take that long—I'll wait until you die. It might even take us longer than that!"* she says brightly.

"But, I won't remember you."

"Bah!" she dismisses my comment with a wave of her hand. *"We'll be friends again, this won't get between us."* She points to a massive wall of white...the Veil that separated my pre-mortal existence from my mortal life.

"I'll bring you up to speed after you die," she assures me, then the memory ends and I find myself looking back at the same face, bearing that same smile. "This is *me* bringing *you* up to speed."

"Oh," I feel a bit disoriented, like after watching a fast-paced 3D movie. The interesting thing is that it's all in my head. Physically I feel nothing, but the memory of feeling dizzy makes me wobble a bit. "I see," I look from one expectant face to another, and I muster a smile. "I would love to be your—your...Issa'ahot then. Nothing will make me happier!" I say with breathless enthusiasm.

Dayspring purses up her lips, unconvinced. "Well, it's the best I can hope for, given the circumstances."

She turns to Kerubiel and pushes him back. "You!" she orders, "make sure your Cherubs sound the trumpets." Her face softens, and a beaming smile crosses her face. "We're finally getting married!"

The moment that Dayspring unfurls her leathery bat wings and places me on her back, I know I'm in for the ride of my life—or after-life in this case. Soon I find myself being whisked away from my spirit realm and into outer space.

Drymus, my new babysitter, casts suspicious glances at me now and then as he flies like Superman next to Kerubiel. The three of them look like a force to be reckoned with, like a Heavenly Justice League. They're all very competitive, and before long, I find myself caught in the middle of a fierce flying race through space—one that Dayspring seems to be wining. Constellations, planets, moons, suns, whole galaxies even, zoom past us like shooting stars. I see things that I've only seen at the planetarium, and things that I've never seen before. I'd like to see these things in more detail, but Dayspring is flying so fast that everything melts into a shiny blur. In spite of the speed, on Dayspring's back, I feel like I'm on a leisurely pony ride. There is no jostling, no bumpiness, no turbulence, just smooth flying through space. The oddest part about this is that, as fantastic as all of this is, it feels very familiar, like I was born among these stars, like this is my long lost home and just now I'm coming back to it.

Finally, we enter the atmosphere of a huge planet, and from above, it looks very different than from Earth. While our planet is mostly blue, this one is mostly green. It looks foreign, *alien*, as well it should, I suppose, since it is a foreign planet.

As we make our descent and get closer to the landmass, I see why it looks so green from above. There are no oceans here, but there are lots and lots of ponds, pools, and lakes that are completely surrounded by the greenest tallest trees I've ever seen. It's like the Redwood forest on steroids here. This planet has mountains, hills, valleys, and it looks like an endless forested Paradise of green.

"I suppose you're taking her," Drymus says possessively as he makes a smooth landing on the Seraph mossy turf.

"I won't let her out of my sight," Dayspring says with a roll of her eyes. Drymus grunts and, before leaving, casts a warning look in my direction. What does he think I'm going to do? Start an alien war? Kerubiel follows him, but turns and winks at Dayspring before disappearing into the thick forest.

"The Cherub planet is very different from ours," Dayspring says wistfully as she watches her fiancé get swallowed by the woods. "They barely have any trees at all. Their planet is mostly jagged rocks with a patch of grass here and a bush there," she sighs.

"That sounds dismal," I say, conversationally. It feels easy to talk to her, even though we haven't said much to each other.

"Well, it is pretty in its own way, of course. The rocks are translucent, like what you'd call a diamond. When the sun is out, its light bounces off and makes beautiful rainbows and patterns on the ground, or anything solid for that matter. You should see it dance around Kerubiel's body when he stands still—it's really mesmerizing. I used to think he was so...well...white, until I saw him in his own planet. I was alive then, or I should say, we were both alive. We were trying to sign a truce between the two worlds, so he invited me to his. When I stepped inside his house, the sun was just setting, and the light that filtered through touched the side of his face and arms, and danced right on his skin. I was speechless, and I'm pretty sure that my mouth fell open." She shakes her head, and her golden dreadlocks bounce off my arm. "I felt like such an idiot. I got angry with him because I found him attractive, and that almost cost my world its peace."

"What happened next?"

"Kerubiel, as always, was gracious and ignored my rudeness. He had prepared a meal that was a combination of traditional meals from the two worlds. He personally cooked some of the dishes. It was hilarious. We laughed for the rest of the evening and gagged on most of his half-and-half creations. There were a few things that actually tasted decent and we're serving those at our wedding."

"What a great idea!"

"Here we are," she announces as we land on a mossy hilltop that is decorated for a huge wedding—huge as in Cherub and Seraph size— with rows of tall stools on one side of the isle for the Cherubs to sit on, and plush pillows on the other made for Seraph comfort. They are all facing the edge of the cliff, but there is no altar, or arbor, or anything really where the actual ceremony would take place.

"Where's the gazebo?" I ask.

"The what?"

"You know...the place where the officiator stands and pronounces you man and wife?"

She chuckles. "You're thinking like a human. We'll be over there." She points to thin air, and I frown perplexed.

She takes out one of her wings and shakes it slightly. "We can fly, Tess, both of us! Our officiator too." She looks smug, then saunters away.

"Who will officiate?" I call after her. "A Cherub or a Seraph? And won't it be kind of uncomfortable to hover there, flapping your wings in mid-air throughout the whole ceremony?" I say logically.

"If you had wings, you'd understand, " she snubs over her shoulder. "But, no, it won't be uncomfortable. We're proud of our wings and as to the officiator...you'll see," she taunts while suppressing a smile. "We will hover there, *flapping our wings*, as you so well put it," she says and points to a spot way off the edge of the cliff. "And there will be one row of Seraphs and one row of Cherubs, right here." She moves both her arms up and down in parallel lines, like a landing signal officer helping a plane to a safe landing. "Also *flapping their wings*," she adds with sarcasm. "And making arches out of fruiting zayit branches. The altar will also be *hovering* in mid-air, and my nephews who are my altar boys will hold it up. There, the officiator will marry us." She pointed to a spot, still further out. She stood erect and pensive looking at the spot that would soon make her a bride.

"What are zayit branches, and why all the mystery about the officiator? Who will it be?" I ask, full of curiosity now.

"Zayit is a holy plant that is used in all religious ceremonies in Seraph culture. I couldn't get married without it. As to the officiator, my lips are sealed, you'll just have to wait and see." She smiles, then suddenly sobers. "It's time to get serious now, I saved one last crucial detail for you and you alone."

"What's that?"

"Will you design me a dress?"

Chapter 7

I struggle to know what's real anymore. I know I've heard her; she sounded like she used to sound. I felt that old familiar feeling I used to feel when I dreamed of her in life.

Somehow, I still feel like that boy in high school, the one that thought he was going crazy. I was by all intents and purposes the all-American guy—football player, student government, popular, rich, cute girlfriend—I used to think I had it all. But then one day, one look from her changed everything. I tried to convince myself that there was no such thing as 'love at first sight', that it was all for books and stories. My parents even disagreed on this point. My dad swore that he fell in love the moment he saw my mother's eyes, and my mom always alleged that she didn't know she was in love until much later. As always with my mom, there was some dream and a drawing involved, her life always revolved around her dreams...and her drawings!

When I first saw Tess, I didn't know what had happened to me. It was odd, unlike anything I had ever experienced, and it made me feel uncertain of myself—something I've always hated. Her eyes held me captive. They were both gray and green, but they were more than that, they held a memory inside. I felt bound to them—to her—I knew that I always would be hers. The helplessness I felt over those new feelings made me recoil from her at first, and I felt a little trapped, like I had no choice but to be with her.

I felt unnaturally compelled toward her, forcefully magnetized to a girl I hardly knew. But try as I might to ignore those feelings, I couldn't stay away for long. Every time I saw her, that same feeling of being tied to her with invisible cords, came back. Still, I fought those feelings every day, and every day she won. Had she put a spell on me? Why was she invading my life—my dreams?

Everywhere I turned, her presence could be felt or seen. I felt her every time I smelled something fresh, like jasmine or mint—her scent. I saw her eyes every time I saw the sage-green moss that covered all our trees. I would think of her hair whenever I saw a black bird preening its wings. She was everywhere!

At one point I thought I could even hear her breathing while she sat at her desk. From my seat I could see the rising and falling of her chest with every breath she took. I could hear the air going into her throat, down her lungs and back out her mouth, over and over again, like the ticking of the clock. She reminded me of what I loved most—the ocean—her rhythmic breathing was like the waves, constantly washing up on to my mind.

I tried to avoid her all-together, but it was impossible; I felt sick without her, and better when I saw her. She brought sunshine and fresh air with her smile. Her lips…they curved into a smile every time she saw me, they touched her eyes, and she would bring order to my head for that moment. Then that order would leave, and all that was left was confusion.

One day I found her alone, in the rain, shaking, and lost. How I found her is still a mystery to me. How did I know where she would be? I never told her this in life, but that night, I knew I was going to find her. I was coming back from football practice; the way home has always been one way, and a straight shot at that. But that night, I turned and started driving in the opposite direction. I drove downtown instead, not knowing why or what was possessing me. All I know is that I was thinking of her, and, just as my mind was dwelling on a smile she had given me that day, I heard her in my head! Her voice sounded strained, scared, and pleading. *"Alex, help me, please!"* It was like an echo, reverberating in my head over and over again.

I sped up, feeling the urgency in her voice. I could feel how scared she felt, how wretched, miserable, and alone. She had no one, yet somehow, she knew she had *me*. I made turns as if I knew where I was going. I cut through traffic and found myself on the freeway. I exited somewhere and made a series of turns into an industrial part of town, until finally, in the distance, I saw her. She was being spot-lighted by a streetlight. The rain was pelting her, the drops looked like vicious little knives that stabbed her as she sat curled up in a ball. I felt her fear more keenly; I knew that she might take off running at any moment. But when she heard my voice she rushed to me as if she were expecting me!

Words could never explain what I felt when I held her in my arms for the first time. She was mine, simple as that. She belonged in my arms and together we were…home. The rest of that night was bitter-sweet for me. I kept oscillating between keeping her and letting her go. She needed to focus on school, she needed to get those scholarships and get to college on her own. I knew that if I got involved, I would get in her way and be a distraction.

My grandfather's advice—that when it comes to young love, "too good too soon," would spoil things—revolved in my head. "Relationships," he would say, "need to be developed at the right time. Otherwise you might ruin it by simply being too young and reckless."

For a moment there, that evening, we were so close. I felt her lips brushing against my own, and the proximity of her body made me greedy. So after I dropped her off at her foster home, I drove home, determined to call Eugenia and break up with her.

To my complete dismay, Eugenia was already waiting for me at home. She was talking with Katie my sister, and smiling with that fake smile of hers. Eugenia was pretending to give a crap about my sister, when in reality I knew she didn't. Katie looked up gratefully when she saw me, as though she couldn't wait for me to get home and relieve her of this tedious duty that she'd been sent to fulfill.

Why did I ever date Eugenia at all? I guess it was the idea of her that appealed to my vanity. Our parents were friends and we grew up together, in fact, I don't think I ever asked her out. We were pegged as a couple in kindergarten, and had been paired up ever since. She had always been spoiled, throwing tantrums when she didn't get her way, but I didn't seem to notice this until we were in high school. That's when I saw how mean-spirited and selfish she was, only concerned with how she could get what she wanted without having to work for it.

Ironically, what attracted me to Tess that night at my grandfather's house, was how unselfish she was. As he talked about her life with her foster brother, and how she had made the decision to take care of him—that's when it hit me! Not all girls are like Genie! Tess was only fifteen, yet she had taken on an immense responsibility and was *doing* something about it. Tess was selfless, kind, and ready to sacrifice her own comfort for the sake of her foster brother.

The contrast between the two became stark that night, and it woke me up from some sort of deep sleep. If I had felt anything for Tess before, after that night, it was solidified. I was in love. Nothing, no one would ever change that.

So when I saw Genie's fake, condescending smile the moment I got home, I knew that it was over. She knew it too, and panicked. She used all her powers of persuasion, but nothing worked. She became background noise to me from then on. She threw all kinds of fits, she cried, she begged, she even resorted to her parents and had them intervene. The end result was a last promise to take her to prom—which I did under duress.

Well, it wasn't the only result. Eugenia did go to school that next day and tried to bully Tess. I had no idea she was going to do that, or I would have been ready. My plan was actually to ask Tess out that day, but Genie got to Tess first, and apparently pretended that we hadn't broken up at all. Tess was mad, I could see it in her eyes. She thought I was weak and had no backbone. She did something stupid too; she went and got herself a boyfriend. Wes was a decent guy, but from that day on, I couldn't stand him. My pride was wounded, I wanted to explain, but at the same time I didn't want to waste my breath. I spent the rest of that school year trying to forget her. I failed, of course.

If my resolve was ever strong, it failed me completely while at Prom. When I saw her that night, there weren't words in our vocabulary that could describe her beauty. She was ethereal and earthly, all bound into one. A fairy and a goddess, fantasy made real! I knew I wouldn't be able to resist her, and I knew I wouldn't go home without a kiss from her, even if it meant upsetting Wes. A selfish thought crept up in me. Tess was mine, not his! He didn't dream about her almost every night, I did! Some mysterious force didn't lead him to her when she was alone and scared in the rain! He didn't know her at all, but I did!

Much later, and to my complete surprise, I found out she dreamed of me, too. If I was crazy, she was crazy too, and for some reason that made me feel better. The dreams were real, at least for us they were. Inexplicably, we had some sort of telepathic link that I was perfectly fine with. I should have been freaked out by it, but I wasn't. It felt... natural. We never lost it either, not even after we were married, not after I died and, well...haunted her. There was a long period though, when the connection seemed feeble, and only because I didn't want her to worry, I tried not to reach for her on purpose. I wanted her to live the rest of her life in peace. Did I do wrong? Did that change things for her? She might have remarried. Wes maybe. As disturbing as that thought is, it might be a possibility. That might explain what just happened here.

She was here. I felt her presence. I saw her! But my eyes often deceive me so I can't trust them. The link is unique though. It can't be madeup, so I can say with certainty that Tess is dead, and that she was here. I heard her mind, there's no mistake about that. I know I've been living inside my head for a long time here, but *that was Tess*. But for some reason she didn't want me to go to her. She wanted me to stay here. Stuck. Alone. Damned.

The deal made to Eugenia had been, "deliver Tess, and I'll free you from this place." But of course, Agatha didn't keep her end of the bargain; she took Tess instead and left Eugenia to rot in Hell.

"Figures," Eugenia mumbled under her breath when the rift closed right in front of her face. But as she turned, she saw, to her immense pleasure, that Alex was standing some distance away, looking like he had just been slapped. The two Hellhounds were retreating back into the shadows, leaving no evidence of the impending danger that they had posed to him, or the sacrifice that Tess made in his behalf.

"Good," Eugenia thought genially, suddenly forgetting her previous disappointment. "I'll stay here, with him." She straightened, fixed her most alluring smile on her face, and started to go straight to him to console him in his dark hour. Also, she wanted to reassure him of Tess' betrayal, not just of her betrayal to him, but to her as well. In her mind, it was now Tess who had broken the promise, not Agatha. "Fine friend, that Tess!" Eugenia muttered under her breath, with a crooked smile as she glided toward Alex in the darkness.

Just as she was about to reach Alex's petrified form, she realized one crucial point—she looked hideous! This stopped her dead in her tracks. Meanwhile, Alex seemed to regain enough of his senses to glide away, so Eugenia followed him instead, curious to see what would happen to him now that his precious Tess was gone.

It didn't take long for him to form a bubble again and start reviewing every aspect of her face and the ordeal that he had just gone through. Grimly, Eugenia watched as Alex's mind tried to reconcile his present with his past. She was about to leave when a familiar face caught her attention—her own—and quickly, she became engrossed in Alex's memories.

"So that's how he saw me?" she concluded, as she saw herself through his eyes. She had been standing in his living room pitching a fit because he was breaking up with her. She hated that night. It had been a slap to the face. She never imagined that he would dump her half way through senior year.

It was with more curiosity still that she saw what his best memory of her was. They had been eight or nine years old, it had been raining for days and her mom's lawn was getting swampy. They had been playing video games inside, but on a whim they took off running and went straight for the muddiest part of the yard. They jumped and sloshed in the muck until they tore up the grass and made a proper mud pit. They were like hogs in the mire and it had been fun—that is until their moms found them and got mad at them.

Eugenia had forgotten all about that day, never thought of it again in her life, until now. Yet Alex had held that memory as his best of her. Why? What was it about her that day that made him remember her with fondness?

Looking away, she felt a pang of guilt, remorse, and anger, all mixed together. She was responsible for his death and the weight of this hung heavy on her, like an anvil on her chest that restricted her breathing—an odd sensation to have, since she had no body—yet the feeling was quite keen and poignant. She hadn't meant to, it was a moment of stupidity—okay maybe not just one moment, several perhaps—but she had not meant to cause *him* harm. Yet the facts remained, she had ended the life of the one person who had been a true friend to her. Even if the hired gunman had gotten the intended target—Tess—she would have still ended his life. She could see that now; he didn't just love Tess, he adored her.

"Why couldn't I be loved like that?" she thought bitterly and her hate for Tess came back threefold. "Why couldn't I find someone who adored me? I was pretty, intelligent, rich. Even Agatha found someone, cold as she was, average looking, and creepy to boot! Yet she found someone who worshiped her! But not me, why? What was wrong with me? What *is* wrong with me?"

Anger boiled inside until she was filled with it. "To Hell with Alex and Tess! To Hell with all of them!" she cursed out loud, wanting to give in to the fullness of her rage, yet she couldn't, not fully. There was another part of her, a small part, wedged somewhere deep inside of her that ached. She didn't know why or what it was. But that twinge of guilt, or remorse or…whatever it was, made the whole thing simply unbearable.

While she was alive, she could numb or alleviate those feelings with medication, or alcohol—something she resorted to often. But now, there was nothing of that sort to rely on. She had to deal with her conscience head on, or go back to making her own bubble. But even that bubble didn't count as an escape, because deep down she always knew she was daydreaming. She was tired of pretending, she was tired of escaping, and she was ready to move on. The question was, how?

"My bubble is very thin so I heard you. Are you okay?" a man called from a floating living room. He looked rough, long hair, long beard, a leather vest, and tattoos all up and down his bare arms. The man's "living room" looked incongruent with his looks; it was refined, high class, with red velvet high-back chairs, a library full of books, a roaring fire on an stone hearth, and a full length mirror perched off to one side.

Eugenia looked at him and snubbed him at once with a shrug of her shoulder, just like she would have when a guy she thought was way below her standards paid her any attention. Quickly, though, she remembered that her standards should perhaps be a lot lower now. Maybe she should change her position on who she befriended. Giving one last look at Alex's bubble, she bitterly glided over to the man's side. "As fine as anyone could be here," she answered dryly.

"Aye," the man acknowledged with an accent that caught Eugenia by surprise. "Been 'ere long?"

"Don't know. It sure feels that way."

"Please come in," the man said, with a sweeping motion into his make-believe living room.

"Was this your home in life?"

"No," the man said, pronouncing the 'o' with the hint of an Irish accent. "But it's what I would have liked to have if I could have afforded it."

"Mm," Eugenia instinctively said with derision, and once again had to check herself because things were different now. She was no longer pretty, she was no longer rich, and she was no longer anything special.

"How come you were just standing there? Didn't you protect yourself?"

"If by protecting myself you mean forming a bubble, I did. But reality burst it," Eugenia said bitterly.

"Ah! Reality," the man turned to the mirror and looked in it. "I often wonder what that is."

"Are you obsessed with yourself or what?"

The man smiled and looked just a bit handsome for a moment. "I'm not checking to see if I look pretty."

"Then what?"

"Tell me, what do you see when you look at me?"

"A man."

"Obviously," he said impatiently. "But what else?"

"I see…" Eugenia stood up from one of the velvet chairs and glided up to him for a better inspection. She rattled off all the obvious faults that the man had—his long hair, his unkempt beard, his ugly vest, his many tattoos—but then, when she looked into his eyes she saw something else. "I see, I see…"

"What? What do you see?" the man asked eagerly.

"That there's more to you."

The man looked back at Eugenia and said nothing for a while. "There's more to you too," he finally concluded. Surprised, Eugenia took a step back, catching her breath, more out of habit than physical necessity.

"I deserve to be here, you know. I hired a man to take the life of another person," Eugenia confessed and her new friend sat on one of his chairs, looking interested in whatever she had to say. "I never gave death and the afterlife much thought while alive, none at all actually, but the moment I passed and felt that darkness was engulfing me, I knew," she laughed cynically. "I knew I was in for it, then. This was reckoning time for me. Somehow I managed to fall far below even my own expectations. How did I do it?"

"I ask myself that question all the time," the man muttered dryly. They both stared at each other in silence for a long time, each secretly wondering if something good could ever come out of this Hell.

Chapter 8

Talk about expanding my horizons! Dayspring gives me the honor of designing her dress and the wedding is to take place at sunset. At sunset!

In her planet, they keep time much like on Earth, by the rotations of their planet around the sun. The only difference is that their sun is much larger, and their planet is also much bigger than Earth, so their days have thirty hours in them instead of twenty-four. It is now noon by their time, and somehow I have to design, make, and fit her dress all before nightfall.

I have to account for wings, hind legs, and a tail. I have to take into consideration the cultural traditions of two species, Cherubs and Seraphs. And most importantly, I have to make her look stunning for her big day. And when I say big, I mean BIG! Thousands of Cherubs and Seraphs have been invited; this is to be the equivalent of a royal wedding. Yep. No pressure.

"Stop pacing! You're making me nervous," Dayspring barks.

"Nervous! You just sprang this on me!"

"You don't think you can do it?" she challenges, and I stare at her for a while, simmering in my own frustration.

I pace in silence a few more times, when suddenly it hits me! Narrowing my eyes, I walk in circles all around her to make sure that my idea would fit all the…requirements.

"What? What is it? Did you get an idea?"

"Shush…I'm thinking!"

"Did she just shush me?" Dayspring asks someone from her entourage. "I've never been shushed before."

"Hush!"

I have to admit it when I'm brilliant. Once I was able to convey my idea to the Seraph seamstresses that Dayspring had appointed to help me, we set out to work. I was able to show them my idea, by projecting my vision of the dress—in the same way that people who made-up those bubbles back in Prison did—by way of a 3D version of Dayspring, wearing my imaginary dress. When the seamstresses saw what I was thinking, they stood openmouthed for a few Seraph minutes, which are much longer than ours, then finally got to work. They were amazingly fast at their task, and before too long they had a template for my idea. Meanwhile I sent out a couple of Cherubs who Dayspring had left on hand, to find me the specific items that I needed. They looked at me like I had fallen off my rocker when they heard my requests, but they obeyed nonetheless.

Now, all I have to do is fit the bride with her dress.

"So?" Dayspring saunters in, her curiosity piqued by all the rumors she's been hearing all afternoon about my odd requests and the total secrecy that I put everyone under. The minute I had my idea, I had banished Dayspring from the room. I told her to go take care of all the other final details, and that I had this under control. She left reluctantly, but now she's back, a bundle of nerves, with a good dose of elation mixed in.

"Stand right here." I order.

She stands on a little pedestal and I call for my assistants to fly in with the dress. Upon seeing it, Dayspring gasps.

"It's—it's—" We all look at her expectantly. "It's beautiful! Out of this world!"

"That's right. You hire an alien; you get out of this world," I proclaim.

A few of the assistants giggle, and I know that I just made fashion history in this planet. The seamstresses help Dayspring into her dress, and she looks radiant, even better than what I had envisioned.

"When I heard a rumor that you had Cherubs flying all over the Universe trying to find you a specific thread…I thought you were going overboard. And you did! But wow!"

"You know, it really helps to have this new ability, to project whatever I can think of. Can you still do it once you resurrect?"

"With a lot of practice you can," she assures me as she checks herself in the mirror.

"It came in handy when she was trying to tell us what to do," one of the Seraph seamstresses affirms. "We've never done this kind of thing before. She really has opened a new door to fashion here."

"Yeah! Thread made from a moth? I would have never thought of that!" another pipes in.

"Silk," I correct. "The thread is called silk, and it's made from a caterpillar. I'm so glad that the bugs were willing to donate. I never thought of caterpillars as the giving, or the understanding type." I had asked the Cherubs to go to Earth to get me some silk thread, but they refused to infiltrate the mortal realm for such a trivial thing. So I asked if they had silk and they knew nothing of the sort. So I sent them to find an expert on caterpillars from either of their planets. They were amazed to find that, indeed, a type of caterpillar existed on the Seraph planet that spun a silky cocoon. The entomologist directed them to some of these caterpillars, and the Cherubs asked them personally to give of their silk for Dayspring's wedding dress. Miraculously, the caterpillars agreed and personally spun a pile of thread for her dress. Katie would willingly die again for a chance to talk to these caterpillars!

Once I had the silk thread, I was able to start my end of the project. Immortal matter had substance to me, so I was able to handle every-thing they brought to me. I could also move my hands as fast as I could think of them to move, so once I had all the items I needed, I worked swiftly.

The dress is completely covered in snowy, white feathers, freshly plucked from a rare bird that is native to the Cherub planet. The bird is actually something like a swan mixed with a dinosaur; it's big, and kind of mean, but since their world is now harmonious and millennial-like, the bird let himself be preened for a small price—a squeaky-chew toy. The Cherubs found this request rather unusual, but they agreed to do it, because they were not willing to give up their own feathers for the project.

"These are Cygnus feathers?" Dayspring asks admiringly as she feels the soft, downy feathers that cover her dress.

"Yes. The tips are dipped in spiritual gold paint from Earth's Heaven." I smile. It really looks as good as it sounds. The spiritual ink adds the perfect finishing touch, just like the silk thread. The soft, almost transparent color of the golden spiritual ink was enough to add a light shimmer to the tip of the feathers, but translucent enough to be delicate. I attached each feather myself with the thin silk thread. The embroidery I did was embellished to look like a super-fine, flowering vine, and to a Seraph—tiny, tiny. I guess, to them, I was *The Tailor of Gloucester*—or rather—the mice, which stitched and sowed a fine dress. My needlework looked minute to the Seraphs, and terribly intricate.

The long train is also completely covered with the feathers. From the bust up, the feathers are fanned upward. From the bust down, I placed them so they fanned down—there was no skirt, of course— the front of the bodice was long enough to reach her hind legs, the feathers, giving it a wispy sort of hem. The backside has a heart-shaped opening at the shoulder blades, making room for her wings. The train is not only long, but also wide—so wide that we'll have to enlist extra Seraph bride's maids to hold it up while the couple hovers in mid-air.

"Now make sure that the train is not perfectly straight the whole time, it has to ripple just a bit so that it has more flow, like, like…" I reach for the right description, but it eludes me.

"…Like nothing we've ever seen." Dayspring finishes.

"So, you like it?"

A tear slides down her cheek and that tells me all I need to know.

On cue, twenty Cherubs start sounding their trumpets, and from the horizon, a figure cloaked in brightness floats forward. All around me, I hear gasps and soft pleased murmurs. The light that extends from the figure exceeds that of the sun, and its rays graze us, who are sitting on the hillside, like a soft caress. The moment that one of those rays reaches me, I feel all the love He has for me and I feel completely overwhelmed. I would like to run to Him, get closer, feel more…but I can't. He stands under a single arch made out of the fruiting zayit branch that Dayspring was telling me about. Two floating Cherub children form the arch. The trumpets start playing a different wedding tune—a march of sorts—that is spellbinding. Kerubiel, the groom, floats forward. He calmly saunters, with a huge smile on his face, under the tunnel of the green zayit, followed by Drymus and another Seraph who bears an uncanny resemblance to Dayspring. *"Daystar,"* the name comes to me, it floats to me like a radio wavelength, and the thought that I had a whole life before my actual mortal life hits me anew. I have been told this before, but it never seemed real until now that actual memories are coming to me all on their own. It feels a lot like when I was alive and would remember a part of my forgotten early childhood, fleeting, yet packed with information.

When Kerubiel and his escorts reach the floating arch, they exchange friendly glances with *Him*, then take their places to one side of the floating altar. The music changes again, and now it's my turn to perform my duties as Dayspring's Issa'ahot. I walk in first and start throwing feathers in the air; audible gasps tell me that Dayspring is making her entrance behind me.

I hear a buzz of amazed comments about how beautiful Dayspring looks and how extraordinary her dress is. From the corner of my eye I see that some Seraphs and Cherubs are pointing at me: the human dress-maker and Issa'ahot.

"Is there anything conventional about this wedding?" some murmur astounded.

My instructions are to move aside once I reach the altar, to make way for Dayspring. This I do, but not before sneaking a glance in *His* direction, I want to see Him, finally, see Him. He directs a brief, but purposeful smile my way, and in an instant I'm filled to the brim with His love for me. In the briefest of milliseconds that He takes to acknowledge me, He conveys more information than I can process. He—the one they call the First One, and we on Earth call Jesus Christ— takes the time to tell me of his love, appreciation, thankfulness for my efforts, and willingness to fulfill my mission in life. Yet I also feel rebuked for what I did. His reproof is stern and serious, but has no anger in it. It's more like a warning and a plea to fix my own mess. And before I know it, His attention shifts to Dayspring, but I remain filled with an unspeakable peace.

Once Dayspring reaches the altar, her brother Daystar comes to her side and kisses her on the cheek. He gives her away and the ceremony begins.

His actual voice is both like thunder and a babbling brook. His words are precise and full of meaning, but I find that I'm not listening. My mind is still trying to process all of the previous communication He conveyed to me. All I know right now is peace—complete inner peace.

This peace, however, gets mingled with a foreign feeling—a scream rather—of desperation. It's Alex. His mind is screaming, overloaded with grief and pain, reaching an intolerable point, a breaking point.

"Alex?"

"Tess?" The surprise and alarm in his voice sounds crisp and clear in my head.

"Yes! It's me! I'm sorry, I tried to help but—"

"Get out of my head! I never want to hear from you again, you hear me?"

"Alex, don't say that, please. I'm doing all I can to help you, I promise!" Even as I say those words guilt sweeps through me at the fact

that I'm not telling him the truth, I'm not doing all I can, I'm designing clothes, attending a wedding, enjoying myself, all while he's losing his mind. He sees all this in my head, of course. I can't hide anything from him while we are linked. A sneer forms in his lips, and a swell of bitterness sweeps over him, adding to his torment.

"Alex please, you don't understand, please let me—" It's no use, he shuts me out. All I can see now is bitterness poisoning him, quite literally, from head to toe. *"Don't bother with me, Tess. I'll be fine. You just go and enjoy your after-life, don't let me ruin it for you."* And just like that, he severs our link, and I'm left feeling a blank static-like emptiness that feels like a bucket of ice water has just been poured on me.

In looking up, I realize that not only was the service over, but He's gone too, and with Him, that peaceful feeling. All I have left now is the memory of the warmth, tainted with Alex's unforgiving last words.

The guests are mingling amicably and reminiscing about the bride and groom's long past. I feel completely out of place here. I'm the only human and the only ghost. The previous excitement over the dress and all my accomplishments seem ridiculous to me now and all I want to do is get out of here.

"Great job!" Drymus says conversationally.

"Thanks," I look around for a way out, and I realize that I flew here on Dayspring's back. There is no way I'll ever find my way back to my planet's spirit realm all on my own. I don't think I ever quite figured out how to get to the airport without a GPS back on Earth, so interplanetary travel is definitely out of the question.

"Stranded?" he asks, amusedly, obviously reading my thoughts.

"Yeah, I guess with all the excitement, Dayspring forgot to find me a ride back."

He laughs heartily. "I guess even the mighty Dayspring makes mistakes now and then," he jokes. "I'll give you a ride, don't worry."

"Um, thanks."

He laughs again, then without any further warning, he whisks me up like a rag doll and places me between his wings. His hugeness hits me anew and I quickly wrap my arms around his massive neck for safety.

Unlike Dayspring he flies upright. He only slants forward slightly so I don't slide off. "Hold on!" He flaps his huge wings a few times to gain height, and laughs thunderously at my trepidation. "You humans are always so fond of your earth. Come by it honestly I guess, since you were formed from the element."

"What do you mean? What element where you formed from?"

"Wind," he states with a tinge of pride.

"And Dayspring?" I ask.

"Fire," he laughs as if it were obvious.

"Is there a water?"

"Sure. They are brand new in fact, their first world just now got inhabited by the first beings."

"Really? What do they look like? Mermaids?"

"Not really, not like the mythical creatures from your planet. They are humanoids, like us, but they're aquatic. They have legs and webbed feet and hands, by-dorsal fins on their backs—much like my wings here—but they are small, like my hand." His hand was about a foot long, so not that tiny, but small enough. "They are also incredibly color-ful, shimmery shades of purples, blues, greens, and yellows. They are truly remarkable."

"Can I see them?"

"You can't interfere with other planets. Not unless you are assigned to them."

"Have you interfered?"

"I haven't been assigned to their planet, no. But I did train some of the pre-mortal spirits, just like I trained you."

"I'd like to do that some day," I muse.

"You might just get to—some day." He smirks, and snorts a chuckle.

The speed at which Drymus is traveling is dizzying; I try to picture the water creatures as a diversion, but all I can think of is to hold onto him a little tighter. I wonder what would happen to me if I fell off his back and into empty space? Would I float aimlessly for ever?

"So who's faster, me or Day?"

"Huh?"

"Who's faster? You know, at flying?"

Constellations are zooming by me so fast that even without the threat of actually throwing up, I feel queasy.

"You are," I say dryly.

He catches my drift and slows down. My surroundings start to look less like streaks and more like actual things. I find myself enjoying this pace much better and I tell him this.

"Sorry," he apologizes. "My competitive nature always gets the best of me. I've been told once or twice to, um, how do you say it on Earth? Oh yeah, chill out."

"So even though you're a resurrected being, you are still not perfect," I point out.

"Obviously," he states. "We all have an eternity to work on that, and eternity takes, well, forever!"

We both laugh and I find that I like this big guy.

"I think I remember you, from before."

"Good! I'm glad! Otherwise you're hitching a ride on an alien from another planet who's twice your size, and that would be awkward."

I laugh again, and as my laughter fades, I feel that empty feeling again—the one that Alex's accusations left me with.

"So, are you ready to obey my every command and Open?"

"The sooner the better."

We are quiet for a while and I notice lots of interesting things, things that I know Alex would love to see—colorful cloud formations, debris that floats around a planet's orbit, fiery suns, and distant galaxies.

"You're sure about that?"

"Yes, I am. The High Council says I have to Open before I can go and get Alex, so let's get on with it."

"You're in luck you know," Drymus comments after a short silence.

"How so?" I ask, distracted by how many colors space really has. It's not black at all; it's actually filled with myriads of color, like a strange garden of stars.

"I happen to be an expert at a certain type of Opening."

"What type?" I ask, suddenly very interested because his tone of voice sounds mischievous.

"I'm the only one I know of that dares Open spirits the fast way."

"Dares? What do you mean, 'dares?'"

"Well, I don't know why other Spirit Guides don't try it. It's perfectly safe. It might not be fun…but it's safe."

"What do you mean by, 'not fun?'" I ask, suddenly alarmed.

He doesn't answer. Instead an impish grin stretches across his face, then he extends his wings all the way out, and we start to glide in a downward descent toward Earth. Instead of entering Earth's regular physical atmosphere, we enter a different type of layer, the spiritual realm.

Once I'm safely on spiritual ground, he shakes his wings out slightly and cranks his neck to both sides in a stretch. We are back at the entrance of the huge Parthenon mansion. Spirits are coming and going into the building like it's the most popular mall around. A few Cherubs too, come and go from this building looking like average college professors, some holding scrolls, others holding tablets, all looking very professional and committed. A few of them acknowledge my companion, Drymus, exchanging a few polite words in their native language.

"Why so many Cherubs and no Seraphs?"

He shrugs. "Seraphs are more antisocial that way. They mostly keep to themselves. After you." He sweeps his arm around with a welcoming gesture toward the steps.

"Dayspring doesn't seem antisocial," I say, rooted to the spot.

"Dayspring was assigned to be your personal trainer, back in pre-mortal life. She had to." He pauses then adds with a more subdued tone, "At first, she had to. She quickly found that she really liked you."

"So our friendship is not a common occurrence?"

"No. Not common at all." He makes the same sweeping motion toward the steps, a little annoyed now, so I start moving.

"You never answered my question, earlier. What's not fun about your way of Opening?" I say as I climb a few steps, then realize that I can float all the way up much faster.

"You should show me a little more respect, and confidence too, you know. You've been appointed to do all that I say."

"You are my own form of cruel and unusual punishment, aren't you?"

"I wouldn't say cruel..." he admits with sarcasm.

Unexpectedly, I feel very comfortable around him, like I would around an old friend, yet I do still feel a healthy dose of fear and respect for him. "So, where to Sensei?" I ask, once we're inside the building. The whole thing is marble white; it looks sterile and cold like a hospital. The middle of the hall is open, and Greek columns line the perimeter, forming four hallways that connect with each other. Doors line the walls, all tall and solid white. Off to one side I can see the double doors that I know lead to the High Councilor's court—a place I don't want to go back to unless I have good news to report. Looking up, in the middle of the open hall, I see that there are several stories of the same type of hallways and doors, all perfectly lined up, one after the other. Some doors open, and spirits come out, shake the hands of their Spirit Guides and leave. Some look troubled, others relieved.

"Sensei? What's Sensei?" Drymus mutters. "Oh Yeah, Asian Earth culture, it means teacher, trainer, or master," he recites like a memorized fact.

"Y—yeah..." I bite my lip, and look around.

"So, what do I call you? Xuéshēng?"

I stare at him for a moment. "I don't know what you just said."

We stand there, wordlessly staring at each other for a few awkward moments. And the fact that we're both aliens to each other becomes very obvious.

Chapter 9

We fly straight up to the third floor. No need for elevators here, I guess. I follow him past several doors, until Drymus finally stops at one particular door that isn't marked in any way. He opens it for me, and makes another sweeping motion for me to enter.

Inside, the room is bare, but for one tall stool for Drymus and what looks like a wide screen TV on the wall. Besides these two things there's nothing else.

"What, no couch?"

"Why would you need a couch?" he asks, perplexed.

I shake my head. "Never mind. So what now? What is this special way of Opening spirits that you and only you can do?"

"I didn't say that only I could do it. I just said that only *I* dared do it."

"Why? What is it?"

"Why do you want to Open?"

"I was told I had to by the High Council."

"Why?"

"Because..." *They want me to jump through their hoops, and because they don't trust me after what I did,* I think, but don't say out loud. However, the second I think it, my every thought is displayed on the big screen TV, in movie form. All the images that made up that thought played out instantly, leaving me completely exposed. "Are you kidding me?" I say shrilly. "Is that thing going to display all my thoughts? Who else has access to this, besides you?

"Does it matter?" he responds dispassionately, like a scientist studying a lab rat.

"Yes, it matters," I affirm roundly.

"Don't forget, that even if the Probe wasn't here, I still can read thoughts. I knew what your thoughts were."

"So why that—that Probe thing?" I point to the infernal device, feeling infringed upon.

"It's for your own benefit, really. The Probe will help you see yourself more clearly. It will expose you to...yourself."

I hide my face in frustration, and wish I had that couch to lie on. I see now that there is a good reason for it in a shrink's office, I feel so uncomfortable standing here like a social experiment.

"If you'd like I can have one brought in," Drymus says sensibly, trying to sound accommodating.

"No!" I bark back. "Let's just get on with it." I sigh. "What was your last question?"

"Why did the High Council want you to Open?"

"I don't know exactly, but somehow Opening will help me find Alex or make me ready to find him, or something." I peek over at the screen of the Probe with apprehension, and it remains perfectly blank.

"It only works when you say one thing and mean another."

"Oh." *Probe my—. It should be called the tattler.* And on queue the Probe displays my last stream of consciousness complete with all the visual imagery.

"Okay then," Drymus says, fighting the urge to smile. "Lets move on." He adjusts himself on the stool and his wings quiver reflexively, like a dog's leg when stretched. "Yes, you are right about why the High Council wanted you to Open, but that's not all. You already know that Open spirits have nothing to hide. They are perfectly transparent, not to be confused with perfect," he warns. "You saw your own mother Open right before your eyes."

"Yes."

"You could see that she was not perfect, but you could also see that she had worked through and fixed all the major issues. She's ready for her final trial. If she remains Open, she could be judged right now and she would inherit the highest reward that Heaven has to offer—Earth itself—glorified and purified."

"Same with Dorian and Luz."

"Yes, but they didn't have to work through anything. They were innocents in life, and that gets them an automatic pass in the afterlife."

"Good," I say simply. "They deserve it."

"You, however...have a lot to work through."

I nod, ashamed.

"Most spirits take a long time to Open. They have lots of little sessions like this one where they work through their issues. They do it this way because it's a more natural pace. To do it any faster than that, would be...painful."

"Somehow I get the feeling that you're not going to let me do this at a natural pace."

He affirms. "You expressed an interest in doing it quickly, did you not?"

"Y—yes. I did. I mean, I see no point in delaying it. I figure the longer it takes me to Open, the longer that Alex has to suffer in there, and the longer before I can explain to him what happened."

"That's true," he says, but I can tell that something else is bothering him now. I look at the screen, but the dang Probe is not showing me *his* thoughts. "I haven't said anything I don't mean," he reminds me with a know-it-all, singsong sound to his voice.

I roll my eyes.

"But even if I do help you Open quickly, it doesn't guarantee that you'll be able to get Alex right away. You'll have to ask permission from the High Council first, then—"

"Yes, yes, ask for permission, grovel in pain, and play by the rules. I get it. So can you do it? Can you help me Open quickly?"

"I can, but you understand that it's not going to be pleasant."

"Yes! You've made it abundantly clear, I'll sign the waiver, you won't get sued," I say annoyed. "I do have a question though, how is it that you know so much about this way of Opening? And why are you the only one who dares do it?"

"Because, I'm the only one who has gone through it."

"You Opened fast too?" I ask, incredulously.

"I had to. Like you, I was under a self-imposed deadline. Like you, I felt that the sooner I fixed myself the better for those I loved."

I stare at him, intent on his every word.

"You might find this hard to believe now, but like your Alex, I was stuck in Spirit Prison for a while."

I narrow my eyes and peer into his. "You've been to Spirit Prison?"

"Yes, my planet's of course. Right after my mortal life, I went straight to Hell." He raises one of his eyebrows and exhales. "In life, I wasn't necessarily good." He pauses for a moment, letting that sink in for a second. I never thought that a high-ranking angel like Drymus would ever be anything but good.

"I wasn't terribly bad either," he corrects with an edge to his voice. "I was a warrior, like your Alex. I fought in the same war in which Dayspring fought, but for the other side, the Cherub side. We were enemies then." He crosses his arms around his broad, bare chest and inhales.

"But so was Kerubiel, and look at them now!"

"Yes," he nods grimly, while letting the air out of his lungs slowly. "But they were not me. They fought out of necessity. I on the other hand…" He lets that sentence die, not wanting the Probe to display how ruthless he really had been during that time. I, however, can discern what he means. Bits and pieces of information float my way—calloused, unfeeling, angry—he had been all those things and perhaps more.

"Kerubiel and I are childhood friends. We grew up literally next door to each other and we are like brothers. But I was always the angry one, always getting into trouble. I started fights, and Kerubiel ended them. He always had my back though; he never left me to hang. I always got us into so much trouble, but he never complained, or got angry with me.

"When we grew up, we both joined the military. We were at war with the neighboring planet of the Seraphs. I wanted to kill all the Seraphs; he wanted to bring peace and resolution to the conflict. He moved quickly up the ranks and got promoted, and I served right under him. One day, we had received intelligence that the camp of the Seraph leaders was nearby, so we made our camp for the night and Kerubiel told us to wait until the morning before we attacked. He believed in fighting honorably, I believed in winning at all costs.

"Both sides were tired that night. We had all been fighting for days and were operating on little to no sleep. I didn't agree with his decision to wait. I thought we should attack during the night and get it over with. He pulled rank on me and that made me angry." Drymus shakes his head, and tightens his lips, to imply the extent of his anger. "Well, let's just say that I was very angry. I pushed him aside and told him that this war would never end if we went soft on them. He ordered me to my bunker and I obeyed, but I couldn't sleep. I waited until everyone in my camp was asleep. Then, arming myself with only one weapon, my dagger, I sneaked past the sentry and stealthily infiltrated enemy camp.

"It didn't take me very long to find where the leaders of the rebellion were sleeping. I just had to choose which one I would kill first. I chose him, because I thought that she was weak and that I would be able to overtake her easily if something went wrong with her brother."

"Wait, who are you talking about?"

Drymus sticks his hand out, halting my questions. "They were sleeping in the same tent, so I knew that I would have to be quick and precise. I might be able to kill them both, but I knew that chances were that I would get caught and killed myself. So I crawled into their tent and drove my dagger through his heart."

"What?" I can't believe it! Is he talking about—?

"Yes," he says, reading my thoughts. "I killed Daystar, Dayspring's brother."

His words stuck to the space between us like a thick wall. He murdered the same person who stood next to him at his best friend's wedding!

"It was a long time ago," he reads my mind again. "Daystar has forgiven me, and so has Dayspring."

I can't speak. Memories of Dayspring telling me about her life flash before me. I start to piece together the bits that I remember and group them with what Drymus is telling me.

"In a way, I was responsible for Kerubiel and Dayspring's first meeting," Drymus continues with a sheepish look. "As always, Kerubiel had to clean up my mess. Dayspring woke up and caught me trying to escape. She pounced on me and we struggled. I had underestimated her," he says incredulously. "I was promptly captured and imprisoned."

"Thanks to that, Dayspring and Kerubiel had to meet. They agreed on a prisoner exchange. He wasn't about to let me rot in some Seraph prison, even if I deserved it."

I'm still staring at him; I can't believe that the glorious angel before me is a murderer.

"*Was* a murderer," he rectifies my unspoken thoughts. "And don't forget that it was war. But you're right." He takes in a deep breath, owning my severe judgment of him. "I'm not telling you this to make excuses for myself; I simply want you to understand." He starts pacing the room that now looks ridiculously small for him.

"Needless to say, after the war was over, I wasn't much nicer. I married and was a terrible husband. Later I became a father and was quite inept at that as well. When I died, I simply could not exist among those who were wholesome and guilt-free. My shame imprisoned me, and kept me there for a long, long, time."

"Who got you out?"

He chuckles a mirthless laugh, "As always, Kerubiel."

I nod, understanding.

"Once I was out, I still felt...odd, like I didn't belong. Like you feel right now," he says and I look up, shocked at how well he picked up on that particular feeling that I had been keeping at bay. "I could see the damage and the pain that I had caused my family. Their looks of mistrust were too much to bear, so I decided to put a quick end to it all."

"What did you do?" I gasp.

"I Opened—fast! I don't recommend it to just *anyone*. In fact, I don't recommend it period. But you might be the exception."

"So once you Opened, everyone forgave you?"

"Among those who are Open, forgiveness comes naturally."

"That's nice." I pause to think what that would be like. I have a hard time picturing a world where people don't hold grudges and readily forgive each other. In fact, I can't fathom it, but it does sound lovely. "So...how will it work?"

A wide grin spreads across Drymus' face as he turns and stands right before me, looming over me like a snowy avalanche. He then extends one huge hand toward my face, as if he were going to smother me.

"I thought this would be fast! You said, 'I know the fast way'," I hiss. "But we've been here for—for," I look around the barren room for any signs of time passage, but I see none other than my tired mind screaming that I've been at this for way too long, and want no more of it.

Every time I see that mammoth hand of his plunging its way down toward my head, I know I'd better catch my breath, because the minute those sausage-size fingers make contact with my cranium, I'll be dunked once more into the deep waters of remembrance. Once I'm down there it feels exactly like I'm drowning. Every time I'm plunged into a memory, I feel like my lungs are about to collapse for lack of air. I have to keep reminding myself that I don't need air, that I'm already dead, that I have no need for breathing. Yet, the feeling of drowning remains, and when I come out of the memory I'm gasping and gulping, and wishing I could breathe again.

Retrieving memories is done in the same way as Dayspring did it, when she wanted me to remember my promise to be her Isa'ahot—by placing one huge hand on the side of my face. It reminds me of the Vulcan mind-meld, only that Drymus' hands are so enormous that instead of just touching my temple and my cheek, his hand wraps all the way around my head. I often fear that if he's not careful he's going to rip it off. The Probe—of course—immediately shows my many disturbing fears, mixed with some old Star Trek episodes, where Spock performs this task. To say that Drymus finds this humorous is a complete understatement. He still suppresses a smile every time his hand has to make contact with my head, and once or twice, I've caught him mockingly saying, "My mind to your mind. My thoughts to your thoughts." The jerk! It is one thing to have my every thought revealed to him, it's quite another to see him making fun of them.

"You humans are such thespians," he laughs with a shake of his head.

"Oh yeah? How do Cherubs entertain themselves?"

"Not by dressing up and pretending to be someone else," he says smugly. "We have sports. One in particular is the most entertaining of all. It's a combination of what Earthlings call martial arts, fire dancing, and sword fighting. It's really—"

"Yeah, yeah…really remarkable, a true show of skill and prowess," I mimic mockingly, with my best human thespian skills. When he sees the smirk on my face, he's reminded of his torturous task, and he promptly goes back to it.

Besides this brief respite, the rest of this process has been nothing but painful, shameful, and demoralizing. We are working our way backwards through time, and it's getting harder and harder to recall the events on my own. So he's been bringing the memories forward with the mind-meld thingy, and all I know is that I'm drowning, over and over again the deeper we go.

"Trust me, Tess, this is fast." Drymus assures me, looking like he's mustering some patience from somewhere deep inside.

"But we've been here forever!"

"How long do you think it feels like to Alex?" He eggs me on with that biting remark, just like a personal trainer. By now, Drymus knows me better than anyone in the whole universe. He has seen through that horrible little T.V. all my intentions and all my thoughts, expressed or otherwise. He knows that at this point, the only reason I have to keep going is Alex.

"I'm so tired. I can't—"

"Impossible," he cuts me off with a bark. "You have no physical limitations. Your mind is fighting you because you don't want to deal with the issues at hand."

Right again. But my mind *is* tired—sick and tired. I thought that I had been pretty good in life. I mean, didn't I accomplish my mission on Earth? Wasn't I a pretty good person?

"You were pretty good, Tess, but no one is perfect. You can't fully Open until you realize one crucial point."

"And what is that? Pray, tell me!" I say sarcastically, swinging my arms wide to make my point.

Drymus stands and rakes his long white hair with his fingertips. His hair is thick, like horse's hair, and smooth and straight like fine silk. Only now do I realize that it is nearly to his waist in length. He really is an impressive specimen.

"Thanks," he acknowledges my unspoken complements. "But we are here to talk about you," he tries to sound annoyed, but I know that deep inside he's amused by my mind's constant rambling. "Now focus, Tess," he orders, in a serious tone now. "Tell me, how do you feel right now?"

I think for a moment and try to focus. "I feel...frustrated, ashamed, sorry, disappointed in myself...should I continue?"

"No. Let's focus on one of these. Sorry. What do you feel sorry about?"

"I feel sorry that I did some of those things, that I thought those awful thoughts, that I let them enter my mind and fester there."

"Okay, so you feel sorry for yourself?"

I pause and think about that. For some reason this seems important. "No." I say finally. "I don't feel sorry for myself."

"Then who? Who do you feel sorry for? Why is this sorrow painful to you?"

There is a long silence while I think. I know he can read my every thought, so I don't try to verbalize anything. I simply search and search for some elusive answer I know is edging closer to me.

"*Him!*"

Drymus, who had been swiveling on his stool, turns suddenly toward me with a look of shock in his eyes. No, it isn't shock; it's more like "Eureka!"

Chapter 10

"Him who?" he asks softly and encouragingly.

"Him, the First One. He has many names on Earth."

"Why Him? Why do you feel sorry for Him?" Drymus presses.

"Because...I made Him suffer, for me." The moment those words slip out of my mouth, a torrent of grief pours out of me. Grief so intense that I think I will drown in it! Pain and sorrow so deep that I think my heart will break. Exquisite. That's what it is, exquisite pain, pure and undiluted pain for all my sins and mistakes, whether I meant them or not.

"I'm sorry," I groan as I crumble to the floor in one neat little heap. Why is it that in low times, we reach for the ground? Is it because, like Drymus said, we were made from it? Because we are dust, and my body is buried somewhere deep in the earth whence it came from, and now, even as I'm separated from it, my soul reaches for it?

I start begging for His help to release me from this torment. "I'm sorry," I cry again, and the moment I do, I feel intensely guilty for even asking for release from my pains. I feel immediate shame for even daring to ask for His help. How could I? He, who never did anything wrong! How could I even ask for His help now, when in doing so, I would be adding to His suffering?"

"Yes, Tess," Drymus encourages, looking almost wild with excitement. "Now you're getting it."

I shut my eyes and ignore my Spirit Guide. My mind is buried in shame, real shame this time. Not the shame of having Drymus sifting through all my personal garbage, but the shame of the pain I've caused *Him*. Why would He ever forgive me? I wish I were dust again.

The moment I think that, I feel light coming from somewhere behind me. I open my eyes and turn, only to find that I'm no longer in the little white room, but on a hillside that gently slopes down toward a lake. There's a man sitting near the water. I know Him at once, not from pictures, or even Dayspring's wedding, but from the feeling of familiarity, and from the marks that He bears on His feet and hands.

At that moment, it seems as if He is and has always been an integral part of my life. I feel as if He has been present all along, even while

Drymus was Opening me—only I didn't realize it—just like that poem of the footprints in the sand...*He* has been with me all along!

With a genial wave of the hand, he calls me to Him. I obey, not sure why He would even want me near Him. He smiles broadly and encouragingly.

"I'm sorry. I am so, so sorry," is all I can say as I approach and throw myself at his feet—his pierced feet. He's been with me, so He knows all about me and what I've done. He knows that what's going on out there in the mortal realm is entirely my fault. He knows all of it. But as He lifts my chin with his hand, I see that His gaze has compassion in it. And instead of a verbal answer to my former pleas, He responds in a much more complete way—feelings. His penetrating eyes never look away from my own, even when mine stray to the wounds on his hands.

Then a burning fills me, a very physical burning, and with it, an all-encompassing feeling of love—intense, pure, whole, satisfying—love unlike any other. My whole frame fills with it and purges all the guilt, sorrow, and darkness that has been part of me for so long. As the dross falls away from my soul, His light and love engulf me and I feel like singing.

The exquisite pain. Gone. The shame. Gone. The guilt, the remorse, and the burden—gone! I can't even seem to remember any of it! The sting, the ache, the loneliness, and the fear are all gone. For the first time in my whole existence I know without a doubt that I'm important, and that I matter to Him.

No. Not just me. Everyone. We all matter.

Suddenly I understand. Every single human life that has ever passed through Earth, or will ever pass, however briefly, matters! Good and bad...they all matter! And now my heart yearns for them all! Unknown as they are to me, they matter and *I* love them—even Agatha, Eros, Eugenia and countless others—I love them like I never thought I could. They need to be saved just as much as I needed to be!

I look into His eyes, and He sheds the tears that I can't. How I wish I could join Him! How I wish I could repay Him this marvelous gift and undo all the damage I've unleashed on Earth.

His answer, again, comes in thought form, *"You can..."* He says, and makes me see a way for me to help. I can see it clearly in my mind, and when I look back at Him to thank Him, He's gone. But the feeling remains, the light, the warmth, the message, it all remains, and I thank Him again. Perhaps this is the greatest gift of all—that the peace remains—and is not gone with Him like it was the last time I saw Him.

I can no longer see His face, but I know He smiles in reply to my resolve and my grateful heart. The fact that He is pleased with me fills me with hope and determination.

I turn to walk away from the spot, but in turning back, I find myself back in the room with Drymus, who looks up the moment I materialize.

"I like the way you look," he states, grinning.

I look back at him, not knowing what he means.

"I can see right through you." He laughs, "well, let's just say that your thoughts are as transparent as your form. No Vulcan mind-meld needed," he adds with a crooked smile.

I grin and curtsy.

"I can see now why Dayspring likes you so much," He chuckles, in my head.

I look up at him and stare, a bit shocked to hear him telepathically, just like I used to hear Alex.

"It's called the Link," he explains. *"For some reason, you and your Alex have had a natural Link since, well, I've never known you two not to have it."* He brings up a memory of my existence before mortal life. The moment he alludes to it, I remember it in great detail.

"Is that why we've been able to dream those vivid dreams, and to get into each other's head?"

"Yes."

"Do lots of other people have the same ability?"

"It's rare, but not unheard of. Once you Open, you can connect through the Link with other beings who are Open as well. But it doesn't become really cool until you resurrect and become immortal."

"How so?"

"When your planet and all the beings are judged and resurrected, then..." Drymus nods and sighs approvingly. *"Then it gets really fun!"* He tucks his arms under his wings and starts pacing. *"You see, everything takes back its physical form, people, plants, animals, your whole planet even! When that day comes, you will experience the Link in full force. You will feel what it's like to be a tree or a bird. You will know what it's like to be a planet, to orbit, to quake, and rend, to explode in magma from within. You'll know how the ocean feels when one of its waves crashes against a rocky shore. It's incredible!"* Drymus' eyes look moist, and thanks to the Link,

now I know through him what that feels like too. It's only a portion of what the real feeling of Linking in that manner would feel like, but it's wonderful still.

"What happens to those who never Open?" I was thinking of Agatha, and Drymus nods, understanding what I mean.

"Everyone resurrects, but not everyone will inherit your Earth. Your home planet is only reserved for those who accept Him and Open. If you don't, you still get to live forever, but the place will not be as glorious. It will be some other planet, not your mother Earth. You can never fully feel whole without your mother planet."

"Is that where Hell comes in?"

"Sort of, Hell is eternal guilt and remorse, not a place. Those who choose to carry this guilt around forever will never feel comfortable around a bunch of people who can read minds. It's just nature. They will get a planet more suited to what they feel comfortable with, an imperfect planet that matches their natures. The Eternals don't wish anyone pain. They are just, fair, and merciful. They will deal justly with all." Drymus smiles and breaks the Link. "So, now you're Open!"

"I have one more question for you."

Drymus raises his eyebrows, "It's not like you can't read my mind, but shoot."

"You said that guilt and remorse are our Hells. Why do you still carry yours? You are Open, and immortal, so shouldn't you be rid of that?"

He stares at me unflinchingly for a while; then one corner of his mouth twitches upward. "Nothing gets past you, does it?"

I grin in return.

He nods and then his smile fades.

"I've been forgiven and cleansed, but I carry part of my remorse around as a reminder. I've been told to let it go...but I'm still working on it."

I fly up and wrap my arms around his huge neck, squeezing him tight, then plant a kiss on his cheek. A minute ago I hated him, now I love him.

My screams have no echo. The moment they escape my lips they die. Everything around me is dead, dark, and empty. I question everything now. I no longer know why I even bothered to come here. It was to help her, I think, but I'm not sure any more.

"Alex!"

"Who? What?" I turn at what I think is a sound, and see nothing but darkness. Did someone really call my name or am I hallucinating again?

"Right here! Snap out of it, son!" again that soft sound.

"Uh?" I look around again and vaguely I see a nebulous figure in the distance, then a much brighter one hovering right behind it. I shield my eyes and try to focus again.

"It's me, Leo."

"Leo?"

"Tess' dad. Remember?" The man is whispering and I can hardly hear him. Why bother whispering?

"What are you doing out there?"

"Shush, not so loud!" Leo and the bright light approach me, blinding me in the process.

"I can't see anything. Can't you turn that off, or dim it somehow?"

"Sorry, it doesn't work that way. I'm bright now," a woman says softly. Her voice reminds me of hers. I hate her right away and recoil from them.

"Don't be afraid, it's just my wife, Irene. She's come to get us out."

"Ha!" I laugh, cynically. "What's the point? It's all over now."

"It's not! We can leave! Come on, take my hand." I faintly see a white hand in front of me, but I'm not about to take it. "Vamos! Come on, don't be difficult," he presses raising his voice just an octave, only to be shushed by his wife.

"Mas vajo, they'll hear you," she says hoarsely in Spanglish.

"Who? Who will hear us?" I demand, annoyed.

"The Hellhounds."

"The who?" What kind of ridiculous thing is this?

"Well they're not actual hounds, they're men, but they're known as Hellhounds here." Leo explains.

"Yeah, and who told you this? How do you know?"

"Because, they tortured me for a while. I had the unfortunate privilege of running into one of their bubbles when I first got here. They revel in their grossness and still exist to torture the spirits who come here."

"I've never seen one. I've never encountered any such creature. I've seen the bubbles, and what they contain, but no Hellhounds. What makes you think they're around?"

"They're all around you, Alex. You're surrounded by them!"

I drop my own bubble and take a look around. There are other bubbles in the vicinity, but they all contain their own miserable inhabitants. "I don't see anything out of the ordinary."

"No? Look closer," Leo suggests.

"For Heaven's sake, Leo, don't tell him to look in those! They're terrible!"

I ignore her, of course, and focus on one of them. Right away, my stomach turns, or rather, the memory of it turning makes me sick. She was right, they're terrible, and that's putting it mildly.

"You see? She's too bright to be here, we'll get noticed soon enough, and if we're loud to boot..." Leo explains.

"Go then," I tell them dismally.

"No." Leo says firmly. "Not without you."

"I won't go."

"Are you dense, don't you see where you are? It's my fault you're here, and I'm not leaving you behind."

I shake my head and look at his wife. She's beautiful, looks so much like Tess, but darker. "You two go, save yourselves. There's nothing on the other side that interests me."

"But Tess! She's there!" Irene implores, and hearing this feels like a knife just got plunged into my chest and is being twisted and turned in all directions.

"Good for her," I say sourly.

Leo looks back at me with shock, like he simply can't believe his ears.

"She's doing all she can to come back for you," Irene pleads.

"That's a laugh, because the last time I saw her, she told me to stay away from her. To stay here, to not move." I can tell that they are both puzzled by this, and are about to say something, when there's a commotion somewhere behind me.

"The Hellhounds! Quick! We have to get out! Come Alex, please, come!" Irene begs. But I shove Leo back into her and tell him to take her and leave. They do. In a flash, they're gone. And my real nightmare begins.

"Thanks, but where do you think you're going?" Drymus asks, slightly blushing under that marble white skin of his.

"Where? To get Alex of course. I'm Open now, so I can go, right?"

"Yes, technically, but do you see a way out?"

"What?"

"Do you see a way out for him? Do you see how or what to say? Do you hear him calling you, asking you to get him out?"

"N—no," I stammer. "But, I thought—"

Drymus just stares at me with that stone face of his, eyebrows arched, looking high and mighty, and annoying me to no end. But I just Opened, and I do feel a reserve of patience, so I take a deep mental breath. "You said that once I Opened, I'd be ready to go get him!"

"And *you* are, but unfortunately, *he* isn't."

"So what was the point in Opening fast? Why did I even bother?" I whine like a petulant child.

"I thought you wanted to be ready! So that when he is ready to get out, you can just swoop in and get him."

"He is ready Drymus. I've been there, he's torturing himself unnecessarily, and he wants to get out, trust me."

"Not any more," he declares like an all-knowing white wizard. "His bubble has gone dark."

"What?" I ask and exclaim all in one. "How do you know? What does that mean?"

"I know because of the Link, and it can mean a number of things. But I have not been authorized to know what has happened specifically."

"Am I authorized to know?"

"If you don't already know, then you are not."

I bite my lip and try to control my temper. I mean, I just had one of the most amazing experiences ever! I spoke with the First One! I promised Him that I would do anything He asked me to do, that I would help anyone. But...I want to help Alex first! He's in there thinking I deserted him!

"What did you see when you were Opening? You saw something, didn't you? You saw what you needed to do."

"Yes, but...I can do that after I get Alex out."

"Look, Tess," Drymus says as he escorts me out of the room. Once we are out of the building, he takes one look around and then hunches slightly forward so I can hear him better. "Why don't you go meet with some of your family and see how they're doing. Then go to the Angelic department and get signed up; and do what you were asked to do in your vision while you Opened. Before you know it, Alex will be ready and you'll be able to just jump in and get him!" I stare back at him, defiant and angry, I feel like I've been tricked somehow.

"Right then." He nods, knowing that he has not succeeded in changing my mind. "Don't get in trouble. I'll be around," he says with a disapproving shake of his head, then flaps his wings a few times and takes off. Slowly at first, then fast as a bullet. Just as he leaves, I hear him in my head—no, not hear him—I see a picture in my head. It's the image of Alex, squatting inside a dark bubble with nothing but swirling dark smoke inside.

Chapter 11

"Aunt Tess! Aunt Tess!" I look up and see Robyn, of all people. She flings herself toward me with Katie, Jase, Valerie, and Dane in tow. Basically Alex's entire family! Valerie and Dane were Alex's parents in mortality, Katie was his little sister, and Jase later became her husband. Alex and I had custody of Robyn after Katie and Jase passed, so to me she's like a daughter. It's weird seeing everyone like this—all young, about the same age, mid-twenties or so—we're all equals now. No matter what we were to each other in mortality, we are all the same here.

"I was hoping to see you and Uncle Alex when I crossed over, but they told me that you two were indisposed at the moment."

"You could say that," I tell her while I hug her, and think of that last disturbing image of Alex that Drymus shared with me. It must have been significant or important somehow, or he wouldn't have given it to me. I wonder what it means though?

"You're Open! How did you manage it so quickly?" Katie says approvingly. Apparently, in my absence she and Jase had Opened as well. Dane and Valerie had not, but there was something about them that told me that they soon would. There was only one thing holding them back, one regret, or rather, once source of guilt, and it pained me to admit that it was Alex.

"I was told that there was a way to Open fast, so I did it. But...it seems it's not enough."

"What do you mean? You look Open enough to me." Dane noted rationally.

"I am Open, but I was just told that I can't go get Alex."

"What's this business of not getting Alex?" Russell, Alex's grandfather, strides into the group, with his little wife Nancy in tow. She too is Open and looks like a nice, patient woman, the traditional matronly type who could whip up a good southern Gumbo and bake you a pie in under an hour. She reminds me of my aunt Amor, in that sense. Thinking of her, and the rest of my family, makes me groan inwardly. If Alex were here, I would have all my loved ones together in one place. Everyone is finally together, all but the most important one to me. Even in this new state of increased peace, I feel a pang of sadness that seems endless. The image of Alex hunched there in the empty darkness haunts me now, and it will haunt me until I can get him out.

"Dad! You said you'd be Open by now!" Valerie protests, looking at Russell.

"So did you," he counters.

"What's holding you back this time?"

"What's holding *you* back?"

"It's your bickering!" Nancy whines. "Why can't you too get together with your Spirit Guides and—"

"That stinks of therapy," Russell growls defensively, and Valerie concurs heartily.

"Oh you two are a pair!" Nancy throws her hands up in the air. "Not to mention that you're married to a psychiatrist, dear," she turns to her daughter. "You hurt his feelings when you say things like that."

"No I don't," Valerie affirms. "He's used to it."

Dane shrugs and nods unperturbed, and Nancy eyes him fixedly, trying to determine if he was truly okay with this treatment. Upon finding no apparent evidence of hurt feelings in him, she relaxes and assumes a less aggressive stance.

"Dane has known for a number of years now that I have issues with the couch," Valerie says as she tenderly ensconces herself into her husband's arms. As she does this, I'm struck with the fact that she looks different. It's as if Valerie has shed something since she's crossed over. It's hard to say exactly what, but something is missing and something else has been gained.

I sigh, shake my head and change the subject. "So Robyn! I'm so glad that—that—" I'm lost for words. Last time I remember seeing her, I was trying hard to not haunt her.

"It all worked out in the end," she says brightly, saving me the trouble of dredging up the past. "Duncan, my son, he is here too. He's with his Spirit Guide though, but you'll get to meet him later."

"Yes, but in the mean time, we need to figure out how we're going to bust Alex out," Russell says in his take charge, Admiral voice.

"I was told to work as an angel for a while and then…"

"If you were told that, you should do it," Nancy suggests wisely.

"Speaking of angelic duties," Russell looks down at a pendant that is hanging from a long, hair-thin chain. It looks like an odd compass; it has no needle, just a glowing, pearly ball that floats in the middle like a little planet orbiting a miniscule galaxy. Russell sees something in it, because he announces that he has been assigned to Earth to watch over a boy, and with a shrug, he zooms out of sight.

I'm shown to the Angelic department, where I can sign-up and get one of those pendants. This mansion looks like a Hindu monastery, and I half expect to see red-clad monks walking around or practicing some form of martial arts, but I don't. Inside, the spirits are from all different nationalities and they all appear to be doing the same thing I am—signing up for angelic duties.

"Name," a tired sounding angel asks. At least *she's* Asian, but she's wearing a white kimono.

"Tess. Tess DeLeon," I say to the lady, who is busy clanking on a keyboard.

"I don't need your last name," she drones without looking up from her speed typing. I venture a look around, while she types away on a sleek, white, laptop computer. Some spirits are clustered around a big screen that reminds me of the Probe. I shiver involuntarily and look away, not wanting to ever be near that device again. "It's not a Probe," she guesses, still not looking up from her unyielding inputting. "It's just a T.V. that plays updates from Earth."

"Really? What's going on?"

"See for yourself," she lifts one hand and points a tiny finger toward the screen.

The scenes are not much different from some of the things I remember seeing on the news while I was alive—wars, fires, and explosions—the only difference is, that while I lived, all those things happened far away from me. These images, however, were from all the major U.S. cities and Europe!

"Here you go," the woman says loudly and dangles from her fist the same type of pendant I saw Russell wearing. She looks rather impatient as she gives the pendant a little shake. "Come on, take it."

"Oh, thanks. How long has this been going on?" I ask, about the war updates on the screen.

"A few years now. There's a new world government that is really oppressive."

"A world government?"

"Yes. It's called ROWE," she says as she quickly taps her fingers on the keyboard a few more times. "All set," she taps one final key and then looks up with a smile. "Next!" she calls, and I move away, draping the chain around my neck. The second the pendant hangs safely from my collar, it starts to glow, just like Russell's did. I pick it up and squint, trying to focus on the tiny writing on the floating pearl. *"Samantha,"* it says, and below her name, an address—my old address—where Alex and I used to live when we were married. It was a lovely little bunga-low style home downtown; it had been close to work, school, and later, my trendy little shop. But after Alex passed, I never set foot in it again. Dane and Valerie moved Robyn and me in with them. To the best of my knowledge, all our personal things were put in the attic for storage and the house was used as a rental. I had it willed it to Robyn, but I never knew what she did with it. Now, I was going back there, to watch over someone named Samantha.

Passing to the mortal realm legally, as a full-fledged angel, is like passing through customs. I have to say my name, show my pendant, my instructions, and sign out. Then, and only then, an elevator type door opens up, and I can step through to the other side. Fortunately, I don't have far to go because the moment I set foot in the mortal realm I'm standing right in front of my old house. It looks battered and old, haunted by the elements. With sadness, I glide toward it and see noth-ing but piled up rubbish, and the decomposing dregs of years of neglect right where my flowerbeds used to be. The front porch's paint is practi-cally all peeled off and the wood underneath is rotting. The roof looks like a colander and the whole place looks more like a shelter for squat-ters than a home. My whole neighborhood, in fact, that once was so trendy and beautiful, is now reduced to nothing but a ghost town. What ever happened here?

It's nighttime, and the light that emanates from my person is the only light that there is. All the streetlights are out—broken in half—as if Godzilla had been set loose and had crushed whatever was in its path to pieces. Power lines, homes, and old cars, all seem to have been destroyed by some attack, leaving only a few things intact, like my old house. Besides my light, the only other source of light is a faint distant light that shines over a tiny little spot, like a checkpoint or something. My eyesight is perfect now, and I can tell that there is one uniformed person pacing in the spot of light, as if he were on guard.

Stepping through the closed front door, I light my old entryway with the glow that I emanate. There's furniture inside, dusty, broken, ruined by time and the leaky roof. The furniture looks familiar; they are the pieces that Alex and I bought when we first moved in here. It's ironic to see them this decayed, like our relationship. How I wish I could be trying to fix that right now, instead of here, helping a perfect stranger.

"Hello? Is there anyone there?" a mortal girl calls. A creaky floorboard startles me—me—the ghost! I laugh inwardly and go toward the sound. The girl looks to be about sixteen or so. She's pretty dirty, her clothes are threadbare, and her face has dirt smudges all over. She has scraggly long blond hair and a haunted look to her light blue eyes.

"Hello?" she asks again, tremulously. "Who's there?" Her eyes are wide as she scans the darkness. She's barely breathing she's so scared, so I too freeze in my spot and watch her for a while. Can she hear me? Does she have a special gift like I did?

"No, not again, not again!" She presses her hands against her temples, as if trying to squeeze a headache away. "Please leave me alone, go away, go away, go away."

"Can you hear me?" I whisper.

She doesn't acknowledge my question; instead she covers her face with her hands and tries to stifle a scream. "Okay, relax," she tells herself. "There's nothing to be afraid of, they can't hurt you, relax, relax," she keeps murmuring to herself.

When nothing happens after a few minutes, she relaxes a bit, but still casts suspicious looks around as she goes to the kitchen and looks through the cupboards. What could she possibly hope to find here after all these years? She shivers and tries to warm her torso with her arms. I see a puff of fog come out of her mouth as she breathes out, so it must be really cold here. She looks around for something, probably something to warm herself, but there's nothing—nothing to eat in the cupboards, nothing to wrap herself with, and nothing to light the few logs that sit cold inside the cobwebby fireplace. She gazes at those logs longingly and scans the room once more, letting out a long, tired, sigh. Then she shivers again and rubs her arms with her hands.

Something on the mantle of the hearth catches her eye and she reaches for it. It's a box of matches. She grabs it, and seems to deliberate something before she kneels down and starts a small fire.

I move closer to her, wanting to take a closer look, because something about her seems familiar, but the moment I get closer, she freezes instantly, sensing my presence perhaps, or maybe even seeing me. The sound of the front door creaking open makes us both jump and she dashes behind the sofa for protection.

"Sam? Are you here?" a tremulous voice calls from a crack in the door. At the sound of his voice, she relaxes immediately.

"Pete, you freaked me out! What happened to our secret knock?"

"Oh, that's right!" he says laughing slightly. "I forgot."

Samantha hits him in the arm, and he rubs the spot absentmindedly as he looks around the room, taking in all the details of the place, with a look of worry etched in his face. "You shouldn't have made a fire," he states, but goes to warm himself by it anyway.

"I was freezing, and I found this!" She shows him the small box of matches like a prized treasure. "I couldn't resist. Who knows what else is here?" She takes another sidelong glance at the place as if it held hidden treasures. "Besides, it is my house," she says proudly. Like an apparition, another ghostly figure passes suddenly through the front door of the house. As if he were part of a swat team invading a suspect's house, Russell points a sword in front of him and takes a few swipes in my direction. When he realizes it's me, he brightens up, and is about to boom his customary lively welcome when I shush him and I grab him by the elbow, lifting him up, straight up, through the second story and onto the attic floor.

"I think she can see me, or hear me, or sense me, and I don't want you to scare her. What are you doing with that?"

"It's a Flaming Sword," Russell says, matter-of-factly. "Didn't you get one before coming down?"

"No," I whine. "They're for Cherubs only."

"No, not for Cherubs *only*. Any angel can carry one, as long as there is sufficient reason and need, and I'd say that there is sufficient reason and need at this point in time."

I narrow my eyes and look at him shrewdly.

"Don't you give me that look; my wife gave me that same look when she saw me leaving with it. You'll be glad I took this sword, you'll see."

"So Cherubs are just lending out their swords to any angel who wants one?"

"Yes, lots of angels have one, and I suggest you go get one. You might need it."

"For what?"

"Haven't you seen all those cast-outs and all those dark spirits roaming around? Our instructions are to watch over our mortals, help them fight the war, and return any escaped dark spirit back to Prison. How else are we going to accomplish all that without a sword?"

"I—I wasn't told that, I was just told to watch over my mortal."

"Didn't you read the disclaimer at the entrance of the Angelic Building? It says so right there, very clearly."

"I must have missed that. I was a little preoccupied."

"Yeah, thinking about Alex and how you should be getting him out, instead of your mission?"

I nod in reply.

"Well, it's probably just as well. You wouldn't be able to appreciate a sword like this," he says tenderly as he looks his over. "Not to mention that you're too small to carry one anyway."

"You're barely big enough yourself," I tell him, as he holds the sword by the hilt and gives it a few spins, making it light up like a torch. The sword is almost as long as he is tall, certainly about my own size. "It's exactly the same height as my wife, Nancy, five foot four. It's kind of funny to pick it up and fling it around like this," he says as he spins the sword like a Polynesian fire dancer. "It's kind of like spinning my wife." Sure enough, he's hardly done saying those words, when he loses control of the sword, and it slips out of his hands, knocking over a pile of old boxes and spilling their contents on to the attic rafters. "Uh-oh." He looks up at me with a pouty look.

"How on earth?" I start to marvel, when I remember Samantha and her friend downstairs. So I hit Russell on the shoulder, forgetting that he's not really my age, as he looks, but my senior—my husband's grandfather—and that I should probably treat him with more respect. But he's acting like a child, so I'm a little confused.

"The Flaming Swords can affect mortal, spiritual, and resurrected matter at the same time," he whispers, a little too late, now that we've spooked our mortals.

Not moving a muscle, we both stand stock still, as we hear our two mortals scampering up the stairs and opening the attic door. Once they're up, they take a moment to look around, using a log from the fireplace like a torch.

The boy, Pete, crouches on the rafters and helps Samantha up. They both look around with fear imprinted on their faces. "You heard that, right?"

Samantha nods in reply. "Look! Over there, those boxes! That must have been what we heard."

Bending down to avoid hitting her head, she makes her way toward the boxes, and us. When she gets closer, she pauses and looks around, shivering again. Suspiciously, she lets her gaze rest almost right on my person, leaving me wondering if she can see me. "I feel strange here, like we're being watched," she says as she turns her attention back to the boxes that have been knocked over.

"Nonsense," Pete affirms. "There can't possibly be any cameras here," he says as he looks around the cramped space. "So, who did all these things belong to?" Pete asks, as he makes his way to the boxes that Russell whacked with the sword.

"I have no idea. This house has been in my family for generations. It was rented out for many years, so it could be anyone's, I guess."

"As long as we can find something of use, I don't care. They're all dead anyway." Pete says dryly as he ransacks the contents of the boxes.

"She's one of my descendants?" Russell asks, suddenly shocked. This is now a total game changer for him.

I shrug. "She must be."

"Let's exchange! I want to be her angel."

"Are you kidding me? I'm not breaking any more rules. You were assigned to him, I'm assigned to her. I'm not switching. Besides, he'll be kin to you soon enough."

"What? That—. You think my little, great-great-great—whatever—granddaughter will marry this individual?"

"She likes him," I point out. "Oh, come on, Russell, he can't be that bad!"

Russell deliberates for a moment, filtering all he knows about his mortal through new fatherly eyes. "I suppose he's not *all* that bad. He's just—just."

"What?"

"He's too much like me. Too eager to fight, to take on these ROWE soldiers, and take on a lost cause. He can't do that and take care of her."

"Don't worry, I'll take care of her. I won't let anything bad happen to her. I'll go get a sword and I'll do what it takes," I assure him. Russell's head starts shaking. "What? Why can't I? You don't think I can protect her?"

"You really just showed up, didn't you? You didn't read a single disclaimer, or take a class, or anything."

"No," I say, defensively. "Why?"

"Keeping them alive is no longer our mission. It's not any angel's mission."

"Then what is?"

"We just have to keep them safe from the cast-outs and the dark spirits. All we can do is help our mortals be strong enough to not be fooled by the evil spirits. We are just trying to keep them good, so when they die, they can go straight to Paradise, not Prison."

I look at him incredulously. "Really? That's the best we can hope for them?"

Russell nods, grimly. "I'm afraid that this is a battle they will not win."

"It can't be. Good will prevail, it always does," I say, shaking my head emphatically.

"Good will prevail, but this war will not be ended with guns, or bombs, or civil combat. It'll end when all the escaped dark spirits go back to prison, and all the cast-out spirits along with their leader are captured and bound. This war is more spiritual than mortal, even for them." He points to our two little mortals, no older than sixteen, both of them. "If they want to win, they'll have to be good. And by good I mean, moral, up right, kind-hearted. The last thing we want for them is to become hardened fighters, cynical, calloused, or cruel."

"I see," I say, feeling that old guilt come back, remembering that thanks to me, all of this is happening. But the guilt doesn't crush me this time, not like it used to. *He* lifted that weight from my shoulders. Sadly, *He* carries it for me now, and all I can do is what I promised Him I would do. I take comfort in knowing that if I do my part, small as it may be, it's enough for Him. Still, my heart aches and I feel slightly queasy as I watch these two poor souls shiver with cold, rummaging through our old things, trying to find something useful.

Pete opens one box, and finds a trove of Alex's High School things, trophies, report cards, yearbooks, pictures, his graduation cap, and his diploma. Pete goes through it with mild curiosity, since none of those things are any use to him now. "Alexander Dane Preston," he reads the diploma then turns to the P's in the yearbook. "So that's you...isn't it weird?" he says, as Samantha cranes her neck to look at the picture. "He probably lived to a ripe old age, then died. But he's immortalized in this picture as a kid our age forever," he remarks as he looks at the picture of Alex when he was a junior in High School."Who was he to you, again?"

Samantha shrugs. "I don't know, I think I had a great, great grandmother with that last name. Her parents died when she was young and she was raised by her aunt and uncle."

"Maybe this guy grew up to be your great-great-grandmother's uncle."

Sam stares at the immobile picture of Alex for a moment. "Maybe," she finally says, with a sigh.

"He did, but he never did live to a ripe old age," I clarify.

"No," Russell agrees, with sadness. "I blame myself, you know. That's why I can't Open. Well, one of the reasons anyway."

"What do you blame yourself for?"

"His death, and my inability to explain things better to him. I'm always too...too, short with explanations. I reverted back to Admiral mode, when I should have been more thoughtful, more understanding. Death to me was welcomed. I should have understood him better," Russell says glumly as he shakes his head.

"We can't change the past, Russell, we can only hope to change the future," I say trying to muster hope, but feeling an empty void inside of me, the void left by Alex. "For some reason, they are our responsibility right now. They might be the key that unlocks Alex's prison door."

"I hope you're right," he says dejectedly. I too could understand that feeling of helplessness when it comes to Alex. How could *he* of all people get lost like that?

"What's wrong? You okay?" Pete asks concerned. "Do you hear something?"

"No, no."

"Then what?"

Sam presses her lips together. "It's more like, feeling," she admits tentatively.

"Feeling? Feeling what?"

"I don't know...a presence?"

"Like a ghost?"

She looks at him with fear in her eyes, fear that he will think her weird and then leave her. Suddenly, I can sense all her feelings pouring out to me—all her fears, all her hopes, everything she's been mulling around in her head in that precise moment—they all come to me with a flood-like force, and I finally understand. She has my mother's gift, the ability to sense spirits. I had learned from my mother that when she was growing up, she thought she was cursed in some way. My mother could feel the presence of all the cast-out spirits and she called them the shadows. She also felt the guiding presence of her grandmother, and that soothed her. This poor girl! With all the spirits that are going around nowadays—cast-outs, escaped prisoners, and us—she must be very paranoid.

"M—maybe," she hesitates and looks at him with pleading eyes.

"Believe her," Russell whispers in Pete's ear. Suddenly, Pete's face changes from total disbelief to the possibility. "Well, we are going through dead people's things. Your family's things no less." He looks

around the small attic and exhales a long held in breath. "But if they are here, I think they want us to go through their things, or they wouldn't have tipped over these boxes for us to find—this!" He says as he pulls out an old ham radio from one of the fallen boxes.

"I gave that to Alex when he was ten!" Russell shouts, excited at the sight of the old thing. "To play with! I told him I would try to contact him while I was deployed."

"What is that?" Sam asks, both relieved at Pete's response and happy to see something of use.

"I'm not sure, but it looks old enough to work for us." He leans in closer to Sam and whispers, as if he were telling a secret. "You know how I went underground to find the resistance." Samantha nods encouragingly. "Well, I found them. And they are not only organized, but they have found a way to communicate with other organized rebellions from other parts of the country, and the world even!"

"How?" Both Samantha and Russell ask in unison.

"A primitive way of communicating, called Morse code."

"Primitive?" Russell echoes with outrage, while Sam stares at Pete with rapt interest.

"Is this a Morse code?" Sam asks incredulously.

"No, this looks like a radio of sorts. See? He shows her the small print. "Ham radio. The Morse code contraption looks like a button that you tap. It was found in someone's house, in much the same way we found this." Pete sets the radio down, and frantically now, starts opening all the other boxes, ransacking through all our old things, looking for more treasures.

"Look!" Pete holds up Alex's old Navy uniform and his dog tags. "Alexander Preston," he reads. "The mystery of Alex Preston's life keeps unfolding! He became a soldier." Pete looks excitedly back at Sam, who is holding one of my favorite dresses that I designed. She too looks excited, but not so much about the uniform as she does about the dress. I can read her thoughts more easily now, and I can see that she's having a brief daydream. She's wearing that dress, and Pete is dressed in Alex's old uniform, both looking dashing as they dance.

"Whose do you think this was?" She holds up my dress.

"Not his, I hope." They both laugh and keep opening boxes. They find warm coats, and they don't hesitate to put those on. Sam finds many of my dress sketches, mixed with some of Dorian's pictures that he drew for me. I lean over her shoulder and observe with melancholy the things that used to be so dear to me in life. Some of those drawings

I kept as my private treasure trove for years under my bed, hidden in a little valise. Over time, I filled the little thing full of these earthly gems that meant nothing to anyone else, but meant the world to me.

Sam pauses at the picture that Dorian drew of me, sitting under the relentless rain, hands covering my face, hiding the fear I felt. Shadowy figures are floating behind me, and Alex is approaching cautiously from in front of me. She studies this decaying picture with great interest. She knows it's special, and the presence of those shadows does not go unnoticed by her.

"They exist, Sam. Good spirits and bad," I whisper in her ear. "I'm her," I say, pointing to the picture of the girl hiding her face, scared of the unseen, just like her. "I'm here to help you."

She shivers, and I know she hears, or at least understands me. Her heart is racing, but I feel no fear coming from her. She knows this picture is relevant to her, she knows it proves something, but she's not sure what yet. The girl in the picture could be her, or it could be someone else, just like her. She folds Dorian's prophetic relic carefully and puts it in my old coat pocket—her coat pocket now.

Chapter 12

"Are you okay?" Pete asks, looking up from his treasure hunting.

"Yes, it's nothing," Samantha says, preoccupied, as she studies the rest of Dorian's old pictures.

Pete tries to read her face for a minute, then, seeing nothing out of the ordinary, goes back to a neat pile of yearbooks and things that belonged to Alex. "Well, I think I can put together this guy's life pretty well. Do you want to hear it?"

"Sure!" Sam says, trying to sound excited, as she puzzles over my own life, with all the odds and ends she has found in my little valise and boxes.

"Okay, here it goes. Alex was a pretty lucky guy of his time. He was student body president, apparently something important," Pete adds as a side note. "He played a sport called football, something that only a select group of guys got to play, then married his high school sweetheart, Eugenia." He looks up triumphantly. "He then enrolled in the military and was a soldier until he retired. Then he ran for political office, see?" He holds up one of Alex's old campaign pins and flyers. "He must have had a nice cushy life. Probably had a few kids, and because he was a good guy, he took in your great-great-grandmother and raised her. He got old, then he died, probably in his sleep after a good meal." Pete summed up taking great pleasure in his sleuthing skills.

"I wouldn't be so sure, Pete," Samantha reproves. "Besides, you say all that as if having a good life is a bad thing. And what makes you think that his wife's name was Eugenia?"

"These pictures right here." He holds all the yearbooks that had prom pictures of Alex with Eugenia next to him, the two of them, always being awarded as the "Cutest Couple," "Prom King and Queen," or "Homecoming Royalty."

"See? They went to every single dance together every year, and won some sort of contest every year. You can't tell me that those two didn't end up together."

"Well, what about her?" Sam holds up one of my dresses as evidence. Pete fails to see the connection. "See the tag on this dress?" She points out.

"What about it?"

"It says, DeLeon. All these dresses say DeLeon." She points to the strewn contents of one of the boxes that contained some of the inventory from my boutique's dress line.

"So?"

"Look!" She holds up my fashion sketches with my signature scribbled at the bottom. "Same signature. Tess DeLeon."

"So, maybe it's a made up name for her dresses."

"I don't think so. Look at this last picture." She points to Alex's senior prom picture with Eugenia. Alex looked like he was merely enduring the night, and Eugenia looked like a spoiled child who was getting her way. "Why don't you look her up? Tess DeLeon. See if she's there."

With grave intensity, I watch as Pete turns the pages of the yearbook looking for me. I want them to get this right, I want to be found. I need them to know that Alex married *me*, not Eugenia.

"I'll be," Pete murmurs. "Tess DeLeon."

Samantha scoots next to him and leans into the book, looking at my picture carefully. "She's pretty," she mumbles. But she frowns, perplexed. "I wonder who this is, then." She places the sketch of Celeste that Dorian had drawn for me—my mystery ghost—at the time. When Dorian had drawn that picture of Celeste, I knew that she was the presence that I had felt since childhood, but I didn't know for sure who she was until much later.

"Where did you find it?"

"With her things." She points to my junior year picture.

"Well then it must be someone she knew."

"Must be," Sam says absentmindedly. "I wonder how Alex and Tess ended up together? Obviously, things didn't work out with Eugenia, and he ended up marrying Tess, who was a year younger."

"Well, I think we've wasted enough time with this guessing game. I'm tired," Pete declares, slamming the yearbooks shut and sending a puff of dust flying up in the air.

"Yeah," Sam agrees with a sense of forlornness. She liked the escape; she had enjoyed looking at my dresses and my sketches. Part of her wanted to be me, the girl who got to wear all the pretty dresses she could dream up. In her mind I did nothing but play with clothes and attend parties, where I displayed my many dresses. I feel sorry for her. My life wasn't what she imagines at all, yet I had comforts that she doesn't have. I had a home until I was eighteen, I had Dorian, and even though I didn't know it then, I had Alex.

A few weak rays of slanted sunlight filters through the dirty windows, and Pete winces reflexively the minute they touch his eyelids. I feel sorry for him. Something about light shining into his eyes triggers a nightmare that he doesn't want to relive, so he opens his eyes wide and looks around the room in a panic.

"Sam?" He asks suddenly, pushing back the sudden feeling of anxiety that the nightmare has triggered.

Samantha stirs, and sleepily stretches. Then, awareness dawns on her and she starts up. She looks around the room with her eyes open wide, yet still glossy with sleep. "What? What's wrong?" She asks.

"Um…" Pete holds up the dusty blanket and an expired can of pork and beans. "Someone knows we're here!"

They had curled up by the embers of the fire, like a litter of puppies, and slept soundly in spite of the obvious cold they felt. Russell and I took pity on them, so we took turns looking for more earthly comforts for them. I found an old blanket that we draped over them with the sword. It was a tedious job, but we managed, without damaging anyone or anything. Then we set out to find them breakfast. All we could find was an old can of pork and beans that had long expired, but we hoped was still edible.

Holding their breath, they look around the empty room, but nothing seems to be disturbed. There are no footprints on the sooty floor other than their own, and the door is still locked from the inside. Their breaths are so shallow, that I fear they might pass out. I can tell that their senses are on full alert as they try to pick up the faintest of sounds or movements.

The ham radio is still there, untouched. The fire is cold and ashy.

"I think it's her," Sam says, taking a paper and unfolding it with cold, stiff, fingers. It was a torn page from the yearbook, the page that contained my picture.

Rubbing the sleep from his eyes, Pete takes the paper and focuses on my small portrait. "Why her? Maybe it's him, Alex." He shakes his head, and hands her back the paper. "Besides, it's crazy to think that ghosts are helping us, or that they exist, even!"

"But you said so yourself, last night. When the boxes tipped over." Sam says defensively.

Pete rubs his face and takes in a deep breath. "I don't know what to think anymore. Sometimes I just feel like screaming."

Samantha nods understandingly, and gently folds the paper back and sticks my picture in her coat pocket. "Well, we have something to eat. Lets eat it!" With a pocketknife they poke jagged holes into the can and take turns gulping down the meager contents.

"So what exactly do they do?" I ask Russell, who is studying his sword with loving interest.

"Well I don't know what Sam does all day, but Pete here will probably try to infiltrate the underground once more and show off his new-found radio."

"Is it safe?"

"Is what safe? The infiltrating or the underground?"

"Both, I guess."

"Once he's underground, he'll be safe." Russell swipes the sword a few times, making the thing light up like a fiery torch. "I'll make sure he makes it."

"This house has to remain as shut up as possible. We should do our best to not arouse any suspicions about it." Pete wipes his mouth with the back of his hand, and picks up the radio to inspect it for the hundredth time.

"Oh, Pete, I don't want to leave it. I feel good here."

"In a spooky kind of way, I feel good here too." He sighs. "But we need to keep a low profile."

"Where are we going to sleep tonight?"

"The shelters."

Samantha's shoulder slump down, and she looks miserably back at Pete. "No! Not the shelter! That's the whole reason why we came here!" she protests.

"I know, but now we have a plan; we have a purpose. You don't want the officers to ransack and destroy this place, do you?"

Samantha shakes her head and sighs. "Fine! I'll go back to the shelter, but every once in a while I want to come back here."

"We will, I promise." He slides his hand under her disheveled blond hair, and kisses her forehead—his first sign of affection ever! She blushes at this unprecedented act of tenderness and looks down, gracing her high cheekbones with her thick eyelashes. Pete seems hesitant to let go of her. He's having an internal battle between wanting to get closer, and knowing that getting close to people has only brought him grief, pain, and eventually death to those he has loved.

Not privy to his thoughts as I am, Sam looks disappointed and puzzled, as Pete clears his throat, and pulls away from her rather suddenly. She was expecting something more, a proper kiss, or even a longer caress, but she remains disappointed in this hope. Her mind immediately flashes back to the first time she met Pete at the shelter. She had been the only one from her family to survive an epidemic that swept through the shelter like the plague. Pete and his sister came right after that, not knowing of the plague. Apparently, they had come to be with an aunt and uncle, but when they got there, they only found their cold dead bodies, stacked up in a heap, ready to be burned. Sam's whole family was in that heap too, and together they sadly watched the gruesome sight.

As the infernal flames danced across their faces, they exchanged blank stares, and noticed each other for the first time. After this ordeal, they kept seeing each other at the soup line, at the sleeping hall, and just in passing. They never spoke; they simply exchanged silent, vacant gazes, until after the night a soldier took Pete's older sister. When Pete realized what was going on, he took off after the soldier that was dragging his sister away, and was about to lunge at him, when a strong pair of hands gripped him from behind and dragged him into the shadows.

"No sense in you dying too," the man who grabbed him said to him.

"I'd rather die, than live like you!" Pete spat, and the man stopped his mouth and dragged him even further out of the way. Sam had silently followed them, curious, and ready to help if it was needed, though she had no clue how this would be done.

"Your time for dying will come, just not tonight. Not like this," the man growled, quietly through his gritted teeth.

"That's my sister!" Pete spat.

"And she would want you to live to do something that really matters."

"What do you mean?" Pete asked, his nose flaring, trying to rein in his anger.

The man put his index finger to Pete's lips, signaling him to be quiet. "Not here, not tonight," he said mysteriously. He then left Pete panting on the floor. That's when Sam ventured out of her hiding spot and went up to him, quiet as a mouse. Pete saw her come and said nothing as she sat next to him. They sat there in that hallway, side-by-side, not touching, not talking, both staring out at nothing, then quietly crying themselves to sleep.

They stuck together after that. It was an unspoken mutual agreement they had for days. When they finally spoke, it was as if they needed no introduction.

While still remembering this and pondering what it would be like to be kissed, really kissed—Pete calls her attention back to the present and to another, more practical and pressing thought—how to leave the house undetected, and how to come back undetected. This call to reality promptly squelched the other, more frivolous thoughts, to the extent that she felt silly for entertaining such trivial daydreams as kissing.

While the two of them made plans, the two of us made plans also. "First off," Russell enumerated with transparent fingers. "I'll have to go make sure that the coast is clear. Cast-outs and prisoners are just as bad as the ROWE soldiers; in fact they are the masterminds behind every ROWE soldier. If the spirits from Prison get wind that there are two kids holing up here, they'll alert the soldiers and these two are done for."

"What if the coast isn't clear and they go out while there are bad spirits about? How do we tell them to hide?"

Russell sighs. "Just remember, their soul is more important than their life, right now. Whatever the circumstance, just make sure you save their soul."

They have to make it to the underground by different ways, by themselves, and each undetected by both mortals and spirits. To accomplish this, I find myself flying in all directions, trying to spy out the area beforehand, and then going back to tell her which way to go. Fortunately, she is very intuitive and listens well. Every time I speak to her and tell her which way to go, or whether to hide and be still—she smiles inwardly—like she knows I'm here, guiding her, and she tightens her hold on my picture that she keeps in her pocket, as if it were my hand.

Somehow, we manage to make it to the underground in one piece. Pete had given her specific directions on how to get there. If he hadn't, we would have never found it since I have always been so directionally challenged. The entrance is a boarded-up door to an old commuter train station. A dilapidated, old sign that reads "Caution. High Voltage Area" hangs precariously above the door by one nail. Sam knocks and the sign rattles unsteadily. Looking all around, afraid of being seen, Sam hurries up and knocks again making the same exact rhythmic pattern. From inside a different knock responds and Sam knocks again in a particular way—a secret code, I surmise.

Two boards part slightly from the inside, and a pair of eyes inspect Sam for a few seconds. "Who sent you?"

"Pete," Samantha says, then she clears her throat and speaks slightly louder. "Pete Moore," she adds. A few seconds later what first looked like a boarded-up door opens up on invisible hinges and a hand pulls Sam briskly in. Inside, the darkness is complete, and it takes us both a moment to adjust our eyes to it. It's cramped too, literally like a small closet of sorts.

"Is he here yet?"

"Who?"

"My—Pete, Pete Moore, did he make it yet?"

"No. *Your* Pete's not back yet." The voice belongs to a husky girl, who, unlike Sam, looks like she could defend herself against any soldier, any time, and come out unscathed. She's holding a large antique handgun, and has it casually resting on her shoulder, with a finger on the trigger and another on the hammer. "Who are you?"

"Samantha Feltz."

The doorkeeper shakes her head. "I don't recall Pete ever mentioning a Samantha Feltz," she says with a challenging smirk on her face.

"Well, he didn't know I would end up coming so soon, but we found something."

"Oh yeah," the doorkeeper says with mock interest. "What did you find?"

Samantha looks around nervously, not sure if she should trust this burly gal or not. "He—he better show you himself," Sam finally says, and the brawny girl laughs at Sam's insecurities. Chuckling still to herself, the doorkeeper lifts a latch revealing a tunnel, then leads Sam down the dark, muddy, and slippery shaft. Sam presses her hands against the walls and roof of the passageway for support, and still manages to slip a few times. The doorkeeper, however, walks briskly down without slipping once.

"Wait here," the girl instructs. "Someone will come for you soon."

"Who?" Sam asks, suddenly alarmed.

The girl laughs again. "Don't worry, there are no ROWE soldiers here. This is the rebellion, we don't hurt our own." She smiles a forced smile, and then disappears up the same tunnel they just came from.

This holding area is nothing but a muddy, wet, carved-out hole deep underground. There's only one torch here, providing both light and warmth. Samantha takes advantage of this and puts her hands up toward the flame to warm her frozen fingers.

"Sam, is it?" a man's voice surprises her.

"Yes, Samantha Feltz." The moment she says her name she realizes she knows that man. It's the same man that pulled Pete back that night, and kept him from getting killed by the soldier who took his sister. The man watches as this realization registers on her face, then smiles.

"Miles," he says stretching his hand affably. "Welcome to the rebellion, Samantha."

Chapter 13

The rebellion headquarters is at the heart of several narrow tunnels that snake their way to an old dried up sewer holding tank for the old city. Apparently, each tunnel leads to a different exit, so as to not attract attention by coming and going from a single location.

The main area is full of people who turn and stare as Samantha passes with Miles in the lead. Apparently he's one of the leaders, because they all salute him with reverence, and study the new face he's brought. Most of the mortals present have angels who, like me, are assigned to watch over them. As I pass by, the angels acknowledge me in turn by a cordial wave of the hand, or a nod. Every mortal and spirit has a workstation of sorts, and they all seem to be busy doing something. Etched on the ground, in the middle of the room are the words, "If not me, who? If not now, when?"

"Sorry about your family, Sam. Your dad was a good friend of mine."

"He was? You knew him?"

"Him and your mom," Miles affirms. "They were both part of the rebellion, so it's no surprise for me to see you here."

"But I never saw you talking," Sam protested.

"You wouldn't have. That's the whole point of being part of a secret organization." He smiles and winks. "Sam, if you join there are a few rules you'll have to abide by." Sam nods slowly. "No one sleeps here unless you have the night-time shift. When you leave, you have to go back to your shelter a different way each time. You will not acknowledge the fact that you know me, or anyone else from this cave—no one!"

"W—w—what about Pete? I already knew him."

Miles stares at her for a few seconds then smiles. "It'd be best if you didn't alert the soldiers to the fact that you have a boyfriend. It'll just remind them that life goes on, and they don't like that. But since you two have been hanging around together for some time now, I guess you should continue as you were. The main point is not to alert anyone that things are different."

Sam nods again and looks over Miles' shoulder. Behind him there's a girl about her age, sitting at a desk next to an odd looking button. She's holding a pencil and had presently paused whatever she was doing to listen in on the conversation. "Sam, this is Gladys. I want you to become an expert at this. It's called—"

"A telegraph," Sam says looking hypnotically at the device.

"Yes, how do you know?"

"Am I to learn Morse code?" Sam asks, trying to avert Miles' attention, for fear of getting Pete into trouble. She had a sneaky suspicion that talking about these things outside of this cave would be one of the rules.

"Yes." Miles narrows his eyes and looks shrewdly at her, and just as he was about to say something, Pete's excited voice diverts his attention.

"What took you guys so long?" I ask Russell as he glides through the cave, sword in hand, looking tense.

"We ran into some trouble," Russell explains. "An escaped dark spirit started tailing us, and I had to use this." He swings the sword around briskly, then tucks it behind his back expertly.

"What happened to the spirit?" One of the other angels asks, moving toward us with haste.

"I temporarily erased its essence, giving us enough time to escape. We really need more good spirits though," he adds, shaking his head wearily. "We need to send these escapees back to Prison, so we can get a handle on this situation. We might be spirits, and we might move fast, but we can't protect our mortals and return dark spirits at the same time. It's one or the other."

"I've been saying this for years!" the angel who came toward us exclaims, as he folds his arms across his chest. He's a short, Open spirit, who is also packing a sword that is way bigger than him, yet he looks quite comfortable with it and not at all bothered by the huge hilt that sticks out from behind him. "Tony." The spirit sticks his stubby fingered hand out for a friendly shake.

While Pete shows a group of rebels his ham radio and Samantha learns how to operate the telegraph from Gladys, Tony shows us around and introduces us to the other spirits in the cave. Most of these spirits are veterans of this war and are the original spirits who helped organize this rebellion. They were around when ROWE was first created, and they chose to stay and extend their missions to help mortals organize a stable rebellion against this oppressive world order.

"We've had to teach them how to operate the telegraph, and we taught them how to read Morse code and how to send encrypted messages," one spirit explains. "I used to be a spy in my day. I'm a World War II veteran." The spirit puffs out his chest with pride.

"Admiral in the United States Navy," Russell states, saluting the fellow soldier.

"Good, good, we need as many trained soldiers as possible," the veteran says, then looks at me with hopeful eyes.

"Fashion designer. Sorry," I apologize with a shrug. "But I am a discerner."

"And a very good discerner, I might add," Russell avows.

"Well, the rebellion is made up of all kinds of ex-this or ex-that's," Tony interjects. "I myself am a fellow with a dubious past on earth, but as you can see, I've mended my ways, and have managed to Open at last. Now the important thing is to work together and use any skills we can bring to the table."

"So how *did* this all start?" Russell asks conversationally.

"The rebellion started when the current president went to a secret summit and hatched out this brilliant plan with the leaders of the other world powers at the time. They wrote out a template for a Re-Organized World Empire, which would stabilize the world's economy. They claimed that this new world order would end world hunger and poverty, do away with current evil world leaders, and unify the world in peace and harmony. There would be no more world wars, no more civil wars, and no more oppressive and inhumane policies based on absurd religious practices. In short, they packaged crap, tied a pretty bow around it, and shoved it down everyone's throat by way of a massive ad campaign."

"Oh, they were good," Tony recalls. "They made heartwarming TV ads promoting world peace, and persuasive billboards encouraging people to vote for Prop. ROWE at the next election. They also sent out representatives door-to-door, giving out pamphlets as well as gifts of every kind. They were armed too, which I always found interesting."

"Yeah, I remember. I was alive when one of them offered my family a gift certificate for the local grocery store with a week's worth of food," one of the spirits, a woman, stated in agreement. "When I told them to take their gift certificate and stick it where the sun-don't-shine, I promptly got a gun pointed at my head, was arrested over trumped up charges, and then was sent to prison. My husband was given an ultimatum: 'vote for ROWE or watch me die.'"

"You can't be serious?" I gasp. "Here? In this country?"

"Right here in this country," she maintains. "I told him not to cave in, and he didn't. I was murdered shortly after in what they called 'an accidental prison incident'. That's my daughter over there." She points to the girl who's teaching Sam to operate the telegraph. "The only surviving member of my family. She was a baby when I was killed. She doesn't remember me, or even know I'm right here next to her," she says with longing in her eyes. It reminds me of that same look my mother had when I saw her for the first time.

"How awful for you," I say, mortified by the fact that all of this has to do with me. ME! I let Agatha loose on this planet. I let her join forces with the Second One. I opened the rift and upset the spiritual balance of my world. *Me.*

What would all these spirits who have suffered so much say to me if they knew what I have done? But what am I saying? I'm Open. They can see it, can't they? I look at Tony, the short spirit who said he had a dubious life on earth. He's Open, but I can't quite tell what his mistakes had been. They have been erased, as mine have. Yet...I know. Even if they don't show, I know what I've done.

"It was inevitable," the veteran continues, eyeing me cautiously. "We all knew that the world would come to an end sooner or later, *one way* or another," he says meaningfully, tilting his head toward me. Maybe he's a discerner, like me. "No one can stop that from happening, but we can save as many souls as possible in the process. Life in the shelters is no life at all. Mortals need to fight for their convictions and they need to stand for something. Even if they can't win, they have to keep fighting."

"But they will win in the end, and there are small victories every day," the woman who was murdered says. "My death was a victory. Their lives are a victory, this rebellion is victory, and when the world ends that will be a victory for all those who fought."

"Well said, Carmen, well said." Tony reaches up and pats her on the arm. "Now let's get back to work. We need more spirits from Heaven, and when I say more, I mean, lots more!"

"Two per mortal, I suggest," Russell states. "One to protect and guide the mortal, the other to fight the cast-outs and send the escaped prisoners back to their realm."

"But how can we get more spirits?" I ask. "I mean, don't we need to have special permission for that or something?"

"Yes we do," Tony says, stabbing the air between us with a stubby finger. "The High Council will want a specific plan. What we need to do is come up with a good plan of attack, something that the High Council will not be able to refuse."

"Yes!" the veteran says enthusiastically, then calls everyone's attention to a plan he's hatched out in the last minute or so. Russell nods with interest as he hears the details. He adds a few comments, and everyone agrees with him. Suddenly, the two ex-military guys are going back and forth coming up with a strategy that, even I must admit, sounds perfect. But I'm only half listening to them; another part of me is still dwelling on what Tony said about the High Council not refusing a good plan. What if I came up with a good plan of my own, one that would involve rescuing Alex and fulfilling my current mission? What if I didn't have to neglect either one? What if I could do them both?

"I'll do it!" I say loudly, raising my hand like an eager schoolgirl. "I'll go talk to the High Council...again," I add under my breath.

Tony has a look of uncertainty on his face, while Russell looks suspicious, and the rest are just plain shocked by my sudden eagerness to go back. I know what they're thinking, too. They think I don't like my mission here, that I find Earth too changed, too difficult and that I want to go back to Heaven. But that's not true at all. Well...part of it is true, I do find it changed and sad, but I would never leave Sam behind.

The only one who suspects my true motives is Russell, who wants the same thing I do—Alex's speedy release from Prison. We haven't shared this with each other, but we both fear seeing Alex among the escaped prisoners' faces. We're both afraid of having to be the ones who have to escort Alex back to Prison, by force, or worse...having to use the sword on him.

With his eyes trained on mine, Russell clears his throat. "I think it's a good idea," he says with authority. "Tess is good with words and quite diplomatic. I think she'll be a great choice to send to speak to the High Council."

"Are you sure?" Tony leans into Russell and mutters under his breath, misgiving showing clearly on his face. Unfortunately, Russell is so much taller than Tony that instead of being level with his ear—as Tony intended to be—he's practically level with Russell's bellybutton, and I have to bite my lip to suppress a smile.

"Sure I'm sure!" Russell leans down and whispers back.

"But she's said so herself, she was a tailor or something," Tony insists.

"I know of a carpenter that did great things," the woman says reproachfully. "I was a simple housewife, and look at me now!"

"Yes, but—"

"What Tony is trying to say," the veteran interjects. "Is that whoever goes to speak with the High Council has to be very passionate. Has not only to be persuasive, but also truly invested in this plight."

"You don't think I'm invested?" I ask, both stunned and hurt.

"Well..." the veteran shrugs. "Not like the rest of us who still have people here who we care about."

I'm about to respond with a few choice words and an example of exactly how invested I really am, when Russell sticks his hand out and stops me. "What you may not know is that Tess and I are family. What you may also not know is that Samantha, over there, is one of our descendants and has a very special bond with Tess. What you might also not know is that Tess, here, has a more intimate knowledge of what is going on here on Earth than the whole of you combined, and while I'm not going to give you the details of this knowledge, or why she has it, I will simply say this: Tess is better qualified than any of you to speak in our behalf to the Council. In fact, if there is one spirit who could ever convince them of taking any sort of increased measures toward this war, Tess is it."

With such high recommendations from Russell, the rest of the spirits have no choice but to send me to the High Council with a detailed plan of attack. I have to admit that I don't feel as "uniquely qualified" as Russell put it, other than it's my fault that this is going on to begin with, and the responsibility of fixing this mess sort of falls on my shoulders.

As long as Sam stays underground with Gladys, her new friend, and the rest of the rebellion, she should be safe. So I leave her temporarily, with the eyes of every spiritual member of the rebellion trained on me. They don't wish me luck, they just stare in dumb amazement, baffled over Russell's words and wondering why *I* would be so uniquely qualified for this task.

"There is a time assigned for all," one of the High Councilors says after I make my second appeal. My first request of sending more Heavenly forces down has been readily accepted. All the spirits from the rebellion can now relax and know that all their plans will soon begin to take fruition. But I'm not done with the High Council, or with my requests.

"All angelic duties are timed perfectly," another adds.

"You mean to say that if I don't perform my assigned angelic duties, no one else can?"

"No. Someone will be sent in your place, but it will not be the same. There is a purpose for everything, not just for those who you'd help, but also for your own benefit."

"But what about Alex? Besides, the moment I get back with him, I'll come right back to my post and happily continue it. Can't we just postpone those same lessons until I get back?" There is some deliberation among them through the link. I can't read them, but I can tell that they are in the middle of a discussion because they look at each other, and nod, or shake their heads now and then in civil agreement. They do this for some time. Finally one of them looks up and addresses me. "The problem here is twofold. You have a mortal charge that needs you, and you want to pluck a plant that has no roots."

"What does that mean?" I ask.

"You might be able to remove a spirit from Prison, but the spirit might still remain there," another councilor explains.

"We all know he doesn't belong there, and that he made an error in judgment. He's paid for his mistakes long enough, he deserves to be forgiven and to be set free," I maintain.

"Forgiveness has been available to him all along," One says.

"But he hasn't sought it," another adds.

"He's lost in there! It's oppressive and disheartening! Please let me take him out. He will see things more clearly once he's out."

They don't respond to my last comment. Instead they exchange a series of glances and do a great deal of nodding again. Finally, after another long period of silent discussions, they all snap to attention, and sit perfectly still. I think they are receiving some sort of communication from the Eternals, because a thick blanket of peace falls over the whole room. Even I feel it.

One of the High Councilors rises and delivers the verdict solemnly yet with a piercing, kind eye that seems to convey fatherly love. "The Eternals have granted you permission. But," he lifts one admonitory finger. "There is one condition." He pauses and looks at me significantly, making sure I know that what he's about to tell me is of grave importance.

"Okay," I say.

"That you bring back with you anyone you encounter along the way."

"Anyone?"

"Anyone."

"Who crosses your way," another clarifies.

"Very well," I agree and they nod with approval.

"Ah!" one of them exclaims as I turn to leave. "One more thing."

"Yes?"

"You must find a replacement to watch over your charge. She must not be left alone at this critical time."

"Anyone?"

"Someone qualified, but of your choosing."

I don't even make it all the way out the building when I find a large gathering of familiar spirits that surround a female Cherub, who is holding a scroll. As I approach, Valerie turns and looks at me, then elbows Dane in the ribs to get his attention. He feels nothing and takes no notice of the jab; he's too intent on what the Cherub is saying. Finally, Valerie turns his face toward me and a broad smile crosses his face as he beckons me with a jerk of his head.

"What's going on?" I whisper in Valerie's ear, not wanting to disrupt the Cherub.

"They want one of us to go get Henry out of Prison."

"Who's Henry?"

"He was Estelle's husband, you know, Russell's father, my grandfather, Alex's great grandfather..." She looks toward Estelle who is holding fast to a tall, distinguished man who is dressed like he just stepped out of a Jane Austen movie set. Estelle herself looks radiant, with her dark red hair and chocolate eyes.

"He looks like Mr. Darcy," I whisper in Valerie's ear.

"I know!" She elbows me in the stomach amiably. "I've been saying that all along. Anyway, they've been dating now for a while," Valerie leans over and explains. "He lived in Ireland in the 1800's. He heard her sing and..."

"The rest is history," I finish.

"Yep. Pretty much. His name is James."

"A match made in Heaven?"

"Literally," we both giggle, and the Cherub holding the scroll gives us a reproving, sharp look. It's a bit strange to be with Valerie like this—giggling. In life, she struggled with depression, and each day was a battle for her. Though I seldom saw her laughing, I always got along with her, and we enjoyed a good relationship. But now, I find myself being taken back when I see her laugh or smile. She looks unencumbered, light, and free—like a burden has been removed from her personality—and she's finally able to be herself.

"What is she talking about?" I lean over again and ask her in a low whisper.

"Henry is apparently ready to leave Spirit Prison and one of us has to go get him. The only problem is that no one wants to."

"So what is the Cherub going on about?"

"Our duties, blah, blah, blah." Valerie rolls her eyes. "The problem is that none of us is Open, so we can't go get him. Our own issues with him are the ones keeping us from Opening. So you see, it's a quandary."

"Ahem!" the Cherub woman says loudly and looks at me. "Perhaps you should go, since you seem to be the only one from this clan who is Open."

"Clan?"

"That's what she calls us, a clan. Not a family, a clan."

"Better than a coven," I say, then we both chuckle once more. The female Cherub is not impressed and she looks at me expectantly. "It just so happens that I am going that way, so if he can find me, I'll bring him back."

"Really?" Estelle says jubilantly, and comes to my side to hug me. "That would be so nice of you."

"I'm going in after Alex, but I promised to help anyone who crosses my path. Let's just hope he does. Otherwise, I don't know how I'll find him."

"He is ready," the Cherub says. "He will naturally seek your light."

"Good! But I do need help with my mortal charge." I turn to Valerie with pleading eyes. "You are trained as an angel, aren't you?"

"Well, yes, but..."

"Don't worry, she's very sweet—one of your descendants. Robyn's great-great granddaughter or something. Russell is there too! She senses spirits so don't spook her. Just keep her safe until I get back." I rattle in a hurry.

"O-kay," Valerie says, a little overwhelmed.

"Can you do this for me? I was told that I could go get Alex, but only if I found someone to watch over Samantha." I ask, biting my lip and looking at her expectantly.

"We'll do it!" Dane volunteered. "We'll do it together! I've always wanted to watch over a descendant. It'd be an honor."

I look at Valerie for a moment, and she nods in agreement. Her eyes are big and still full of shock. "Sorry to just dump this on you, but I do want to go get Alex as soon as possible."

"Of course, of course," Valerie nods again, and looks at me steadily with her violet eyes.

"Oh! And while you're there, tell Russell and the others that I did get approval from the High Council, and that they will start sending more reinforcements." I say as I start gliding away.

Valerie is still nodding and looking fixedly at me with her piercing violet eyes, making me feel self-conscious. "What?" I ask, floating back down toward her a little.

Those intense looks from Valerie are never a good sign. But she says nothing; she simply bites her lip and shakes her head. "Nothing. Just...good luck Tess," she says with consternation, then stretches a forced smile across her face. Both Valerie and Dane nod numbly as I fly away, toward the dividing line between Heaven and Hell.

Chapter 14

The transitional space between the two states of being is not like a well marked dividing line; it's simply an edge. On one side there is nothing but light, on the other, nothing but darkness. It's like a State line, you step over, and you're there—no signs, no gates, or roadblocks. Anyone can come in or come out of either one. So what holds all those spirits anchored to the darkness? What kept me there? Ignorance, guilt, my own blindness?

I hate being back here. It's dark and dismal, and even in my Open state, I feel that oppressive feeling that I felt the moment I first came—wrong place, wrong time, wrong side of town. The only light that shines here is my own. I'm like a beacon and it scares me. What if they start coming at me again? The place looks oddly deserted, though, and the bubbles that assailed me the last time I was here are nowhere in sight. This creeps me out even more, and I wish I weren't alone. I wish I had Dorian with me, but he's gone on some top-secret mission on Earth—he's big-time now.

Drifting forward, I try to focus on Alex and I try to channel all my energy into thinking of him and the good times we had together back on Earth, but thoughts of that Henry guy keep intruding. I've never seen him, not a picture, not a description, nothing. I've never even heard anything about him. Russell once mentioned his childhood, but had simply said that his mom was a single mother. I never asked any questions, and he never volunteered any information. How bad had Henry been to keep Russell, Estelle, and Valerie back from Opening? He alone was responsible for holding all those spirits back. I held my own mother back unintentionally, because of my lack of forgiveness. I wonder what key this Henry character holds that will help all those spirits move on?

"You're back! And you look much better I might add. You're real, right, or did I think you up?" The haggard looking man with the long hair and the long beard, which I had met on my last stay in Spirit Prison, approaches me. In the distance I see a bubble—his, I presume. I wonder why he's out of it?

"I'm real, and yes, I'm back. Is that your bubble over there?"

He turns and looks behind him, then suddenly the bubble speeds up to meet up with us. I wince, not wanting to get stuck in a bubble at all. "Yes, that's my imaginary home. It is as it's always been, remember?" He turns and looks at me with eagerness. "We've been hoping to see something, a way out, or a light, or something that would help us get out. We think we're ready to leave." He looks down, and stroking his beard, he smiles. "Well, as ready as we'll ever be while we're here."

"Who's we?" I ask and peer inside his bubble. There's the distinct possibility that he's made up a friend and he thinks that he's not alone. But his bubble is as I remember it—the fire, the high back chairs, and the mirror. All is intact, and there's no one inside.

"Oh, I met a lass," he says, his Irish accent in full swing—and that's when it dawns on me.

"What's your name?" I ask curiously.

"Henry," he responds without guile. "What's yours?"

"Tess." I say, my voice barely above a whisper. This guy is Henry! *The* Henry! It all makes sense, the accent, what he said last time I was here about his wife not risking her eternal salvation for him. How he had been a jerk his whole life, how I found my way to him, when I wanted to be in a familiar place.

"Tess? Now why does that name ring a bell?" He muses, stroking his beard again. "Oh yes! My friend! Oh…" His eyes open wide and he realizes something. "Oh…" he groans again and starts pacing. "Well, I see how this might be a problem now."

"What? What's a problem? What are you talking about? Who's your friend?"

"Me." Eugenia floats up to us, looking steadily at me, like she's not sure whether she should be here or not.

A grin crosses my face and I shake my head. "Henry, I don't think you should trust this one. She's—she's—"

"She's made a lot of big mistakes. Like me." He says simply, looking steadily in my eyes. "You're probably only talking to me right now because you don't know what I've done. If you knew, you might not be so sure."

He's right. I have no problems with him because I don't know anything about the guy, other than he's Alex's great-grandfather. Yet he's the one who is holding back everyone else's progression back in Paradise. Still, he didn't kill anyone that I know of. "Henry," I say with a sigh. "I'm here looking for your great-grandson. He is dead because of—"

"Me," Eugenia owns up to it with a steady voice. "He knows. Well he didn't know it was his grandson. I didn't know they were related until now."

Henry comes to Eugenia's side and puts his arm around her shoulder. Somehow he has been able to look past the burns, the scabs, the patches of scorched hair, and has accepted Eugenia for who she is. "We are ready to leave," he states. "Will you help us?"

His words remind me of my promise to the High Council, that I would bring back *anyone* who crossed my path. But surely, they didn't mean Eugenia! She—she's the one who started all of this! *"I will forgive whom I will forgive,"* the words fall into my head as if they were raindrops. I nod in reply to the silent reproof. But I can't help feeling a bit mad about this, like I've been tricked into doing something I didn't want to do.

"I am sorry for my part in Alex's death," Eugenia bites the words out, like they're painful to utter. "I never intended to hurt him."

"No, you intended to hurt me," I correct.

She clenches her jaw and does not contradict me. "I don't want to be that person anymore," she admits, after a long, uncomfortable silence.

Suddenly I realize that my promise to the High Council could mean that I bring a whole lot of people back with me. This makes me feel disheartened, because somehow, in my mind, I had envisioned getting Alex and maybe a few more spirits, then getting out. Now I see that this would not be as easy as that.

"Listen, Tess, for the record I still don't like you either," Eugenia says blankly. "But I am sorry for my part in all of this. I know it probably doesn't make any sense to you, but just to prove to you that I'm sincere, I'll show you where he is." I realize what a grand gesture this is coming from her. I can read her intentions, and she's not being devious, nor is she trying to pull anything. For once, Eugenia is being unselfish, in her own way.

I agree to follow her, and when we reach the outside of Alex's bubble, I hover above it, looking down before entering. He is back in that prison cell in Mexico where I found him, all those years ago while still alive. Little did I know then, that busting Alex out of prison would be a recurring event for us.

"Was he a soldier?" Henry asks.

"He was imprisoned by some Central American guerilla fighters," I explain.

"No. It was Eros, Agatha's husband. He was going to sell them to Middle Eastern terrorists."

I look at her stunned.

"Agatha told me," she says in a subdued voice.

I feel anger creeping in, and I can see my light starting to dim.

"Don't upset her!" Henry croaks. "She's our only way out of here!"

"Sorry, I was just...telling the truth," she whispers the last few words and lets them dissolve in the darkness where they belong.

"Think happy thoughts, Tess," Henry encourages.

"Wait here," I tell him and dive down into Alex's bubble before it's too late and I lose my temper altogether, or my nerve, or both.

Alex looks up; he has the same expression he did when I found him all those years ago in the real cell back in Mexico. He looks like he's just seen a ghost. Only this time, I really am a ghost. He blinks and shields his eyes from my light; apparently it's still bright enough to blind him temporarily.

"Alex, it's me."

He winces. The light seems to be too much for him. I crouch down next to him so that I'm eye level with him and cup his face. He recoils as if I were toxic to him. I try to link with him, to prove to him that I'm real, but he's blocked me out. *No, don't let it be too late!* "Alex? Come on, let's get out of here. It's me, Tess—I'm real," I tell him, but I can tell that he's still upset with me. His aura is totally changed, I barely recognize it at all. I can't believe the High Council thought he wasn't ready—he's past being ready—he's lost.

"Please believe me," I beg. He looks up and focuses on something behind me. I turn and realize that he's looking at Eugenia and Henry, who did not heed my advice.

"What are they doing here?"

"They want to leave Spirit Prison too, and they're coming with us."

"Eugenia?"

At the mention of her name, she looks down, embarrassed at her appearance.

"Yes, Eugenia is coming with us, and Henry, your great-grandfather."

Alex stares at the man. No doubt he's remembering what the Admiral had told him about Henry. I wish I knew for sure, but he's still blocking me so I don't know what he's thinking. "Does Russell know about this?"

"He does. Come on." I lift him up by one arm, but he doesn't budge. He's like a sack of potatoes. I've never seen him like this—irresolute, negative, jaded—it's like someone replaced the Alex I know with some empty puppet. I try not to let this growing feeling of dread get hold of me. I need to finish this. I need to get him and these spirits out of here and back to Paradise before my own light dims and I can't find my way back. Otherwise, we'll all be stuck here—again.

"Alex?" Eugenia looks up timidly. Alex frowns and looks back at her, not showing any surprise at her appearance in the least. "I—I'm responsible for you being here," she pauses and fidgets with her hands. I can't believe it, but she looks genuinely remorseful and tormented. "I'm trying to set things right. I want to be the person I should have been, and I can't do that unless I know that you are safe. I know it sounds selfish of me, but if you stay, I can't move forward."

I'm about to snort a derisive reply, but Alex's reaction stops me, catching me by surprise. He believes her! He actually responds to her plea and slowly nods his head, and starts to get up. How is this possible?

Looking from one to the other, I check and double check to make sure I'm getting this right. Eugenia is actually convincing Alex to leave Prison. He's showing emotion to her when he showed none to me. Astounded, I watch as his aura is changing from a dogged determination to stay put, to a conceding nod of forgiveness and, and, something else. He's feeling something for her that he didn't feel before. I try to discern better what that feeling is, but my own emotions are getting in the way, I'm stumbling on them, like I would on huge boulders. One thing is clear, though, he's willing to leave Prison and forgive Eugenia, but not me.

Straightening up, he dissolves his bubble and moves forward on his own accord, leaving me standing alone, in the darkness. "Okay then," he says, and eyes Henry dubiously. "I can see where my mother got her eyes," he adds as he brushes past Henry.

Openmouthed and dumbfounded, I hover in the same spot, watching as the love of my life rejects and ignores me completely. "Well, I thought we were leaving," Alex says, without turning to look at me. This is like a slap to the face. I don't know what just happened, but it feels like a nightmare.

Still stunned, I move, but I feel suddenly lost. I'm not quite sure which way to go.

"I want to come too," a voice says behind me. Turning, I see the boy who I encountered my first time here. He's the one who kept driving off the cliff. Now, he's hovering a distance away, with his hands in his pockets, looking spent. "You're taking them out, aren't you?"

"Yes, I am." Seeing him makes me happy, and brightens my spirit. I hated not being able to help him the first time around. "This way, stay close to me," I say, regaining my sense of purpose. I came here to get Alex at all costs, and to bring with me anyone who wanted to come, and that is what I'm doing, I tell myself. A soul is a soul, and we're all important. Still, it gnaws at me that Eugenia was the one who convinced Alex to come, but who cares? He's coming and that's what counts.

Before we move too far, five or six more spirits ask to join us, then ten or so more. Before we clear the darkness, several more spirits join us. I sigh with relief once we cross into the blinding light. Once our sight adjusts to the brightness, we see a throng of spirits looking at us expectantly. They have all come to welcome those who have come out with me. There's rejoicing the minute they see their loved one and stampede forward to greet them. Alex gets a warm reception from his family, but he hardly seems to notice them or care about their reception. Eugenia too, is busy with her family, but keeps taking nervous looks toward Alex. Henry gets a formal hug from his ex-wife, Estelle, and a shake of the hand from her new suitor. There are others whom I don't know greeting him, and Henry looks genuinely happy to see them. Yet he now and then looks longingly after Russell who left earth momentarily, to greet Alex. Valerie is here also, and both of them seem to be intent on ignoring Henry to the point of being rude.

Alex is still sullen and doesn't look particularly emotional about the reunion. Valerie gives me that look, the look that I always dread from her, the one that says—I've seen this in a vision and it's not good. I simply shrug, but a bitter chill permeates my soul. I wasn't made to be ignored by Alex, my essence does not accept it.

We're all walking on eggshells around Alex. No one is sure of what to say or do. Reluctantly, he follows us as we take him on a tour of Paradise. Most of these scenes are new to me, since I haven't had much time to explore. Alex looks around disinterestedly. I think that part of him still wonders if he's imagining all of this. I ask him this in confidence, but he just looks back at me with that same masked face and doesn't answer. Hurt and stung, I look away, trying to keep the fact that I want to scream hidden from the rest.

After the others show us the highlights of Spirit Paradise they leave us, instinctively sensing that we need time alone. I fly us to a familiar spot, the Heavenly replica of the dock of Cielo Celeste, where we spent our honeymoon. We sit there in silence, dangling our feet over the edge of the dock, technically getting them wet with the spiritual water, but not feeling any of it. The heavenly version of Cielo Celeste is nothing like the real place back on Earth. Here, everything looks pristine and paradisiacal. The St. Augustine grass is lush, thick, and vibrant green. The tall oaks look stately and grand, the Palos Borrachos trees that line the riverbank look equally round and heavy, but the spikes on their trunks look less intimidating than I remember them. Their seedpods are open and their fluffy cottony interior is flying all around us, making it look like it's snowing in spring. It's beautiful, but I can't enjoy it.

"I wish I could feel the water," I say, breaking the long silence.

He doesn't respond. There's a chasm between us and I don't know how to bridge it, or what to do about it. He's said maybe two words since he's been in Paradise, and none of them to me. Inwardly, he's also closed up like a clam, and I can't link with him at all. All I can do is read his new aura that tells me one thing—the Alex I know is gone.

"You know, the first time I went to Prison to get you, I saw Agatha. She threatened that if I didn't help her, she would unleash some spirits she called the—"

"Hellhounds, I know."

I pause. "Yes, the Hellhounds. She promised me that you'd be safe as long as I did what she asked."

Alex gets up and glides away, effectively ending the conversation. I follow him, hopeful that perhaps we can still talk about this on the move.

"I know you saw me leave," I say as I try to catch up to him. "I'm sorry that you thought I was leaving you. I wasn't! I was pulled in! Or out, or—" I say shrilly, but get all tongue-tied for some reason and can't seem to be able to explain myself properly. "Believe it or not I did all that for you."

"Believe it or not, I'm not interested in your platitudes."

"W—what?" I shake my head. How is it that this conversation is going so sideways on me?

"Look, I don't feel like dredging up the things that happened there, so stop trying to psychoanalyze things," he states with a tone of finality in his voice, like he's done talking, yet he's only said two dozen words.

"But we have to talk about this. You have to hear my side of the story!"

"What's there to hear or talk about? I died for you, I went to Hell for you, you left me there with the Hellhounds, end of story."

"I'm sorry, but *he* has to ask."

"But he won't talk to anyone! Not to me, not to Russell, no one! Instead he's been spending all his time with Henry and Eugenia, who he hated in life. He needs some sort of intervention." I plead.

"You were told that he wasn't ready, remember?" Drymus has an infuriating way of pointing out the obvious.

"He was tortured by Hellhounds and *you* know better than anyone what he's going through. You told me that when Kerubiel saved you from Spirit Prison, you felt out of place in Paradise."

"Yes, but I also wanted to leave Prison, it was my choice. And it was my choice to Open."

I'm flying myself in circles, both in actuality and emotionally. I can't think straight, I can't see straight, all I know is that after all this work, after all my efforts and all we've been through, I've lost Alex just as we finally made it to Heaven. It makes no sense, I don't want to admit it, but I'm secretly starting to harbor resentment toward the Eternals now. I'm Open, so people can see this in me, and keep giving me the stink eye for feeling this way. I have no one to confide in or talk to about this because everyone has their own deals that they're working on. Celeste is mixed up in a dramatic affair involving her late husband Max and her second husband Ricardo, and it's something right out of a soap opera. Valerie, Dane, Russell, Katie, and now Robyn are all busy trying to fulfill their angelic duties or Open. Dorian has already taken time off from his busy angelic schedule to listen and give me his advice, and I feel bad pulling him out one more time, just so he can listen to me gripe—again. And Alex...he's lost in a miasma of his own making. Nothing he says or does makes sense to me. It's like we speak a different language now. All he wants to do is hang around Eugenia and Henry. Does he know that Eugenia was the one who hired a killer to kill me, then missed and killed him instead? Yes. He knows this. Does he know that Henry abused his great-grandmother Estelle and never tried to contact them after Russell was born? Yes. He knows this too. Does he care? No.

I wish I could cry—have a good long cry—and get it all out. I would rather endure Agatha's physical torture over and over again, than this. Being physically separated from Alex when he died was hard enough. Being spiritually separated from him while he was in Prison and I in Paradise was awful. But to be purposely ignored by him, it's—it's harrowing, unbearable, and simply heart-rending! Oh, how I would like to wail and scream! But I'm in Heaven, and there are no tears in Heaven. Sure, people struggle still and they have to deal with hard things. Dealing with all your unfinished life problems is not easy. If it were we would have dealt with them in life.

One thing has become clear to me. It's harder to deal with life problems here, in the realm of the dead, than it is while alive. The reason, I think, is because you can't change any of it now. You can't go back to life and say: "I'll make that up to you now." Cravings don't just fade, they stay in your head, telling you that you still need whatever it is you crave. No eye for an eye, no tooth for a tooth. Harm can't be undone, or paid for in any form of sacrifice. Physical comfort can't be given, tears can't be shed, kisses can't be given—life is over.

I try to remind myself that what Alex and I had went beyond the physical. We had a spiritual connection before we even knew each other. We shared dreams, we were able to find our way to each other time and time again—so why not now? Why couldn't I find him on my own when I went looking for him in Prison? Why can't he find his way to me now, like he's done since...since before the world began? Yes. I remember that far now. I've been remembering lots of things from my previous existence. Little by little, locked up memories from before I crossed the Veil have been cropping up in my memory, making it even harder to accept the fact that Alex and I are history.

"Tess, you need to stop pacing. You're making it possible for an immortal being to get a headache." Drymus covers his eyes with his hand and rubs the pressure points right between his eyes.

"Sorry." I stop flying in circles and look at him. I feel like a small child every time I look up at him, he's so huge and so imposing. "Did I Open wrong?"

"What? No. Don't insult me," he snaps.

"I'm not trying to insult you. I'm just wondering what I've done wrong?"

"The High Council advised you that he wasn't ready. You were stubborn and railroaded them into letting you go. This is the result," he states.

"Okay, okay." I try to compose myself. "So what now? What do I do? Tell me and I'll do it."

"I don't know," he shrugs and the tips of his wings pop slightly out like a reflex. "There's no rule book."

"But what would *you* do?"

"I would let him be."

I look at him like a lost puppy dog. Does he know how hard that would be for me?

"As a matter of fact, I do know. I had to do the same thing with my wife and kids once Kerubiel brought me to my Paradise," he answers my thoughts.

I stare at him for a few seconds, "Okay, if you say so," I say, beaten.

"Hey, I'm not telling you to do anything. This has to be your own decision."

"I understand." I'm going to do this. As much as it kills me inside, I'll have to let him be. Besides, I do need to get back to Samantha. I've left Valerie and Dane out there too long; she's not their responsibility. "Keep an eye on him for me?"

"Two," he says pointing to his eyes, then winks.

Chapter 15

"What are you doing here? What is this place?" Henry looks around and takes in the scenery. Before him is a fairytale backyard, complete with a flowering vine covered swing set and not just one pretty little playhouse, but a small neighborhood of them. Heaven's muted colors make it look dreamlike and somewhat enchanted, like the Irish fairy tales he grew up hearing.

"This is where I grew up." Eugenia says matter-of-factly.

"Really? This place existed? I can't believe it! It looks like it came out of a painting."

Eugenia nods absentmindedly. "It did. I mean, my mom found the picture in a book and gave it to a landscape designer who recreated it for my third birthday."

Henry shrugs and sits by Eugenia on one of the red-topped toad-stools. "You must have loved it."

"Yes, I did. But I never told her that. I threw a fit instead."

Henry laughs. "Spoiled, were you?"

Eugenia nods again, then shakes her head. "I was spoiled, but so were the Preston's, and neither Alex nor Katie acted like me. Why did I always have to be such a brat?"

Henry looks out and ponders carefully his reply. He had, in fact, asked himself that question many times before. In life, he had made an art out of complicating things for himself and others to the point that he succeeded in driving everyone he ever loved away, including his wife with his unborn child. "I don't know, some of us seem to have been born hard-wired to be contrary. I guess it's just our natures."

"But how unfair is that? Why would I be naturally hardwired to be whiney, annoying, and spoiled, while Tess was hardwired to be strong, confident, and mature? Alex always looked up to her. I knew he was attracted to her, even though she had nothing and was a nobody. He always thought that everything she did was amazing. Why couldn't I do amazing things, things that others would admire and respect?"

"It's no use comparing yourself to others. We are who we are and just like everyone else we have weaknesses *and* redeeming qualities. I just think that we invested more time and energy into the weaknesses, rather than the good qualities."

Eugenia shakes her head emphatically. "I have no redeeming qualities. All I've ever had was money, beauty, and now…even those things are gone. I have nothing left."

"Ooh, I wouldn't say that. I can see good qualities in you. I'm surprised you don't see any of them."

Eugenia turns and looks at Henry as if she's seeing him for the first time. "What do you see in me, Henry?"

"I see resourcefulness, tenacity, warmth of heart, pluck," he smirks and winks at her.

"Pluck?"

"Yeah, pluck. I just saw you asking the woman you tried to murder to help you bust out of Hell. If that's not pluck, I don't know what is!"

Eugenia grins and shakes her head. "It's desperation, that's what it is." She turns, staring ahead at nothing in particular. "You know, I don't hate her anymore. I used to. Now I secretly admire her and wish that I could be more like her."

"You don't have to try to be more like Tess. You just have to find yourself again, or for the first time!" Henry suggests. "You know, I used to think that I could find myself by doing the things that pleased me and me alone. In the process I let everyone I loved down and lost myself entirely. Since my passing, I've had plenty of time to reflect on my life, my choices, my actions and I've come to the conclusion that I've done nothing but betray myself my whole entire life. Who knows what I could have accomplished had I been less self-centered and lost myself in pleasing others, rather than myself?" Henry lifts one finger and shakes it in warning. "I think that had I done that, I might have found the real me."

"What you just said makes no sense to me," Eugenia admits frankly. "How do you find yourself by losing yourself?"

"Have you been to any of your Opening meetings lately?"

"Yes, all of them! But I have no idea what they're saying. It's like everyone is speaking in riddles or some mysterious code language that I don't understand." Eugenia shakes her head angrily. "Why does everyone get it except for me?"

"I think the mind assimilates things when it's ready to assimilate. You'll understand everything at your own speed."

"How come you're so ahead of the game?" Eugenia snaps cynically.

"You forget that I've been dead for a long time. I lived during the turn of the century—the twentieth century, not the twenty-first."

This realization hits Eugenia anew, not that it matters anymore, but she is talking to a guy who could have been her great-grandfather. The thought should be somewhat creepy to her, but it isn't. He looks as he did in the prime of his life. Henry isn't necessarily what she would call handsome. He's tall, has dark hair, broad shoulders—a precedent to his son, Russell, who turned out even bigger than him. Now that he no longer wears a beard, she can see his features better—a prominent aquiline nose, large brown eyes, and full lips. His jaw line is angular, and his skin has a light golden hue to it. Henry is, after further inspection from Eugenia, not bad. But what surprises her the most is the fact that she doesn't see him for what he looks like on the outside. When she sees Henry, she sees his soul, and she likes his soul. She trusts him and prefers his company to that of anyone else at this point. Not even Alex gives her this sense of serenity. With Henry, she can be herself. Around Alex, she has to be on guard, always on her best behavior, always pretending to be someone else, someone more to his liking. It's debilitating and tiresome.

Instinctively, Eugenia slides her arms around Henry's own and snuggles up to him on the toadstool, resting her head on his shoulder. This takes him by surprise, but he doesn't object. Instead he pats her head with his free arm in a soothing manner and rests his own head on top of hers. "That's right, you just let the creepy old guy comfort you," he says self-deprecatingly.

"I don't see you like that!"

"But I am. I could have been your great-grandfather."

"Well...you weren't. Look at your ex-wife! She's with some guy from the 1800's!" Suddenly realizing that what she had just said could be a sore subject, Eugenia looks up at him with alarm. "Wait, does that bother you?"

Henry shrugs. "I'm happy she's happy." He looks out thoughtfully.

"Do you still love her?" Eugenia asks not sure why all of a sudden she cares, yet she does.

"I will always love Estelle, but I've never deserved her. She was an angel sent to deliver me, and I was a devil hell-bent on making her fail. Now, she looks more like an unattainable goddess that is way out of my reach."

Somehow, this answer does not please Eugenia and a tinge of jealousy creeps up within her. But what did she expect to hear? That he only cared about her now? That he no longer loved his ex-wife? "What if... she wanted you back?" Eugenia asks unexpectedly.

Henry smiles broadly. "She wouldn't," he says flatly. "She'd be crazy to. Just like Alex will never want you, dear."

Eugenia's eyes flair open and she pulls away from him indignantly. What a jerk he is! Why would he say such a hurtful thing?

"What? You think I'm rude for saying that? You see this, Eugenia?" He points to her childhood backyard. "*This* is a dream! *This* is a fairy tale. We might be in Heaven now, but Heaven is not Fantasyland. There are realities you and I have to face and one of them is that no matter how much we change, we have hurt these people and they have moved on. They might have forgiven us, but that doesn't mean that we still get to live with them happily ever after. It's a simple cause and effect fact that we have to live with now and for the rest of our eternal existence."

"But Alex is different now. He doesn't even want Tess anymore. He's finally realized how high and mighty she is. He knows that there are things that she will never understand, they can't even relate to each other anymore," Eugenia challenges.

"He's not one of us, Eugenia. He's going through a phase, and he knows that he needs to go through it alone. Once he clears it, he'll go back to her and that will be the end of it."

"How can you know that? You're wrong," Eugenia objects sharply. "We are closer now than we've ever been."

"That may be so, but that's as close as you two will ever get."

"I can see why your wife left you!" she says indignantly. "You're— you are a total jerk!"

Henry raises his eyebrows and shrugs his shoulders, conceding. "I was actually being nice."

With a huff, Eugenia stands and starts to glide away, but gets stopped by something. Looking down at her arm, she sees that Henry is holding her back with one hand. Is he trying to hurt her? She can't tell, she feels nothing.

"I would never lie to you," Henry says, burrowing his intense eyes into hers.

"Ha!" she laughs hotly then jerks her arm away, much as she would have done in life. Then, she flies off as fast as her mind can take her.

"What did I miss?"

"Oh! Good to have you back!" Tony says approvingly. "Thanks for convincing the High Council of our proposal," he says slyly, knowing now that I had a second agenda to bring up with the council all along. "Did everything go, um…okay?"

"Yes, yes, thank you," I say, uncertain of what to say exactly.

"Well, the added reinforcements have made it a lot easier to work with the other angels, who like us are watching over mortals who want to fight. We are coordinating with them, so that our mortals can communicate by ham radio and the telegraph. Sam became one of our most expert radio operators. It was a great cost to have lost her."

"Lost her? Where? How did she get lost? What do you mean?"

"What? You didn't know? They didn't tell you?"

"Tell me what? What!" I wanted to shake the little man and jiggle the whole story out of him quickly.

"She was taken by the ROWE soldiers from the shelter. Pete is beside himself. He can't seem to snap out of it. It's like someone ripped the soul right out of him."

I look wildly around for Russell or Pete, but I see neither. "Where are they? Where is she?"

"Look lady, I have a job here, and I intend to see it through. I don't know what else you have going on that is more important than Armageddon, but I for one, have to get back to work."

I release him and he floats slowly down, stopping short about a foot off the physical floor, making himself look a bit taller than he really is. Straightening out his robe, he eyes me dubiously, then turns back to his duties. "Russell and the boy are at the shelters," he mumbles over his shoulder, with a tinge of pity in his voice.

"Thanks," I say, "Sorry," I add flatly, then fly out toward the shelter.

It takes forever to find them because there are several different shelters in the area. Apparently once ROWE was voted as the new form of government, poverty started to spread like wildfire. Instead of getting rid of it—as the still standing, yet defiled billboards promised—poverty was actually spread equally throughout all the population. Anyone who dared oppose ROWE was hunted down and taken for interrogation. These people never came back. More and more people disappeared each day and families were left without their providers, and without any means of supporting themselves. Business closed down or were vandalized and forced to close their doors. Homes and personal possessions were ransacked by ROWE soldiers and taken as collateral by them. It was legalized crime. Officers and soldiers lived in luxury while the rest of the people starved and froze to death, and that's how shelters came to be.

Some of the less sanguinary ROWE officers had the idea of turning the empty schools into shelters. If everyone died of hunger, there would be no one left to rule over. They were hailed as benevolent and humane, the epitome of what good leadership should be under ROWE, and their measures were copied and implemented worldwide.

All of this I learned from Tony and the other rebellion angels during my first visit to the underground. And as I fly around, I can see what an anthropologist would see—the remains of a great and prosperous society brought to its knees by a corrupt central government. All of it is apparent in the graffiti on the walls, the broken store windows, the rundown, uninhabited homes, the bullet holes, the garbage, and the desolation of the place. My heart aches for this generation, and my heart aches for Sam, compounding the sadness I already feel for Alex and me.

Finally, in one of the shelters, I see Russell and his sword. He's talking to Dane!

"Where is she?" I ask, without so much as a Hello.

"Oh Tess, I'm so sorry, there was nothing we could do!" Dane exclaims. "We didn't leave her side, not for a minute, but—"

"What? What happened to her?" On the floor, despondent and beat-up, lies Pete.

"She's still alive. Valerie is with her. Sam was trying to save these two little kids from the soldiers," he explains hurriedly. "She went back to the shelter, as she was told, so she wouldn't raise any suspicions, and while she was here, she saw that this soldier was taking that lady's twin boys away." He points to a young girl in her early twenties that looks haunted and sickly. She has two vivacious two-year-olds who are playing around her completely unaware of the misery that surrounds them.

"They were being noisy, and one of the soldiers took notice of them. He snatched one of them and was about to take them to what he called, 'officer training camp,' but Samantha snatched the boy back and tried to make a run for it with the two of them."

"It was impetuous of her," Russell remarks. "Had I been here with my sword, I could have stopped the soldier, but…"

"We tried, Tess, trust me. We tried to stop that soldier tooth and nail, but nothing we did worked. There were two escaped spirits from Prison accompanying the soldier, and they grabbed us and held us back. Some of the other angels that happened to be here came to our rescue, but all we could do was take the dark spirits down and bind them. The mortal soldier took Samantha while we struggled with the dark spirits. There was nothing—"

"Yes, I know. Nothing you could do," I mumble. "And him?" I point to Pete.

"We got here right as they were taking Sam, kicking and screaming. Pete tried to get involved, but the soldier knocked him out. They're coming back for him; he's no longer safe here. I've been trying to convince him to get up and move, but he won't. It's like the life has been sucked out of him."

"I know someone else with that problem," I say under my breath.

"Alex?" Dane asks softly. I nod. "I'm going back up to get some Flaming Swords," he says, "I think it's time to have a talk with my son."

"I don't know that talking would do much good. I think maybe time..."

"Maybe I should go," Russell says, with a twist of the sword. "Maybe I should tell him how I feel about dark spirits."

"I think you need to give Tess that sword and in the mean time, while I go get some more weapons for us, keep this kid out of trouble," Dane orders, in an unprecedented take-charge sort of voice. Both Russell and I look at him, as if we're seeing Dane for the first time. "What?" he grumbles. "I'm assertive, I just choose to sit back and observe," he says defensively. "However, the time for observing is over. Now it's time to act." Russell and I nod in agreement and exchange baffled looks. "Come on," Dane gripes. "We're wasting time." He gestures for Russell to hand me the sword and then Dane and I set off—I to help Samantha, and Dane to get weapons.

Sam is being held in a beautifully furnished room in one of the few mansions that has remained intact. It must be one of the officer's homes, or rather, a home that one of the officers took from a civilian. Samantha looks as if she's finally gotten to shower, and has been given a beautiful gown to wear. As she stares in the mirror, shaking with fear, she can't help but also admire her own reflection. It's as if she's seeing herself for the first time in her life, and for a few minutes she allows herself to be a little vain. Her long blond hair is brushed and it flows smoothly down her back, glinting under the bright lights of the room. But as I get closer to her, she stiffens. "You..." she whispers and turns suddenly. "You're back."

I peer into her eyes, and wave one of my hands in front of her, trying to determine once more if by any chance she sees me. But she doesn't even flinch. "Yes," I finally answer her. "I'm sorry it took me so long to come back. I had some business to take care of," I explain, knowing full well she doesn't understand me.

"Yes, it is you. I can feel you. You feel...familiar to me. I wonder why?" She sits on the foot of the bed and slumps her shoulders. "I don't know what they want with me. I don't know what's going to happen to me. The soldier who brought me here told me to shower and to pick a dress to wear for dinner, so I guess I'll at least get to eat. I'm scared though," she says, then cups her face with her hands and starts to cry. Right then Valerie glides through the door and looks in my direction with alarm.

"Tess! Oh! You scared me."

"I did?"

"Yes, I heard her crying and I thought—well never mind, I'm glad it's you." Valerie looks grim and comes to my side. "How did it go? With Alex, I mean."

I shrug. What can I say? "I got him out."

Valerie nods knowingly. "But *is* he out?"

"No," I admit, then sigh. "He and I..." I shrug again. "I don't know what's going to happen. I'm afraid that I've made things worse."

Valerie looks up at me, her eyes are sad and perceptive. "I was going to tell you that I had a feeling that—. Well, never mind about all that."

"I know," I acknowledge. "I saw that look in your eyes before I left and I ignored it. I wanted to go so badly."

Valerie nods solemnly.

"You know...you look different," I comment. "You look...you look..."

"At ease."

"Yes, at ease."

"It's gone!" she says with a smile. "The cloud that hung over me my whole entire life is finally gone! I can't tell you how wonderful that feels! I'm free! I'm free." Valerie closes her eyes and looks as if she's relishing the feeling. I smile. I'm so happy for her. She suffered from depression her whole life, now in death, she's finally found reprieve.

"Well, we have pressing problems to deal with," she says as if snapping out of a trance. Then she glides over to Samantha and wraps her breezy arms around her. As a consequence, the girl shivers.

"I wish—I wish I could see you both. I know you're there, I know you're trying to help but," Samantha shakes her head. "What if none of this is real? What if I'm making this all up?"

With the tip of my sword I reach for a shawl that is lying across a chair and gently lift it up. Samantha doesn't notice it at first, then from the corner of her eye, she sees the sheer fabric floating up all on it's own and she freezes. Her face turns pale and her lips turn white as chalk as her eyes fill with tears that she tries to blink away. Slowly, she stands up and walks toward the floating fabric and touches a corner of it with a shaking hand. "Wow…" she whispers reverently, as she stares at the shawl, suspended in mid air as if by magic.

Chapter 16

A knock at the door makes her jump, and I drop the shawl on her hand right as the door opens. Startled, she turns back and sees that the shawl is now draped across her forearm. "I was just—just—" she stammers.

A good-looking young man dressed in a tuxedo approaches her with a smug look on his face. "I would think that you'd be happy to be finally clean and dressed in a proper dress," he says acidly. "I'd hoped that you would like my home and all the things I can offer you." He brushes a few strands of hair away from her face, and wipes her tear-stained face with the back of his hand. Samantha flinches when he touches her, and he snorts with derision. "What? You don't like me? In time, you will." He looks unflinchingly into her eyes. His slate gray eyes make her even colder and she shivers. His glossy black hair, combed smoothly back, and his crisp suit give him an air of perfection that seems unnatural. "Come on," he offers her his arm. "My parents are waiting for us downstairs." Hesitantly, she places her hand on his arm, and lets herself be led out of the room, but before they exit, he stops abruptly. "Please don't embarrass me," he cautions acidly. "My father is the head of the ROWE division in this area, and we usually have other officers dine with us. I would hate for you to make a spectacle of yourself with poor table manners," he warns. Samantha stares back at him with a deer-caught-in-the-headlights kind of look. Almost imperceptibly, she nods back at him, and satisfied, he resumes their stiff march toward the dining room.

Like two Sentinels, Valerie and I stand guard right behind her, while dark spirits zoom above the dinner table like pesky flies. The conversation during dinner sickens us. All but Samantha chatter away all through their sumptuous dinner, talking about the ignorance of the people and their own exalted state and higher level of intelligence. They laugh about the misery of the people, and talk about them as if they were nothing but mere animals. Then the subject turns to rumors that an underground movement of rebels is forming, and they discuss whether it's a real threat or not. Samantha, who's been quietly eating, stiffens at the word underground, and this does not go unnoticed by her handsome captor, who keeps a shrewd eye on her at all times.

"Samantha, what do you think about an underground rebellion?" he asks with both amusement and a warning in his voice.

Sam holds her fork loosely in her hand, as she looks up, startled by being put on the spot. "An underground rebellion?" she asks tremulously.

"Yes, what do you think about it?"

Swallowing a lump in her throat, she looks back down at her plate. "I think it's a fable," she says. "A story," she adds, "to share when the lights go out at the shelters."

Everyone around the dinner table stares at Samantha, each trying to form his or her own conjectures about her. Up until now, no one would have guessed that such a lovely creature would have an intimate knowledge of what went on in the shelters once the lights go out.

"Well," the head of the ROWE officials says as he clears his throat, wipes his mouth, and looks from his son, to Samantha, and then back again. "I certainly can't imagine any group of civilians having the resources to arm themselves in any way, shape, or form." He laughs, a low throaty laugh. "How are they going to defend themselves? Stones?" And everyone laughs, except for Samantha who merely smiles, and her captor, whose eyes are trained on her like a hunter ready for the kill.

This whole time I'm holding the huge Cherub Flaming Sword that Dane took from Russell, like a bat, ready to strike at any moment. As soon as dinner ends, the men go into one room and the women into another. The soldier who brought Sam to the dinner grabs her arm by the crook of her elbow and holds her back tightly, while the other ladies, full of themselves, walk happily into the parlor. "Behave now," he warns through gritted teeth in her ear, while still keeping a fake smile across his face. "We wouldn't want to cause a scene now, would we?"

"I don't know what you're talking about," Sam says flatly as she yanks her arm away from his grasp, then walks in after the ladies, leaving him standing stiffly all by himself.

"Martin!" his father barks. "Come on, son, come with the men." His face is hard, unsmiling. Once the rest of the men clear the dining room, he stops his son from crossing the threshold. "I don't understand what your fascination is with dirty, dim-witted, shelter girls, but if you bring them here and mix them with good company, you'd better teach them a thing or two about manners," the old General growls in low tones.

The young officer stares blankly back at his father, then pushes past him into the adjoining room. I almost let my sword fall on the creepy old officer, but Valerie holds my arm, stopping me. "Not now, Tess, not like this. We have to play our cards right or Samantha will be the worse for it."

"I'll be fast. They'll never know what happened."

"What, you intend to kill them all? Come on Tess, you're Open, you're supposed to feel more empathy for everyone, right?"

I think about that for a while and my mind flashes to that scene by the lake, where I saw Him, the First One. I thought about His eyes, the pleading in them, and the promise I made to Him. Slowly I lower the sword like a deflated balloon. "We will have to use this to get her out. We'll have to be willing to get our hands dirty to save her."

"We won't get them dirty if we use this sword for its intended purpose."

"And what is its intended purpose?"

"Justice."

I nod and follow in after the men, while Valerie goes in the opposite direction and stays with Samantha. "Justice," I repeat to myself, "What is justice anyway, when there's nothing just about this whole situation."

"It all depends on what your idea of justice is," someone says from behind. I turn in a whirl and see one of the escaped Prison spirits floating carelessly in mid-air, as if he were daintily lounging on a settee. He looks familiar, but I can't quite place him. "You don't remember me, Tess? Oh...I'm hurt." His face is disfigured beyond recognition, but there's still something familiar about him. "Let me freshen your memory, love." He swings his legs over the invisible sofa and hops down to the ground, landing right in front of me. "YOU KILLED ME!" he screams in my face. Even the mortal men, who were talking amongst themselves stop and look around the room with knitted brows. They mumble something about hearing something, and wait for another sound. When nothing else happens, they resume their conversation. The only one who isn't convinced is Sam's captor, Martin, who keeps himself on alert and starts moving around the room, as if he can smell something in the air.

"Oh, I think I remember you now," I say, recognizing the British accent. "You're that washed up rock star, Marcel, wasn't it?"

Marcel stretches a forced smile across his scarred face and looks at Martin. "I've taken him on, you know. He's my own little puppet. Thanks to you and Agatha, I've got my freedom and I'm investing my time into making anyone who is remotely associated with you as miserable as possible."

"Tess?" Valerie, who had popped her head through the dividing wall at the sound of Marcel's scream, says from behind him. "Remember our last conversation?"

"Yes."

"I believe this would be considered just," she says calmly, and before I even think about it twice, I lift my sword and swing it as fast as possible, missing him by fractions.

"Missed me!" he taunts as he darts away from me to the far side of the room. In the blink of an eye, I zoom to the spot where he is and take another swing. "Missed me again!" His singsong voice is annoying me. "Over here," he calls to me from behind his mortal, Martin. "You can finish us both," he sneers.

"You coward! Come and face me, so I can kill you—again," I say savagely.

Valerie, whose head looks like it's been mounted on the wallpapered wall like taxidermy, looks at me as if she's seeing a side of me she's never seen before. But I don't care, I'm sick of all this crap. My past has a way of cropping up and hurting the ones I love, while I seem to escape unharmed. My parents, Dorian, Alex, now Samantha...enough! I'm catching this ghost and I'm sending him back to oblivion, then I'm going after Agatha and putting an end to this.

"Tess?" Valerie warns. "Don't swing that sword in anger."

Marcel whispers something into his mortal's ear, and he obeys unquestioningly. "Martin? Martin!" his father calls, but Martin ignores his father completely and listens only to his little devil.

"Valerie, get Sam," I shout. And with that, Valerie's head disappears through the wall.

I'm floating between the old General and his son, with my sword still pointed toward the little minion who is hiding behind his living puppet. "Come on Marcel, it's me you want," I call him out, but Marcel simply smiles and drones malicious ideas into Martin's ear. Obeying whatever his little devil says, Martin pulls out a gun he had hidden under his suit coat and walks out of the room where all the men are and into the parlor, pointing the barrel right at the women. As he does this, he frowns and looks temporarily puzzled. The women in the room scream, all but Samantha who's petrified, standing at the opposite end of the room. Valerie is behind her, quietly whispering in her ear, hopefully telling her how to escape.

"Martin!" his father's booming voice startles the young officer, and he swings around to face the sound, involuntarily pulling the trigger. The escaped bullet hits his father square in the chest, and the man collapses to his knees with a look of astonishment in his eyes. More women scream, filling the room with a high-pitched ringing sound. Martin's eyes widen and his minion floats back away from him cursing. Without hesitation, I take advantage of this temporary distraction, and let my flaming blade fall straight down on the minion. Marcel's form splits in two and each side of him hangs there, like a mirror image, inert and torpid.

"Valerie, now!" I yell, and Valerie rushes to the disabled Marcel. She grasps both sides of him with her fingertips, and makes a face, as if she was touching some disgusting thing. "Take him back before he pulls himself together," I order, amidst the disorder of the room. Valerie obeys at once and disappears through the ceiling.

With that done, I focus my attention back onto the mortal scene before me. Martin is still standing there, still pointing the gun at his father, who's on his knees, bleeding, staring at his son with astonishment. All the women are still screaming, except for Samantha who is still frozen with shock. The men are rushing to the scene assessing the situation. "Come on, Sam," I murmur in her ear. "Time for us to leave," I say, then try to grab her arm, but can't. My touch, however, makes her shiver and this brings her to herself.

With the tip of the sword, I manage to move the heavy drapes aside, and frantically try to undo the latch of the window. Sam sees the curtains part all on their own, and stares at the miracle with a mixture of awe and astonishment. "Come on, there's no time!" I tell her, still trying to undo the latch. Finally, I give up and with the hilt of the sword, I smash the glass of the window.

Samantha jumps at the sight of the window suddenly bursting and shivers as she sees the small jagged fragments that are still attached to the frame falling on their own to the ground. "Come on!" I yell again. "It's now or never!" I try pulling at her hand and she clenches her fists, suppressing a violent shiver that seems to travel all the way up her arm and down her torso.

Turning around once to see what is going on in the room, she swings one leg over the window ledge, with difficulty, because of the dress she's wearing. None of the women see her or hear the breaking glass; the noise seems to melt into the general upheaval and the hysteria. None of the other officers notice this either. Only Martin seems to hear it above the commotion, and slowly turns on his heels, with his hand still on the trigger. He and Sam exchange numb looks as she freezes temporarily with half her body hanging out the window.

Somehow, Martin knows that whatever just happened is her fault, and he blames her for it. His cold, hard stare conveys all this brewing hatred to her. He had intended to transform her from a shelter scum to an officer's wife. He had meant for them to have a big house of their own and to live in comfort, but she had ruined all of this. She had made him pull that trigger, she had forced his hand in some way and now....

Raising both his hands at the same time, he aims toward Sam. "No!" I scream. "Go Sam, go! Jump!"

A wicked smile spreads across Martin's face, and his finger starts pulling the trigger. One of the women, his mother, who had temporarily fainted at the sight of her husband being shot, presently stands up, blocking his view of Samantha, and screams. "Martin what have you done?" Her strangled voice sounds more like a croak.

One of the officers present looks up at the sound of the woman and sees that Martin is now pointing the gun toward his own mother. He stands up and pushes Martin's arms up toward the chandelier. The bullet leaves the barrel. At the same time Sam loses her footing and falls, landing on a poky shrub. More screams are heard inside the house. There's a scuffle, men shout orders, and someone hits the ground with a thud— passed out or dead—I don't know, I don't care. Samantha is safe from that maniac.

I tell her to run, but I don't know where I'm going, so mostly I follow her. She seems to possess the sense of direction that I never procured. She stops, catches her breath, making a white puff of air come out of her mouth due to the bitter cold. She's wearing a sleeveless dress, but she doesn't look cold yet since she's running high on adrenaline. One of her legs is bleeding; a shard of glass that I missed must have cut her. It doesn't look too deep though, and for now the crimson of her blood blends in with the crimson of her dress. She takes her shoes off, and holds them up eye level to look at them and pouts. "I bet that you, of all people can relate with me," she says as she gasps for air. "You—you liked nice things. You made nice dresses like this one." She looks down at her dress, now in tatters thanks to the window, the bush, and the run. With a sigh, she chucks the shoes behind her and starts running again.

Finally, she reaches my old house, the house where I first found her, where she met up with Pete. I'm way ahead of her, and I float up to the attic, and with the tip of my sword I start opening boxes, desperately trying to find her some better clothes to wear, something practical and warm. Unfortunately all my practical clothes must have been donated, only some of my dresses remain. I go through some of Alex's things and find some old uniforms of his. They will be huge on her, but better for the cold. I have them all laid out for her when she makes it up the stairs, and she smiles with a sigh. "I see you beat me to it," she says casually.

Upon further inspection, I see that her scratch is a lot deeper than I first anticipated. She's lost a lot of blood and she's now shivering and looking pale. There's no first aid kit, no bandages, nothing. I open one of my boxes and take out one of my old dresses. With the edge of the sword I slice it into strips. "No...not that one," she moans. "Of all the dresses! Seriously?" she whines, obviously harboring a preference to that dress.

"I'll make you another," I tell her, while I drape the strips of fabric over the sword and gently drop them over her wounded leg.

"Thanks," she says dryly, and her attitude reminds me that she's still a teenager and necessity has not taken the attitude away. But, in spite of it all, she rolls up her pant leg and starts wrapping her leg with the strips. "Not exactly how I wanted to wear that particular dress, but..." she sighs. "If I had lived with you, in your time period, I would have made dresses too," she declares, then shudders in spite of herself. The cold is finally sinking in and I see that her lips are turning purple.

From between the rafters I see Valerie's head pop up. "Oh! There you are. So glad I found you," she says with a sigh of relief. "I stopped by the house, just to make sure you made it out. The whole place was in chaos."

"I broke a window and she escaped through there. I'm afraid she got hurt," I say, pointing to the leg she's bandaging. "She needs to sterilize it, or it'll get infected."

"Yes...but I'm afraid that's not the worst of her problems."

"No? What is?" I ask, puzzled. I know things are not ideal, but I figured that now that she is free, it's all a matter of letting Pete know and taking them to the underground.

"Martin was taken to a prison for murdering a ROWE official. He'll probably get special treatment though because the official happened to be his father and...he keeps insisting that the only reason he shot his father was because Sam was a rebellion operative. He's claiming that he was trying to shoot her."

"They're going to believe him?"

"I'm afraid so." Valerie nods grimly. "His mother is hysterical, and afraid of him, so she's going to testify in his favor."

"So what are you saying?"

"Pete and Sam need to leave. Now."

"What's gotten into you? I don't even know you anymore?" Dane says to his son through gritted teeth, not caring so much about being overheard, but mostly to keep his cool down. "You've been reticent to us and downright rude to Tess—to Tess! Did you know that she went back to earth to relieve your mother and me, so she could take back her charge as a guardian angel? She didn't have to, she could have stayed, but she did it to give you some space, because you have done nothing but ignore her. Son, do you realize what she's done for you? Do you realize what she's put at stake, just to save you?" Dane sighed and paced in a circle. "Sure, she went about it all wrong, like you, I might add. But her intentions were sincere."

Alex looks at his father with mild interest. He's never seen his otherwise cool and collected father in such a state of excitement. In life, Dane had been a psychiatrist, a good, methodical man who never pressed his children to talk until they were ready. He would often cross their path in the kitchen or knock at their door and simply state that he was available to talk any time they felt like talking—and he always was. Many times Alex could call or corner his father, even at odd times—day or night—and his dad would always drop whatever he was doing and talk for as long as Alex needed. If he happened to be in with a patient, he would have the kindest way of saying he was otherwise engaged. Dane always knew how to say things the right way. However, Alex had never seen his father agitated or upset, not like this.

Even so, shrugging with indifference, Alex turns away from his father. "I'm not ready to talk," he says drily. He knew he was being rude, but he couldn't help it. Something had broken inside of him, ever since he saw Tess gliding by his bubble, ignoring him completely. Thinking that it was a mistake, he had followed her, and when she finally looked at him, she told him to stay away. Then she disappeared, leaving him to rot in Hell. To add insult to injury, sometime after that, they had briefly linked minds, only to find that Tess was safely enjoying herself in Heaven, attending weddings and designing dresses as if nothing was ever wrong in her world. Everything changed for him then. Something shut down inside him at that moment, and now he was different.

Maybe he had been naïve to believe that love could survive death. Maybe there was a reason why mortals only promise to love each other "'til death do us part". Or maybe it had nothing to do with love, maybe it was something else; but whatever the reason Alex felt nothing—no pity, no guilt, no hate…no love. Half the time he wasn't even sure if any of what was going on around him now was real. For all he knew he was still in that prison imagining all of this.

"So that's it? You don't care anymore?"

Alex stares blankly at his father. If he says anything, it would be something rude, something that would no doubt upset his father and alienate him even further.

"Remember when we used to sail in the Caribbean? Remember what would happen when the wind would die down and there was not so much as a breeze to fill the sails and move us?" Alex looks up at his father, remembering the vacations they used to take with Russell, his grandfather. "What did you guys used to call that?"

"Becalmed," Alex mutters, his voice barely above a whisper.

"Becalmed," Dane nods in agreement. "You're becalmed, just like a sailboat without wind. And you will remain this way until you take out your oars and start paddling. There is no motor here. You'll have to get yourself out of this. Save yourself, or be damned." Dane states with an uncharacteristic tone of finality that Alex has never seen his father have. "I've said what I needed to say to you." He looks at Alex square in the face, there's no trace of anger there, just sadness. "Farewell, son." And with that said, Dane takes off suddenly.

Alex watches his father take off, and sees as he grows in brightness. As he flies away, Dane gets brighter and brighter until, in the distance, he seems to explode in light. Suspended in mid-air, he goes supernova, and Alex silently observes as the brilliant light envelops his father completely. Once he is full of light, Dane takes off just like a shooting star across the night sky, leaving Alex awestruck.

"Wow! What was that?" Henry asks, pointing to Dane's fading light.

"My father."

"Dane? What happened to him?" Eugenia asks with alarm.

"He—he exploded into light."

"You mean he Opened," Henry clarifies. "It was bound to happen. He looked ready. I guess he just had to straighten a few things with you

159

first." He looks down to a gadget he's been fumbling with, and arbitrarily starts pressing buttons, making the object emit all kinds of sounds.

"What does that mean?"

"What?" Henry looks up from the apparatus distractedly, as if he has just been pulled away from another realm of existence.

"What you said, that he 'Opened'. What does that mean?"

"What, you don't know?" Henry murmurs absentmindedly, as he lifts the device eyelevel and squinting takes new inventory of it. Eugenia rips the offending gadget from Henry's hand, as she would from a misbehaving child.

"Pay attention!" she scolds. "He's asking you a question."

"What?" He inquires, baffled by this sudden outburst. "Oh, yeah. Opening." Henry shakes his head as if clearing it. "He...haven't you gone to any of the meetings with your Spirit Guide?"

"Spirit Guide? What's a spirit guide? No, I haven't. Have you?"

"Of course," Henry looks insulted, and Eugenia nods knowingly.

"That was one of the first things they told us about when we got here, didn't you hear?" Eugenia asks delicately, not wanting to make Alex feel like an idiot.

"No, I guess I wasn't paying attention."

"I'd say! They only told us to set up a meeting with a Spirit Guide about a hundred times," Henry blurts out, not worried in the least about Alex's feelings.

"What does that have to do with Opening?"

"That's the whole point of meeting with your Spirit Guide—Opening! It's why you do it."

Rolling her eyes Eugenia pushes Henry out of the way and tosses him his gadget back, turned on and all ready to go, then turns her attention back to Alex. "You saw how your dad exploded in light? You saw how brilliant Tess is?" She bit her tongue the moment she mentioned Tess' name, but no matter, it was done. "Well, they are Open. That means that they have resolved all their issues and they are like an open book. They have nothing to hide, no blemish, no spot, no darkness in them. They've been purified. Not perfect, just pure, like a child."

"Oh, nothing to hide..." he echoes softly, then clamps back up like he has been ever since he got to Paradise.

"This device is incredible! Look at all the things it can do! But I fail to see what its primary function is," Henry murmurs, as he glides back to their side distractedly. "It's something that mortals will invent! It's—it's..."

"It's a smartphone, you idiot!" Eugenia blusters. "It's been invented for ages!"

"Has it really? You—you've had this at your disposal? What is a smartphone? And what else did you have?" Henry asks admiringly, impervious to Eugenia's insults.

Eugenia sweeps a hand over her face, then gets an idea. "I know!" She says enthusiastically. "I heard of a place, a museum of sorts, that has all kinds of relics and devices," she adds, turning to Henry. "Not just modern things but all kinds of artifacts that have been around since the dawn of man."

"Not interested," Henry declares.

"No, you don't understand. It has all things ever invented and yet to be invented!"

"Oh. Okay, I'm in," Henry changes his position once more. "You with us, Alex?" Alex shrugs noncommittally, but follows them. But once they're at the museum, he starts getting interested in the different spiritual objects that are on display, and ends up reading about all of them and their significance.

"Ancient Religious Relics?" Eugenia reads a sign that points toward the right. "Let's go this way," she insists and they follow her down a dimly lit hallway. Each artifact has its own spotlight shining down on it, making it look even more Heavenly.

"I liked the modern relics better," Henry whines as he peers unimpressed at the two tablets before him.

"Are you kidding me? You're looking at the Ten Commandments!" Eugenia protests.

Henry shrugs and walks on. "They're just two stones."

"Written by God," Eugenia clarifies.

"Still two stones."

Eugenia looks at Alex for any sign of commiseration, but sees none. Alex looks impervious to the banter in which Henry and Eugenia are engaged. He simply looks at each object and reads the captions with the same amount of interest as he would at any normal museum.

"The Holy Grail, King Solomon's riches, Sampson's hair, the original Dead Sea Scrolls, very interesting, yes, yes, can we go now?" Henry asks.

"No!" Eugenia barks in annoyance, mostly upset at herself for mentioning Tess' name and ruining this outing.

"Hold on." Henry screeches to a halt right in front of an odd looking pair of white rocks that are attached together like a peculiar pair of glasses. "What are these?" He peers down at the plaque that explains what the rocks were. "The Seer Stones," he says with awe and reads the rest to himself in a low murmur.

"They look like goggles with stone lenses," Eugenia whispers.

"It says here that chosen men, from the time of Adam on, have used these stones to see the future as it would take shape should things continue to proceed as they are at the time the Seer looks into them."

"What, like a crystal ball?" Eugenia asks, frowning as she grabs the spiritual stones and inspects them from all angles.

"Sounds like it," Henry replies. "May I?" He takes the stones from Eugenia and turns the contraption in his hands, looking for some hidden mechanism. On seeing nothing out of the ordinary, he gingerly puts them over his head and slides them down toward his eyes.

"I don't think—" Alex tries to stop him, but he's too late, and Henry freezes in place like a manikin. He and Eugenia exchange puzzled looks, then turn to look back at Henry, who after a few minutes removes the apparatus with a wide, pleased smile on his face.

"Wow! Now that's grand!" Henry's Irish accent comes out genuinely strong and fresh, making the other two smirk.

"How does it work?" Eugenia asks, taking the apparatus from him.

"Well you just—okay, never mind," Henry stops explaining when he sees that his explanations are no longer necessary, because Eugenia places the stones over her eyes and goes rigid at once.

After a few minutes, Eugenia too, takes off the stones and places them slowly back in the display case. She's more quiet and subdued than before, like she's still digesting the information she got from the stones.

"What? What did you guys see?" Alex asks, piqued now with interest.

"It was incredible," Henry says.

"And freaky," Eugenia adds. "But yeah, incredible," she darts her eyes briefly toward Henry, who had his eyes fixed on her. The two hold each other's gaze for a few moments, then look away embarrassed.

"Let me see that." Alex reaches over and starts putting the stones over his head. "If this is all a ruse, I swear…"

"Oh it's real," Henry assures, and Eugenia nods in solemn agreement.

Within seconds Alex's senses are assailed with all kinds of images, all coming at him at once, overwhelming his mind with information. Alex feels as if he were watching several 3-D movies at once, each screen showing a different show. For a while he struggles to focus on just one of the screens, and the moment he does, he regrets choosing this particular show. Rejecting the images altogether, he tries to find other images. He repeats the process and sees another, equally distasteful turn of events. He sifts through several different options until he finds one that he likes better, but then another, and yet another set of events unfold—all running along the same theme—possible consequences to his actions. As if stung by a wasp, he rips the apparatus off his head, and tosses it back in its display case carelessly.

"Crazy, huh?" Henry remarks with a smirk.

Alex stares back, stunned, and still reeling.

"Was it bad?" Eugenia inquires with a frown.

Alex narrows his eyes, and looks uncertainly back at Eugenia, still haunted by the visions that those stones gave him. "I'm done with this," Alex states, then storms away, leaving in his wake distress and torment.

Chapter 17

We run into a snag when Russell fails to get the despondent Pete to leave the shelter, and Samantha cannot be moved from the attic due to her cut. She's lost a lot of blood and she's shaking uncontrollably. Currently she's either asleep, or passed out, looking very pale and in great need of medical treatment. Valerie keeps moving around in a tight circle right in the middle of the attic, the only spot high enough to allow her to stand up straight without having her matter pass through the supporting beams of the roof. "She needs food and she needs that cut cleaned and sewn up." She shakes her head with exasperation. "But anywhere we take her, she's bound to get interrogated."

"Maybe if we take her to a place far enough away," I suggest.

"But how? How do we move her? Without Pete's help, we're sitting ducks."

"So, he's just sitting there?"

"Pretty much," Valerie says, her eyebrows raised high in complete disbelief. "Russell says he's been catatonic since they took Sam." She turns a few more times in her spot then looks up at me. "I can't believe that we're going to lose her like this."

"No." I shake my head. "We're not losing her," I say with renewed determination. Sam trusts me implicitly; she still carries around that picture she ripped from that yearbook as if I were her patron saint. I don't want to be worshipped, but I do want to live up to her expectations of me. I've let so many people down lately. Sam will not be one of them.

I don't notice it, but I'm now pacing too, crowding Valerie on the small spot. She's looking at me with expectant eyes, like she knows that I'm brewing up a plan of sorts.

"We need another mortal," I say as I turn, and start tapping my forehead with my index finger.

"I could go to the underground and see if one of the mortals there…" Valerie volunteers, yet even as she says it, she knows that it would be next to impossible. It's hard enough to get a mortal to follow simple instructions from their guardian angel. It would be ten times that difficult to get someone to deliver a whole message with enough time to actually help Sam. "At the very least we can get some rubbing alcohol and sterile bandages."

"I might be able to get those things with the sword, but how do I manage to move it all undetected? I mean, the minute someone spots a jar of alcohol floating in mid-air, they're bound to get suspicious."

Sam's jaw is now chattering, not just with cold, but uncontrollably, like it would with a fever. Suddenly, a crazy idea pops into my head. "John!"

"Who?"

"John!" I repeat, the whole thing making sense to me now. "He's an Aeoninan. He can see and hear us, and he's mortal...sort of. He'll help!"

"What's an Aeonian, and how can he sort of be mortal?"

"He's like a human-angel hybrid. He's a mortal that doesn't age. He's been here on Earth since—since, well...he's John the Revelator," I say, pleased to have explained things so well.

"John the Revelator? He's still alive? And—and you want to contact him?" Valerie's mind is both stumped and racing at the same time. None of this makes any sense to her.

"Listen, Val, John was there for me. My whole life! He promised my father that he'd keep an eye on me."

"John the Revelator knew your dad?"

"Yes, they went to college together."

"John the Revelator went to college?"

"Well I'm sure he went a whole bunch of times, but one of those times, he met my father and they became good friends."

"Why?"

"I don't know...they just did! Listen Val, I know this makes little sense to you, but I know he can help us. So I need to locate him."

"OK, OK. Let's just say that this—this—John of yours, can help us. How on *Earth* are *you* going to find him?" Her sarcasm wasn't lost on me. And she did raise a good point. How would *I* of all people find him? I never had to find John before, he always found me. He had to keep an eye on me, and that's why he was always around. He knew I was dead, so he'd have no reason to find me now.

"Wait a minute!" I exclaim, suddenly remembering something, as if it were out of a dream. "I've seen him! I—I even think I know where he lives!" I say, flying up into a little jump. "Think Tess, think." I tap my forehead even harder, trying to rattle the memory loose. I saw John when Agatha pulled me out of Prison. I was in a daze then, confused, and trying to get back to the realm of the dead, but failing miserably. Vaguely I seem to remember certain things about the place. I mention this to Valerie and she starts thinking and asking for more details. Finally we narrow the place down to a few hundred possibilities.

"It's useless Val. I'm completely inept at directions. I can't believe that this handicap of mine is going to cost Sam her life!"

Valerie stares at me openmouthed, also in disbelief at the fact that being directionally challenged is costing us so much. She tries to say something comforting, but there's nothing she can say—it's not okay, it will not be fine, we won't find another way.

I look up at her with sheer pain in my eyes. Then I crumble to the floor of the attic next to the shivering Sam. I feel liquid, like I could turn into a puddle if I let myself. Instead of dissolving into fluid form, I groan an inner plea for help. *"Don't let her die because of me. Please, help me know how to help her!"* I pray, and while I do so, I'm well aware of the fact that my plea is not just for Sam, but for Alex as well. My need to help Sam right now is not purely selfless—I need her to survive because I need to succeed at something right now.

In the midst of my wallowing in self-pity, a sudden change comes over Valerie, and her old sassiness comes out full force. "For crying out loud Tess, you're an Angel! Pull yourself together and start acting like one! In life you had all sorts of abilities that helped us! You found Alex in some hole in Mexico! You talked to him after he died and you could hear your dead grandmother your entire life! Can't you use any of those gifts now to find this John character?" Valerie yells and Sam stirs, shivers, and mumbles something.

"The Link..." I mutter, in the faintest of whispers. "I could talk with Alex because of the Link. Drymus! He spoke to me through the Link, too."

"Good, see? Use this Link thingy and talk to him!" Val orders.

"Easier said than done," I grumble, as I close my eyes and try to focus on John. Linking with Alex used to be easy; it was more a matter of wanting to talk with him and simply connecting. It was almost like the line to him was always active, only now, he refuses to answer. Pushing aside the pain that this thought brings me, I re focus my attention on John. I think of the first time I saw him, dressed like a police detective, investigating Agatha's disappearance. Then I think of all the other times, culminating with the last time I saw him, in that nondescript apartment, coming and going as I lingered inert and lost in a foggy stupor.

"Tess? Is that you?" A voice sounds clear as a bell in my head.

"Yes!" I respond, opening my eyes with excitement. *"John?"*

"Yes, who else? This is not like a phone line, where anyone in the house can pick up, you know."

I smile and chuckle. Valerie shoots me a quizzical look, and I wave her off. *"Good I'm glad, because I wasn't sure how to connect with you."* There was a long pause, where I could see a bit of impatience in his mind. He wasn't annoyed that I had called, but I can see that he's pressed for time, he has to be somewhere and he's already running late. *"Did I catch you at a bad time?"*

"No, no. I'm just trying to hurry. We are having our first Aeonian council today at my place, and I've already heard from two of them, saying that they are there already. When you first linked with me, I thought it was one of the other Aeonians wondering where I was."

"How many of you are there?" I ask, then remember that there are more pressing things. *"Never mind. Listen John, I'm sorry this is not a good time, but I—we need your help."* I show him my memories of all the events, including Pete's despondent state. *"Now, I know they're not your charges, and that you have bigger things to worry about, but is there a way at all that you could help us?"*

"Well, actually, it might just work for both of us. Hold on," he says, and puts me on hold or something. It's the weirdest feeling, like I'm still connected with him and hear his subconscious but in a paused state. I even think I can hear him humming, just as if I'd been put on hold with elevator music in the background. *"Okay,"* he says, putting me off hold. *"I've just contacted the other Aeonians, and they are on their way to you. I'm going to get Pete. We'll all meet back at my place. John out."* He hangs up on me and my brain goes perfectly blank for a second. Valerie's aggravated face brings me back to reality.

"So?" she asks impatiently. "Did you talk to him? Is he coming?"

I nod. "With reinforcements," I add. "We're about to meet the Aeonian Council."

"You're coming with me," a uniformed soldier growls and bends down to lift Pete up by one arm. "Come on, don't make me angry. Cooperate, or I'll use force." The soldier struggles with a listless Pete who keeps slipping from his grasp, only by sheer lack of willpower.

"Come on Pete, wake up son! Fight! Don't let them take you! I'm telling you, things are not as grim as you think." Russell yells in Pete's ear.

A combination of Russell's words and the soldier's rough handling, wakes Pete up from his lethargy, and he starts to struggle. "Put me down, put me down! I've done nothing! Put me down, you filthy scum!"

"Oh now, that's no way of talking to an armed soldier, boy. If I had no cause to arrest you, I do now," the soldier says good-humoredly, as if he was finally starting to enjoy his job.

"Where are you taking him?" one of the soldiers standing guard over the shelter, asks with mild interest.

"You know where."

"That bad, huh?" the guard responds, lifting Pete's head by the roots of his hair, and staring into his horror stricken face. "What have you been up to?" he says sarcastically.

"Is he at all involved with that incident at the Prefect's house?" the other guard asks, conversationally.

"Don't know, don't care," the soldier who's got Pete in cuffs says gruffly. "Come on, he's a squirmy one, open the doors."

The guards do as they're asked and as soon as they close the doors behind them, Pete arches his back forcefully and hits the soldier in the teeth, with the back of his head. The soldier groans and relaxes his grip. Taking advantage of this, and inspired by Russell's instructions, Pete swings his cuffed hands up and hits the soldier in the jaw. While the soldier is still reeling from the blow, Pete kicks him in the stomach and doubles him over, then takes to his heels and starts running.

"Stop!" croaks the soldier through the pain. "If you ever want to see Sam again, you'll be smart and stop right now!"

This makes Pete stop and reconsider his actions. If they had Sam and they knew about the rebellion, perhaps he'd be able to convince them that she had nothing to do with that, and take him instead. "I know where she is," the soldier groans, still recovering from the blows.

"I want to see her," Pete demands from a safe distance.

"I'll take you to her right now." The soldier says as he takes in a few deep breaths, and lets them out slowly. Once Pete is within arm's length, the soldier pulls him closer to him and secures his grip while he opens the back door of a limousine. Pete had only seen a limousine pull up when the Prefect himself came by to do inspections. He would parade around the shelters like a lord, and look down on the people who had been forced to live there, as if they were sewer rats. Wordlessly, the soldier takes his cuffs off, and pushes Pete into the car. Briskly he jumps in after him—something highly unusual—and shuts the door. "Let's go," the soldier orders, and the car peels out in a hurry.

Pete's eyes had to adjust to the darkness inside the vehicle, and once he did, he realized that there were other people in there with him. "Pete?" a soft, pain-filled voice says from the darkness.

"Sam?"

"Yes." Sam nods and her head feels dizzy by that simple movement.

Meanwhile the soldier sitting next to him starts to take off his uniform, tossing it in the seat across from him. "You have a mean left hook," the soldier says amicably. Pete says nothing; he simply stares and looks alternatively from Sam to the soldier, who looks more like a normal person without the uniform.

"What's this all about?"

"Your rescue," the soldier says. "By the way, my name is John." He extends his right hand and leaves it there for a long while, until Pete decides to go ahead and shake it.

"Pete," he says, with bewilderment.

"Nice to meet you," replies John as he shakes the boy's hand vigorously.

"Who are you, John, and where are you taking us?" demands Pete, still leery.

"I'm a friend of a friend," John explains elusively. "And that is Mathoniaha." He points to the man driving the limo.

"Matt for short, if you'd prefer," Mathoniaha says, tipping his soldier's cap forward just a bit.

"You'll have to leave us around back, Matt, there's no camera there," John instructs, as he leans forward. "I trust you'll be okay dropping off this car by yourself."

"Don't worry about me. I've done this before." Matt grins and chuckles.

"She's bleeding!" Pete shouts, when he finally gets a good look at Sam. "What's happened to her?"

"I—I escaped the Prefect's house through a window," Sam says weakly.

"Did you happen to break the glass first, or did you just jump?"

"The window was broken, but I missed a shard."

"What were you doing at the Prefect's house? And why are you dressed like that?"

Through a dry mouth and shallow breaths, Sam tells him her whole story, culminating with her retreat into her old home, where she changed into Alex's old military clothes that she found in the attic.

"Wow! It's a miracle you escaped at all. Why would that officer shoot his own father?" Pete mused.

"I don't know," Sam says feebly and leans her head back in the seat.

The limo pulls up to the back of a run-down apartment building that looks completely abandoned. John helps Pete move Sam out of the car and up the stairs. John's apartment is a dump, and to make matters worse, it's crammed with people.

"Are all these people Aeonians?" I ask John quietly.

"Yes ma'am," John responds as he helps lay Sam on his dusty futon.

Pete looks up, furrowing his eyebrows and looks around the crowded room. "Who were you just talking to?"

"An angel, of course," John says matter-of-factly, then winks genially at Pete, leaving him more bewildered than ever.

Pete looks down at Sam with consternation and she shrugs in reply.

"As soon as Mathoniaha gets back we can begin," John states to the assorted group that is standing uncomfortably around his studio apartment. There's a long pause in which no one speaks. Finally a tall and slender woman with shaved short hair, ebony skin, and a choker that takes up the length of her neck, steps out from the crowd and comes close to Sam.

"I'm a healer. I can help," she says with a thick South African accent. She then rattles off a list of items that she needs and John scoots his way toward his pantry to fill the order. Before too long, Sam's wound is cleaned and bandaged, and she is peacefully sleeping.

"Thank you," I whisper, not sure if all Aeonians are like John and can see angels.

"Karibu," she says with a white, toothy, smile.

Pete thought she had been talking to him, so he cleared his throat. "Um…what?"

"I said, you're welcome."

"Oh! Um. Thank you?" Pete responds, awkwardly.

The woman smiles, then chuckles, and her laughter grows in crescendo for a minute, then dies down to a more subdued sigh. "She should sleep now for a while. She lost a lot of blood, so she'll need nourishment when she wakes up. You have food in this…dwelling of yours, John?" She teases.

"Yes, Eshe. At least enough to nourish the lot of you while you're here."

A few of the other standing Aeonians utter some comments in low murmurs, then the front door swings wide open and Mathoniaha strides in confidently. "Okay, what did I miss?"

"John here says he has food for all of us," one of the Aeonians, who is standing toward the back says jovially. He's big, like Russell, blond, with an equally blond bushy beard.

"Enough to feed Tor and Atonga?" Mathoniaha quips.

"Are you—?" Russell says with awe as he floats closer to the blond man.

"Thor?" the large guy guesses. "Noooo…well…yesss. I suppose I am. I'm no God mind you, just a legend," Tor says humbly in singsong, Scandinavian tones. "Hard to keep it under wraps when you can't be killed."

"How about the rest of you?" Russell asks, excited now to see what other legends are gathered here.

"I'm Atonga," says the other big guy, in a booming bass, while bowing his head slightly. He looks Polynesian, and like he could give Tor a run for his money. "In my culture they think of me as half human, half spirit, and all because I made a canoe," the big guy explains with a shrug.

"Onamuji," says a small Asian man, dressed in a white robe with long, wide sleeves and red pants. "Though I tried to discourage them, legends have been told about me among my original people of Japan."

Pete is staring at these odd people, as they speak to what appears to be thin air. His head turns from one to the other and to the empty space they are talking to, as if he were watching a tennis match. "Has everyone lost their mind, or have I?" Pete finally says with exasperation.

"These are uncommon times, Pete," John says casually, as he produces chairs and mugs filled with some hot liquid, for all the corporeal beings present. "Normally, a mortal boy such as yourself would never see or hear of us. You might pass us on the street and think we are just regular people, when in reality we're not."

"No," asserts Atonga, leaning forward on his chair. "There might be legends told of us, greatly exaggerated, but those only came about at the time of our transition."

"Transition?" Pete asks.

"When we chose to remain on Earth until the bitter end. You see, all our family members aged normally yet we did not. That's when the legends and the rumors started. Many of us had to leave them behind, so as to not call attention to ourselves." Mathoniaha explains. "Some of us have been hunted and thrown in pits full of wild beasts."

"Like Daniel," I say.

"Yes, like Daniel," Mathoniaha responds, and Pete turns suddenly around to see who Matt was talking to. "We can see and hear angels, Pete," Mathoniaha explains.

"A—angels?" Pete stammers.

"Yes, my son," Onamuji says soothingly. "Angels. It's one of the perks of this mission of ours."

"I—I don't understand."

Eshe, who's sitting on the futon next to the sleeping Samantha, leans toward Pete and pats his hand. "It is a lot to throw at you, and believe us, we would have never revealed ourselves to you," she says, casting a sharp look toward John. "Except, well, this is a unique situation, isn't it?"

"Yes, it is unique," John says defensively. "I made a solemn vow to Tess' father that I would watch over her in life. How's your tea, Pete?"

"Good, thank you." Pete frowns and takes another sip. "Who—who's Tess?" he asks, annoyed now by the many pieces of information that he's lacking.

"Tess is Samantha's guardian angel," John says simply, like it's an obvious fact.

"Is she—" Pete swallows, but his throat seems extremely dry. "Is she the one that drew all those dresses?"

"Yes!" I say eagerly, and John nods toward Pete.

"Sam carries a picture of her everywhere she goes. She thought that—that there was a presence with us."

"She was right about that," Tor nods and his eyes drift toward the three of us spirits, who are floating behind Pete.

"How many—um—of them are there?"

John looks up at us as well, as if he had to count again. "Three. One of them is yours."

"M—mine?"

"Hey, don't act so surprised! I've been with you for a long time now." Russell protests. "You have no idea how hard I've worked at keeping you alive!"

Atonga and Tor chuckle and Pete's head jerks up to look at what they're laughing at.

"His name is Russell," John explains. "And he would like a little more appreciation from you. He has done a great job with you thus far. He's the one responsible for you joining the rebellion, and finding Sam, and keeping you safe all this time."

"Who's the third?" Pete asks drily.

"Valerie," John responds. "She came to help temporarily, and because of her sense of duty, never left."

"Thanks, I..." Valerie started to say, but Pete talked over her. "Am I related to any of these people?"

"No, not you. But Sam is." I say, and John relays the message.

"Are these the people that used to own that house where we found the radio?" Pete inquires.

"It's Tess' house and her husband's."

"Alex," Pete adds, putting the puzzle together.

"Yes, Alex." John affirms.

"But why isn't he here too?"

"Well...that's a long story. But his mother and his grandfather are here."

"Valerie and Russell?" he guesses and rubs his eyes as if trying to get his bearings.

"Precisely!"

"Now that he knows, can we get on with the meeting?" Onamuji says patiently. "It was a great sacrifice to leave our countries to come here. I suggest we get on with it."

"Agreed," echo the others.

"Pete," John says to the boy. "Are you tired yet?"

Pete frowns and opens his mouth to say something. "What? Yes," he says, rubbing his eyes and fighting the urge to close them.

"Good. Then go to sleep," John orders as Pete starts to sway unsteadily in his chair.

Mathoniaha and Eshe catch him before he falls, and they lay him next to Sam on the futon.

"Right on time. That herb never fails." John says with a shake of his head and a twinkle in his eye.

Chapter 18

The Aeonian council works swiftly and well together, discussing briefly the state of affairs in their various parts of the world and quickly deciding what needs to be done to aid the mortals in this last great battle. They promptly divide the work amongst themselves, and receive the approval from the Heavenly High Council right on the spot. They then adjourn and get to work. That's it. There's no delaying, no lingering, no hanging out, small talk, or chitchat; they just finish and go.

Because we are present while the High Council speaks, and because Sam and Pete are out of immediate danger, Russell and I get reassigned back to Heaven. Valerie alone is left in charge of our two mortals—much against my own will.

John, however, convinces me to relent due to the fact that Pete now knows that they are being watched over by angels, so he'll be more apt to listen. The kids are moved to another rebellion headquarters in another part of the continent, where they will be far away from Martin, the crazy officer, and his deadly vendetta against Sam. They are put under the custody of Mathoniaha who is—by design—the most underestimated rebel of his underground rebellion group. He admonishes Sam and Pete to not bring attention to him and to never—ever—mention anything of what they know about him and his Aeonian status.

So, under the guise of being distant relatives of "Matt", as he's called among the rebels from this part of the country, Sam and Pete regain a semblance of a life. I say my goodbyes and leave them with Valerie and Mathoniaha, feeling at peace with the fact that I did my small part in their lives. Then I fly straight back to Heaven where I catch up with Russell, who went up directly.

"Russell!" I call out over a sea of spirits as soon as I spot him.

"Tess! Good, you made it back! How did our kids get settled?" He winks with a teasing smile.

"Good, good. They fit right in due to all the knowledge they had from the previous rebellion group to which they belonged. They were put on the radio and the telegraph right away, and made contact with their old rebellion group. Miles and the others were glad to hear they were still alive, and sad to lose them, but it's a great resource to all of them to have allies in that part of the country." I report, then sigh. "So this is it, then?" I say casually, taking a quick look around. "The last battle, as the Aeonians called it."

"It looks that way," Russell says and looks about him. There are millions of spirits hanging around the High Council building, all Open, all waiting for instructions from their glowing pendants that called them here.

"Hey! You're Open!" I exclaim, finally realizing what's different about him.

"Took you long enough! What, it isn't that noticeable?"

I chuckle. "You blend in so well with the rest of the spirits that I guess I didn't think about it."

"Yeah, well…it's done. Finally done dealing with all my baggage! It feels good—freer, lighter, unburdened—it's amazing that I didn't do it sooner, a shame really."

"So you made up with your father, Henry?"

"Well," he shrugs, "I let go of the anger, once and for all. Then I told him that I no longer hated him and he thanked me for that. He's not what you call the sensitive type, but I guess neither am I." Russell nods to himself and looks around absentmindedly. "I don't think we're that different, actually. I was just lucky to have had Estelle as a mother. Being raised by an angel gave me a clear advantage."

"That is so sweet, Russell," I croon. Embarrassed, Russell punches me jovially in the arm. "I do mean it! Anyway," he changes the subject. "I've been looking for Nancy to tell her the good news. She should be around here somewhere. I also heard Dane was Open, so I'd like to find him."

"Have you heard anything about…?"

"Alex? No." He shakes his head and looks away, trying to hide his clear disappointment. "I tell you, of all people to end up like this," he reflects, then a small shrill voice catches his attention and he starts looking through the crowds.

"Russell!" a singsong voice with a southern drawl calls, then Nancy's little black head appears through the throng, bobbing up and down with childish excitement. She leaps into her husband's arms and they twirl around blissfully. Smiling, I turn and give them privacy, at least from my eyes. Part of me feels like I've been punched in the stomach. All loving displays remind me of the woeful state of affairs between Alex and me, and I feel bitter.

In turning I'm able to see that Dorian and Luz are in the distance. They are busy organizing spirits and directing them to different areas. I float up above the crowd and start waving my arms. Dorian sees me and he brightens up, then waves me to him. Russell and Nancy follow me, and when we get to Dorian I find my parents there with Dane. All are Open, looking bright, beautiful, and unencumbered by unsolved issues. I inquire after Celeste and Max. They assure me that they too have opened and that they must be somewhere around here.

My father and I have a short reunion of sorts, and because we are Open, we link briefly, and—as I had experienced with my mother—in the blink of an eye, I get to see and feel his love for me. It's remarkable how being Open facilitates communication with others who are also Open. Words are not necessary; linking becomes easier and almost second nature. I see my father's whole life, complete with intentions, feelings, and his perspective. Our bonding is immediate and, though a bit overwhelming, in a matter of minutes I no longer feel like an orphan. Part of my life has just been given back to me, thanks to this concise, yet powerful experience.

Like a small flame tied around our necks, our pendants start to blink—in fact everyone's pendants start to glow with new instructions as my parents and I chat amicably.

"Recruiter." Mine says, and I find that out of my group, I'm the only one with those instructions. All the rest say *"Active Duty."*

"Well, not much has changed for Russell, has it?" Nancy notes jovially. "Only difference is that I get to go with you this time, honey," she says coyly.

Leo, my father, looks excited. Finally, he gets to join the action with permission. He's done taking matters into his own hands; he's done mistrusting the Eternals. He is now ready to prove himself as a true follower. My mother is beaming too, and she is so happy to have us both like this—safe, Open, and together. Heaven is finally a Heaven to her.

"If we're going back down there to fight, I'd like to get another one of those swords. We left the only one we had with Val, just in case she might need it." Russell says, turning to the group. My father agrees with Russell and they start talking about how to get one. Dorian says he knows someone and the three of them start making plans.

Irene, my mom, opens her mouth so say something to me, but she gets cut off by the sonorous sound of a female Cherub who is speaking in my head. "All recruiters, please come this way and follow me," she says needlessly loud, through the Link.

"What? What is it?" My mom asks, suddenly worried.

"Nothing," I assure her, "It's just that Cherub," I point to the giant figure in the distance. "She's calling me through the Link—all recruiters I mean. I have to go."

I say goodbye, and float up to follow the few spirits that have been called as recruiters. We all look vastly different—all from different ethnic groups and periods of time. We exchange curious glances with each other, noticing the fact that we are all very diverse, and we all silently speculate as to the reason for this. There are probably a few hundred of us, but we are a small number in comparison to the innumerable host of spirits that were called to active duty.

"Recruiters," the female Cherub says out loud, now that we are all gathered. "Please follow me." This Cherub is thin and tall, and looks more scholarly than athletic—an interesting distinction—since all Cherubs look like gladiators to me. She takes us to the building where Drymus helped me Open. We stand in the center, where there is more room. Still, some of us have to float in mid-air, while some others arrange themselves on the second and third floor corridors.

The Cherub is holding a bunch of tiny scrolls that she passes out to us. Once I get mine I realize that, in my hands, the scrolls are big, yet in her hand they looked like toys. "You are all Open," she observes. "Which means that the other spirits who have not Opened yet will be able to see the truth in you. Your instructions are on the scrolls. You are to study them, and bring yourself up to speed on what is happening on your planet right now. *This is it!*" she adds with emphasis, and looks at us shrewdly. "This is the last battle that your planet will ever fight as mortals. This is the end, the time when all Earthlings have to choose on which side they'll fight. This is as much an individual war as it is a collective war. Scribes will take record of what happens today, in the Book of Earth Life. Your whole planet will be held accountable for what happens now. Win this, and you win it all, lose this and your planet will be lost."

"But—how can that be? Why would *we* be accountable for what others do?" A spirit who looks like he lived in the fourteenth century asks, and several others nod in agreement.

"You *are* your brother's keeper," the Cherub says. "You cannot wash your hands clean unless you do your part. If you do your part—each of you—with all you have to give and offer, you will win. If one of you fails to do so, you will all lose."

"And then what?" a squaw, who looks like she just stepped out of a teepee, asks.

"There was a prophecy given that says..." she opens up one of the scrolls and peers into it, squinting to see what, to her, is miniscule writing. "The righteous will inherit the Earth." She looks up to see if we follow. We don't. "That means that if you want the Earth to be restored and given back to you as it was first intended to be, then you need to fight for it. If not, you will be given another place to inhabit, and trust me—it will not be the same."

"Why?"

"You are of Earth, you were formed from its dust, you were all made from it; *you are all* earth. You will not be complete nor achieve full happiness unless you return to your mother planet from whence you came from."

Her words remind me of what Drymus told me about the Link and resurrection. He had mentioned how glorious it felt to be linked not to just his fellow beings, but also to his planet. Briefly, he had shown me how wonderful it felt to know what a tree felt like, or the ocean, the waves, the grass, and everything that is alive. For a split second I got to feel what he felt when he first set foot on his planet as an immortal being, and what an immense joy it was to be linked to all of it.

I could see that the other spirits present were having a hard time understanding this, so I thought I'd share this memory. We're all Open after all, so I can technically link with all of them. I've never tried such an ambitious task, but for time's sake I figure I should give it a go. If it's that important that we—the few who have been chosen as recruiters—should understand what is at stake here, then I should at least try.

So, closing my eyes, I focus all my senses on one thing: sharing this memory with all the spirits around me. There are a few hundred of us, I didn't count, but it shouldn't matter either—link with one, link with all—right?

Suddenly, an echo of what sounds like several muted voices, starts ringing in my head. All types of stray conversations and thoughts flood my own mind at once, a few at first, then more, and more. For sanity's sake I tune them out entirely and instead, I focus on that one memory that Drymus had given me. My own mind temporarily scrambles to find the exact moment the memory starts, the whole time keeping the other voices at bay. As soon as I find the memory, I start replaying it at a point where those, whose thoughts I have just interrupted, could understand. But I overshoot the context, and I give them more personal information than I initially intend. This is the first time that I've ever attempted to link with several different minds at once, so I scramble to skip forward, but I can't seem to stop the memory from moving forward. I feel like I just hit the "reply to all" button accidentally, and I can't go back and change it!

"It's called the Link," Drymus explains in my memory. *"For some reason, you and your Alex have had a natural Link since, well...I've never known you two not to have it."* I'm so embarrassed, but I simply can't stop the memory from rolling onward, so it keeps replaying exactly as it happened right after I Open. So in essence, everyone who I'm currently linked with gets to see my life before life, with Alex. I even hear a few spirits sighing as they see how we've shared this amazing ability all the way from our pre-mortality.

"Is that why we've been able to dream those vivid dreams, and get into each other's head?"

"Yes." Drymus says in my memory, and again, everyone linked with me gets to see how we dreamed of each other during our mortal life. If I had epidermis, it'd be flushed right now.

"Do lots of other people have the same ability?"

"It's rare, but not unheard of. Once you Open, you can connect through the Link with other beings who are Open as well. But it doesn't become really cool until you resurrect and become immortal." Now, this is what I intended to share. Here we go. I brace myself and hope that everyone understands.

"How so?"

"When your planet and all the beings are judged and resurrected, then," Drymus nods and sighs approvingly. *"Then it gets really fun! You see, everything takes back its physical form—people, plants, animals— your whole planet even! When that day comes, you will experience the Link in full force. You will feel what it's like to be a tree or a bird. You will know what it's like to be a planet, to orbit, to quake, and rend, to explode in magma from within. You'll know how the ocean feels when one of its waves crashes against a rocky shore. It's incredible!"* The amazing part of this moment is that because I was linked with Drymus when he gave me his memory, I was also able to feel what he felt when he first experienced this, back on his own planet. Now many spirits from my planet hopefully understand this as well. I meant to leave the memory at that, but for some reason, those that I'm linked with refuse to unlink with me. They want to see what happened next, so they listened to my next question to Drymus.

"What happens to those who don't make it out of Spirit Prison?" At the time I was thinking of Agatha, and how I let her escape, but I

was also thinking of Alex and all the other spirits that I thought should not be there. Now, due to this Link of mine, everyone knows about Agatha, and how I released her, and how Alex was stuck there, along with my father. I'm not sure what effect this information will have on the spirits that I'm Linked to, but for better or worse, they now know all about it!

"Everyone resurrects," Drymus continues in the memory. *"But not everyone will inherit your Earth. Your home planet is always reserved for those who accept Him and Open. If you don't, you still get to live forever, but the place will not be as glorious."*

"Is that where Hell comes in?"

"Sort of, Hell is eternal guilt and remorse, not a place. Those who choose to carry this guilt around forever will never feel comfortable around a bunch of people who can read minds. It's just nature. They will get a planet more suited to what they feel comfortable with." Okay. That was it. I shut my mind down, I unplug the cord, and send everyone home. But before the link is severed, I can hear a few complainers, lamenting the fact that I cut them short. I can also feel the general sense that they now understand a little better what's at stake. Before I have a chance to regain my composure, someone starts shouting something, and all the recruiters that are gathered in the hall, rush to the entrance and look out. "Ooo's" and "Ahh's" are uttered as they stare at something that seems to be amazing.

Outside the building, we can still see the throngs of Open spirits that were already gathered there, but beyond them, the span of the rest of Heaven can be seen as well. It looks as if all other unopened spirits are flocking toward us and as they do, bursts of light pop up here and there like kernels of corn on a fire. Pop, pop, pop, a light here and a light there, all bright, yet all slightly different in color. A glorious chorus of lights rise up from the surface of Heaven. Even in far away places lights shoot up, like laser fingers of muted, rainbow colored lights, further illuminating the hazy brightness of this realm. It's indescribably beautiful, and just like the turning of a switch, I'm sucked back into the Link, only this time, I'm not the one who started it.

Immediately, I feel a unity that I've never felt before. It's a kinship with my fellow Earthlings that I've never experienced. We are as one. Rooting for one team—the only team that's ever counted—team Earth. *We,* the unified host of Heaven, are going to save our planet! *We* are going to fight for it like we've never fought for anything before. We are going to beat the forces of evil that might cause us to lose our beloved Mother Earth, so we can link with it, and be one with it, the way it was meant to be. We all finally understand, and the realization spreads like wildfire through the link—Earth will be Heaven, not some far away place that we've never known. Earth! Good old planet Earth! And we need to save her now. We need to save our future Heaven.

It suddenly dawns on us what has been the Second One's plan all along. It all boiled down to this one fact. If we didn't save our brothers and sisters, we didn't save Earth. If we didn't save Earth, we didn't get Heaven. If we didn't get Heaven, we would all end up in a lower form of eternal existence, and that would be Hell. The Second One was counting on us not being able to unite; he was banking on us not being our brother's keeper. But he figured wrong!

This new understanding spreads as well through the Link, and we all now understand what we are fighting for. We are not just fighting for the ones we love, but for everyone and everything. None of us will be complete without each other, and that encompasses everything—humans, plants, animals, and the earth itself from where we sprang—we have to save every living thing or none will be saved. When that thought is shared, more lights shoot out from the empty spaces of Heaven and from every angle.

I look up and see a bird overhead, bursting into light as it flies. I run outside the building and step on the turf, the spiritual grass beneath my feet is glowing, and I notice that all the spiritual plant life of Paradise starts to glow too. A wave of color sweeps through Paradise, engulfing everything in its path. As I look and marvel, I catch a glimpse of the Cherub who had been giving us instructions. She's out of the building too and looking fixedly at me. "Well done," she mouths at me. Then she turns, spreads her downy white wings, and flies away.

I notice that my pendant is glowing. It's a miracle that I notice this at all, really. Everything is aglow, and so bright that I might have missed it altogether, but as I lift it, I notice that others have shining pendants as well and because we are still Linked, all the other spirits notice their pendants, and lift them up to see what they say. Connected as we are, we feel not only each other's consciousness, but also that of other beings we've never felt before—animals, plants, and other intelligences we don't understand—but now we know exist. Together we read the same thing.

Fight.

Chapter 19

"Tess, I want you to see this. Come join me," my good friend, John the Revelator, calls me personally through a separate Link, putting the other Link on hold for me, so that I can hear him.

"Right now?" I ask. I'm actually enjoying myself; I don't want to leave Heaven. Something big is about to happen and I want to be part of it.

"Yes, right now! You won't regret it. I want you to see what I'm about to see."

"Fine," I say petulantly. I owe John, so I break off the Link with the rest of Heaven, and start for mortal Earth. John is kind enough to show me a mental path to follow, so I won't get lost. I laugh at this, because he knows how directionally challenged I am. Something interesting happens, though, as I enter the mortal realm and start to follow the map—it's making sense! I'm not just blindly following the map anymore; I'm actually oriented! I know where I am, and I know where I'm headed. I feel a pull, like a magnet—it's the north—I feel the north pulling me like it pulls the needle in a compass. It's not like a physical pull; it's more like an awareness that it's there, like how you feel someone's presence when they enter a room. It's an amazing feeling; it's grounding, and gives me a sense of security and assurance that I've never experienced before.

Looking below, I see landmasses, rivers, oceans, and I'm able to recognize what is what, as if looking at a map. Right now, I'm flying over Asia, and now Europe. I know where I'm going! *"John?"* I ask him telepathically.

"Yes, dear."

"I know where I'm going!"

"Good for you!"

"You don't understand! I know where I'm going. I'm not lost anymore."

"It's your gift, I suppose."

"Gift for what?"

"That's what I wanted you to see."

Right then another voice, or rather, a feeling, is deposited in my head. *"You're welcome,"* it says, soft and gentle, like a breeze.

"Thank you," I respond to *Him*. It had been a simple wish, nothing that I ever really expected to get or have, yet He gives it to me as a token, I suppose, of his love.

And I love it! What an awesome gift! Immediately my mind starts to race, thinking of all the places I could go. Hawaii? That way! South America? That way. Every place I can think of; I now know how to get there, all by myself. Awesome!

A few moments later I land on top of John's Basilica in Turkey. He's just standing there, looking out toward the Aegean Sea. *"Must be nice having your own Basilica."* I say jovially, and he shoots me a wry look. *"What did you want me to see?"* I ask, looking all around the old ruins of the place.

"Not down here. There!" From our vantage point we have a good view of the ocean and the land. Fires and smoke dot the horizon indicating the burning of several cities. "It's like this everywhere," John voices. "The rebels have all communicated, they have rallied together across the world, and today—of all days—they've chosen to rise up.

"Sam and Pete?" I ask with alarm.

"They're part of it. They're fighting."

I am anxious for them and feel the sudden urge to go check on them. I'm about to move out, but John stops me. "You're needed elsewhere. They need to fight their battles, and you need to fight yours," he warns sagely.

"But I can help them! I can go get a sword and…"

"You'll fight, just not with them."

"Why am I here then, John?"

"Look!" He says with a strangled cry. *"This* is what I saw." The moment he says that, a great earthquake shakes the earth violently, forcing a cry out of the mortals who are fighting in the streets. I can see them from above as if looking down an ant pile. But these are people, not ants, and they scatter as they try to hold on to something firm, yet they can't. Some are swallowed by the gashes formed in the ground, others are crushed by the buildings and other structures that fall on them. John's Basilica shakes too, but does not crumble.

The moment the people below us die, their spirits rise. Some look disoriented for a second, then quickly fly to join the ranks of the dead. Some move up and toward the light, while others go straight toward a massive gathering darkness.

The ocean has joined in the destruction, and its waves heave themselves further and further inland, swallowing whole cities. Whole continents start moving toward each other at incredible speed, only to crash into each other, forming new mountains and producing new valleys. Lightning pelts the ground, starting fires and striking whole buildings that explode at once. Mortals disperse to and fro, but have nowhere to hide. My heart aches for them—this generation has known nothing but pain.

"What now?" I ask with a desperate groan.

"Look," John says, pointing to a far distant spot in the middle of the Atlantic Ocean. I look and see that same gathering darkness that I saw earlier, the place where all the dark spirits seemed to be assembling. "And the woman was arrayed in purple and scarlet colour, and decked with gold and precious stones and pearls, having a golden cup in her hand full of abominations and filthiness of her fornication..." John mumbles softly, almost to himself.

"Revelations 17:4," I whisper, and John nods.

"At the time I saw this in a vision," he explains. "I didn't understand a lot of things. I hadn't seen the world. There was no technology. I was limited by my short existence on this planet. But now I understand better what I saw."

"What are you seeing?" I ask, craning my neck to see what he's seeing. I certainly have no clue what he's talking about.

"Look!" He says again, and points once more to the darkness. I focus more intently on the spot, and then start seeing the red and purple, as he mentioned. I fly forward a little, and focus more fixedly on the spot; then I see it! A colossal, snake-like creature is floating on the surface of the ocean. On further inspection, I realize that it's not just a snake; it's a human with a long snake-like torso, dressed in a red dress, with a purple cloak around its' shoulders. It's hideous of course. The red dress is inlaid with golden scales just like the skin of a reptile. The head of this serpent thing is that of a human—a woman—blond, with a crown, and an excessive amount of jewelry. Coco Chanel would disapprove roundly of how many accessories this serpentine woman is wearing—but then again—she would disapprove of so many things with this picture. It doesn't take an eye for fashion to see that clearly.

In one of her ring-laden hands, she's holding a huge cup that is filled with a red liquid that looks like blood. Suddenly, all of this starts to remind me of someone, who? And then it clicks! The cup, the red liquid, the dress, the jewelry, the unnatural buttery blond hair—Agatha—pretending to be beautiful and imposing at the same time.

Her arms are covered in tattoos, not pictures, but illegible words as in a weird foreign language—not of this world. The pleasant, alluring features that she worked so hard to muster while she was in Prison were now distorted and she no longer looks like a model, but rather like a snake-human hybrid. Her mass keeps growing bit by bit as the dark spirits that she released from Prison and the ones that have recently passed, whose souls she bought, heave themselves into her. They look like they are putting together a puzzle, and they only have a few more pieces left to finish it off. Agatha, the giant snake, has no legs as she floats on top of the water, just like a massive, red, oil tanker. Her arms are long and she is waving them around impatiently telling her followers to hurry up.

"What does this mean?" I ask John, aghast.

"It means that this is not yet over. Look!" He points up, toward the sky, and I follow my gaze up to where he's pointing.

Right then, I start hearing the faint droning sound of clarions breaking through the angry clouds. The sound is both glorious and ominous; it swells and fills the air with the dissonant call to arms of a prodigious army. It's the sound of the host of Heaven all rolling forward, out of the spiritual realm and entering the mortal realm at full speed. But from this vantage point nothing but gathering bulbous clouds can be seen. Only the war cry can be heard, I wonder if mortals hear it too? The clarions call to me, and I want to join the ranks. I want to be with them, I want to fight! But John holds me back still.

Hearing the Heavenly call to arms, the serpent looks up and hisses. Her split snake tongue licks the air, emitting a low, guttural sound. If I had flesh, I'd have goose bumps right now. The last few dark spirits hurry up and fling themselves into her, finishing her off. As soon as this happens, she lifts a scorpion-like tail, and slams it down on the surface of the water. Because the two matters don't mesh up, she produces no waves. Not that it would matter, the ocean is in enough upheaval as it is—upset and protesting at what is happening on its surface.

Lightning strikes and thunder immediately follows, reverberating all through the planet. Right then, another huge creature appears from the south. It's flying low, close to the surface of the water. It is smoky black, with pointy wings, and huge, sharp, talons. It's the dragon—Legion.

I groan from within. "I hate that dragon," I mutter. Memories of barely escaping its clutches come to mind—not just once, but twice—three times now.

"And it won't be the last," John says, reading my mind.

"Are you kidding me?"

"Shh...this is what I wanted you to see." He points up to where the literal host of Heaven is gathering behind the puffy gray clouds. The empyreal war cry of the clarions still resounds sonorously in the distance. Storm clouds move in quickly and fill the whole sky. Behind this mist hides a prodigious army that soon covers the whole span of the Heavens. More and more, and more still come; there seems to be no end to us—our side. The sky is filled with the sound of many clarions, now unified in their call. The four quarters of the earth are filled, only one small area right above the serpent and the dragon remain uncovered by the clouds, forming a downward funnel.

Gradually, the clouds start to evaporate; exposing what I knew would be the most imposing sight ever! Millions upon millions of spirits, humans and animals, all standing side by side impatiently, as if barely being held back by some unseen hand.

"This, my dear, is what you did."

"Me? What, what did I do?" I ask defensively and a little freaked out. What *did* I do now? It's bad enough that I let Agatha loose and all her cronies, who are currently fulfilling one of John's most bewildering prophesies. But now I'm responsible for something else?

"Nothing bad Tess. Good! All good! You see the Heavens?"

"Yes," I say tentatively.

"You are responsible for uniting the host of Heaven."

"No," I shake my head. "I only linked with the recruiters that were with me, and gave them the memory that Drymus shared with me."

"You overshot your reach, Tess," he affirms with a single nod, then looks up, the corners of his mouth curving upwards into a smile. "You didn't just link with the recruiters that were with you, you linked with all the Open spirits that were gathered at that particular place in Heaven, and gave them just the precise memory they all needed in order to understand the enormity of what's at stake here. They in turn, linked with their Open kin scattered all over Heaven, who in turn linked with *their* relations, who in turn also, linked with their un-Open friends and family, who encompassed *all* of Heaven. Those who had not yet Opened, once linked, had a reason to resolve their issues and Open just in the nick of time to join this fight. I know you don't understand the enormity of this," he says, looking at my bewildered face. "I barely understand it myself. I just wanted you to witness this from my perspective, because I saw this in a vision several thousand years ago. I just didn't know it would be *you* who made it all happen."

I stare, stunned. "All of Heaven is Open?"

"All." John nods.

"Alex?"

"Even Alex."

Something that resembles exhilaration and joy washes over me, but then I waver. Does it mean he loves me again, or that he merely forgives me? John looks at me and shrugs, reading my thoughts, and only guessing at the answer.

"What about the animals?" I finally ask, coming back to the scene before me.

"Spirits who have the gift of communicating with them, just like your friend Katie and Jase, linked with them too. In their own way, they understand what's at stake, and they too are ready to fight for their Mother Earth."

"But how? How can spirits fight?"

"Most fights are spiritual in nature. Only a few are physical, and even those have their root in spiritual issues." Having said that, John climbs down from the rooftop of his Basilica, all the way to the ground. "I have to go do my part, now, and you have to go do yours."

I nod and smile, then rush to hug him, but go straight through him. "Soon," I say. "Our matter will mesh again and I'll give you a proper hug."

"Soon," he smiles back, his eyes reflecting the weight of this last heavy burden on his shoulders. He's had a long, long life; and somehow I think the worst is yet to come for him. He climbs down and I lose sight of him as he enters the ruins of this place.

From the corner of my eye I see black smoke covering the land, a lot of it! It's coming out of Legion's mouth instead of fire. It's black and wispy and everything that the smoke reaches erupts into some sort of commotion that I can't quite discern from here.

On further inspection, I see that the black smoke is somehow driving humans crazy, making some of them turn on each other, while reducing others to tears, wailing with utter despair. Through it all, Legion laughs, a low, deep, evil laugh that sends chills through my essence. I feel so discouraged, I too want to cry, but then I hear the clarions and take courage. It's hard to see through the dark, mucky

smoke that Legion is putting out, but I still hear them, so I know
they're there.

When a break in the black smoke clears I see a portion of the rally-
ing spirits. As if on command, the animals dive down toward the ocean
and the surface of the land, and join their mortal counterparts in the
fight. Somehow the spiritual creatures relay a message to their mortal
counterparts, and soon all the live creatures respond to their dead fel-
lows at once by stampeding and moving in one accord, with the purpose of helping the innocent mortals win the battle against those who
are under the dragon's spell.

Stunned mortals take courage as they see dogs, bears, even birds,
coming to their aid—pecking the eyes of their armed enemies, nipping
at their heels, or simply passing by them and charging toward their
oppressors with the obvious goal of rendering aid. Some mortals fall to
their knees, and with tear stained faces, thank their Lord for this miracu-
lous deliverance. Others, imbued with valor, lift whatever weapons they
have on hand and plunge forward, helping the animals finish the job. A
child riding on the back of a black panther passes me by at full speed,
and behind him follow several spiritual forms of the same animal, who
turn and acknowledge my presence with a slight nod of their feline face.
I stare back wide-eyed, then watch as several more mortal animals carry
more children to safety. The children look astounded and overjoyed as
they get this rare opportunity to ride an assortment of large cats—chee-
tahs, lions, jaguars, and leopards. "The lamb and the lion," I whisper
with awe, then watch as a herd of rhinos ram into an army tank.

The clarions stop their call for a moment, and the pause holds a
static kind of tension. Then, in unison, they start to trumpet a call to
arms—a loud, reverberating sound—that calls to me. All at once, those
who are holding swords set them ablaze, and with a yell, start pouring
down toward the surface of the water.

"Bind them!" some shout. "Stop them!" and "For Mother Earth!"
others roar.

They split into two groups; some go for the dragon and some for
the snake. Those who go after Agatha waste no time in plunging their
swords deep into Agatha's slinky, red, torso releasing oozing spirits
from her like putrid blood. Those who come out of her are promptly
apprehended, tied with a thin golden rope, and then escorted back to
their Prison.

I feel a pull, and sudden anxiety grips my frame. They're fighting!
Without me! My family and friends are out there. What if they somehow

get hurt? It's happened before, the first time we faced Legion, Henry almost got sucked in.

"Alex!" I scream. If I know Alex at all, I know one thing: He's going for the jugular.

Chapter 20

Looking all around, as I race toward the half-snake, half-human Agatha, I realize that there are so many spirits that finding just one is like looking for a needle in a haystack.

All the Open, bright spirits, are trying to pull Agatha apart by different means. Some are using the swords, while others are tying her up with ropes. Some spiritual animals are flying, or running on all fours through mid-air, attacking Agatha anyway they can. Prehistoric creatures and contemporary creatures alike have joined forces. Wolves, vultures, eagles, and all kinds of predatory animals are biting, scratching, clawing, stinging, pecking, and doing as much damage as they can. An elephant wraps its trunk around an escaping soul, and after letting out a loud wail, it starts marching the spirit back toward the realm where he belongs. A whale swallows a few and does the same thing as it swims through the air back to Spirit Prison.

Some of the human spirits are wrangling escapees and tying them to the backs of horses. They gallop them back to the dark gates of Prison. I can't help but smile at the sight of this unified effort. I bet Katie is loving this! I wonder where she is? I wonder what team of wild animals she's heading into battle? And Alex, where is he?

"Does this please you, Tess? Do you think that a handful of spirits will tear me down?" Agatha's voice sounds deep and sonorous, like it's coming from the bottom of a barrel.

"Yes, actually," I say, looking at her square in the face—her huge, ugly face. Perhaps she hasn't seen how many spirits are really involved here.

"Don't under estimate *him*," she says boisterously and nudges her head toward Legion, who is heading toward us in spite of the efforts of the spirits who are attacking him. Apparently, they are not being as successful as the spirits who are attacking Agatha. "Earth is under our control! I finally get to do what I've always wanted to do."

"There's no glory waiting for you, Agatha. It's over."

"Oh yeah?" She swings one of her arms unnaturally around and grabs me. Her long, thick, sausage fingers wrap tightly around my torso, totally immobilizing me. "What do you think Legion will do to you?" She smiles venomously and a snake tongue slithers out of her parted lips and whips me in the face with its split end. "You might have overcome the Hellhounds from Spirit Prison, but I bet you're still not strong enough to resist Legion. He has as special way of handling spirits. I might be able to fill you with hate, but he'll suck the soul right out of you. He'll lobotomize your spirit and leave you nice and empty for me. Then I can move in and do my part." Her snaky tongue whips me again and I flinch at the grossness of it. The thought of being lobotomized by Legion is certainly more than just unpleasant; it's downright disturbing, and a very real possibility.

Legion is the combined forces of all the cast-outs put together with the Second One, the devil himself at their head, working in one accord. The cast-outs are the original devils that chose to follow the Second One before the world began. They have had thousands of years to perfect their moves, to unify their wills, to work together, and this is their last chance to wreak as much havoc as possible.

"Tesssss," I can hear Legion calling from the distance. The dragon is fast approaching, beating its leathery wings, and unsheathing its huge, sharp talons, as they eagerly reach for me. Agatha smiles at me, pleased and self-satisfied, and licks me again, taunting me, savoring this moment.

"Ugh, you're so disgusting! You are going to regret this for the rest of eternity, you know," I say, not as a threat, but as a warning. Then I turn my face once more to avoid another lick.

"Regret, eternity, blah, blah, blah...you sound like a broken record. Do you know what I've done? I have managed to control not just one nation, but all of them! Like puppets, I've moved mortals to do my bidding. They have prayed to me like a goddess. I have been worshiped, made into statues, placed in sacred shrines throughout the world. *I am the goddess of this world now! Me!*"

"Yessss, and *I* their god!" Legion says, opening its mouth and breathing out that foul dark smoke that clings to me like the spray from a skunk. Immediately I feel like a wilting plant. My surroundings take on a new, more desperate feel. *It's a lost cause,* I think hopelessly.

A Novocain-like numbness starts to spread through me, like someone is anesthetizing me with a small needle, before the big shot comes, the one that is sure to hurt in spite of the numbness. As expected, the big shot comes in the form of harrowing doubt and fear. *"We are going to lose,"* I think, or is it a whisper? *"Alex is not here like I thought he would be. Maybe John was wrong, and not everyone came? Maybe he doesn't care. Maybe, he's joined them. Yes! He has joined them! He's currently part of Agatha. He is fighting, but not with you. He's fighting against you!"* Desperately I start looking for signs of Alex inside of Agatha. *"What if he fell in love with Eugenia? What if he realized the he had more in common with her than with me? What if together they left Heaven and joined Agatha?"* Thoughts of doubt and fear start to take root and they sound more and more logical.

As I look around, I see no one I recognize. Where's my family? *"Oh wait! I have no family, I'm a foster child, I have no one."* Now, I'm in that place again—small, alone, and afraid—mortal Agatha sneers at me, Charlotte doesn't care. I've been deserted. I refuse to think of my parents, so I forget them entirely. I feel cold, hollow, and my head feels dizzy.

Someone is shouting, but I can't tell what they're saying. Something's blocking my ears, or my hearing. A bright swooshing light slices the air in front of me, and I find myself being released from Agatha's grip, then falling, and falling...

Next to me, I see three huge fingers falling with me toward the water. My mind struggles to identify what these huge log-like fingers are doing. Then I remember—Agatha is big! Those are her fingers! Someone cut me loose!

Right before the big fingers hit the surface of the water, they explode into a shower of confetti made up of dark spirits, who zoom out in all directions. Some are captured right away, while others look like they're in a hurry to go back to Agatha, and re-enter her mass.

I'm dazed and disoriented and from what I can tell, still falling. Or am I? No, I'm not falling, but rather hovering right over the ocean in a horizontal position. Nothing makes sense; I still feel drugged or something, I no longer seem to care which team to join, or which way to go, who to believe, or even what to do.

"Go! Get away from here Tess!" A voice orders. I turn towards the sound and see him. The way he looks takes me back to another time, another place. I smile like a drunken schoolgirl, I feel silly—giggly. He opens his eyes big, like I'm an idiot. "Go Tess! What's wrong with you? Go!"

But I don't obey. I feel firmly rooted to this particular spot in mid air, in his arms. "Ha!" I laugh. "I'm floating above water!"

He shakes his head and purses his lips like he's mad, and releases me from his grasp. "Stay here," he commands, with an admonitory finger, and starts to float backward, away from me. I smile goofily, his face is so pretty, so nice to look at. Suddenly, something strikes me as funny and I start to laugh. It's Agatha; she's so big and ugly! As I look around me, everything looks funny, even that huge black dragon that is trying to...to.... "Alex!" I shout, sobering up all at once.

Alex is now looking back at me with a muddled look on his face, like he too just got numbed, and doesn't see that the dragon is opening its mouth and is about to swallow him whole. My newly cleared mind snaps back into action, even though I still feel a bit woozy, and I zip straight for him.

"Oh no you don't," I hear Agatha's booming voice say, and I see that she's trying to catch me with her other hand; but she looks clumsy, like a toddler trying to grasp a tiny raisin with thick, chubby fingers.

I weave my way through her fat fingers and barely reach Alex, but Agatha's pinky brushes against me, knocking me just out of Alex's grasp. I regain my balance and duck to avoid another swipe of her lumbering limbs, not a second before Legion opens his mouth again, and starts to blow his Novocain toward me as well. I'm barely able to grab the stunned Alex by the hand and pull him down, straight down, barely missing the dark dragon's breath.

I pull him to me and hug him tight, but he still has that bewildered look to him, like he's drunk. I don't have much time to sober him up, though, because Legion's claw is fast approaching and it doesn't seem to suffer from the same awkwardness that Agatha's hand did.

Clutched in one fist, Alex has managed to hold fast to his flaming sword. I try to pry off his fingers, but he's got a death grip on it. "Come on Alex," I croon. "Let me have the sword," I say as I would a child who is unwilling to share. I barely have it in my grasp before I get to use it on the descending claw. I slice it right at the talon, then again at the ankle—or whatever you call that part in a dragon. A loud shrieking noise issues from the creature and wispy dark forms start oozing out from the cuts, like tar blood. The screeching is so loud and awful, it's haunting—like something out of a horror movie. This noise seems to finally snap Alex out of his drunkenness and he looks around, startled, like he's just waking up from a nightmare.

"W—what happened?" he asks looking all around him, then checks his hand for the sword.

I start to explain, but I see Agatha reaching for us again. "No time! Fly!" I order. But in the second that it takes for Alex to look back and see what's going on, Agatha stretches and lunges forward, with her mouth wide open, gleaming teeth bared. Her canines are oddly long and sharp looking, and her slit tongue unfurls right before us.

"That's disgusting!" we hear someone yell, who seems to be flying at top speed. We back out of the way and see, to our amazement, Eugenia raising a Flaming Sword with both hands high above her head, and then forcefully brings it down on Agatha's slithery tongue. "Take this, you revolting creature!" she says, and her voice reminds me of when she used to complain about her acrylic nails breaking.

Right behind her, Henry is hacking away at other parts of Agatha, like he's having the time of his life. Each blow from his Flaming Sword delivers a devastating gash that oozes spirits out of the snake-woman. Behind him, unarmed Open spirits are waiting to apprehend the unlawful inmates, bind them, and send them back to Spirit Prison.

"...And that!" Eugenia keeps swinging and looks so hilarious to us, that we have to laugh at her. She looks just like she used to, devastatingly beautiful, but with a new vendetta.

"Eugenia?" Agatha's voice sounds odd, like a record that is set at the wrong speed, low and distorted. "Wha-a-a-at?" Agatha growls in surprise.

"That's right! I'm on their side now," Eugenia boasts smugly, then smiles. "Thanks to someone," she smiles toward Henry, who can no longer be seen.

"And so am I!" Henry yells from somewhere behind Agatha's head. He only comes into view as he floats around Agatha's shoulder, sword held at three o' clock, ready to strike at her neck. What he doesn't see is her snake torso rearing up with her scorpion's tail, ready to strike.

"NO!" Russell yells from a distance, and like a flash, he flies straight for the tail. On hearing this, Eugenia turns and looks. She, too, yells and goes toward the unsuspecting Henry, who has already started his move.

Henry strikes Agatha's neck, right when her stinger is about to crush down on him, then turns distractedly to see who objected to his move. Upon seeing his estranged son ready to protect him, Henry smiles, and instead of moving, he takes another swing at Agatha. Eugenia reaches Henry just as the stinger drops down, but instead of falling straight on his head, it tumbles inert to the side thanks to Russell's timely blow.

As the scorpion's tail falls, hundreds of dark spirits pour out, and a horde of Harpy Eagles swoop down, capturing each one with their claws. They fly their hostages straight back to where they belong, as if the prisoners didn't weigh any more than their usual meal. On seeing themselves being picked up by the huge birds, they writhe and squirm but to no avail.

Meanwhile, Alex reaches for the sword I'm holding, and with a wink, takes it from my hands. "I think it's time for the three of us to do some male bonding." And soon, Henry, Alex, and Russell are all hacking away at Agatha's neck, as if they were cutting down a particularly thick tree.

Eugenia and I watch mutely, looking out for other possible dangers that might assail them while they decapitate Agatha.

"By the way," I say without turning. "You look better than you did the last time I saw you."

"Thanks," she responds frankly, and whips a strand of hair off her forehead. "I'm trying something new."

"Oh yeah?" I say with interest. "What's that?"

"Selflessness," she says matter-of-factly. "I heard this revolutionary idea, that if you lose yourself in helping others, you'll find yourself."

I smile. Then I pat her shoulder amicably. She looks at the spot where I touched her, not with disgust, as she once would have, but with something else. Gratefulness.

"You know, I am really sorry for all I've done to you and Alex. I know that you won't—"

I turn to see why she stopped talking, Legion, who has been engaged elsewhere, has now come back to us and is sweeping spirits into its grasp in a desperate, heedless, manner—Eugenia among them. The Dragon is bound by golden cords on all sides and is being reined in by a host of Open spirits, one of them Dorian.

"Genie!" Henry screams, when he sees her being taken.

"I've got her!" Katie responds, perched on the back of a brachiosaurus, of all creatures.

Rearing up, the prehistoric beast swings its long tail at the claw that is holding Eugenia and several other spirits captive. At the same time, Katie releases a golden rope that lassoes one of the dragon's claws. Several similar lassoes are released and trap the other five digits that make up that claw, and now the Dragon seems to be quite incapacitated. "Hop on!" Katie says to the group that was just released. And they all do, by jumping on the brachiosaurus' back with Katie—Eugenia among them.

All those who are holding the golden cords fly around the beast, effectively bringing that leg flush with its torso. With desperate sweeping motions, and filled with fury, Legion twists and thrashes about in frantic attempts to free itself. But more, strong, golden cords are being thrown at it from every angle, rendering it immobile. Meanwhile, Agatha is literally being torn apart piece by piece, and her constituents are being marshaled, much against their wills, back to Spirit Prison.

Below me, the mortal realm is still in upheaval. A noisy battle is raging, complete with the unceasing noise of all kinds of firearms; planes dropping bombs, and fires…fires are everywhere! They dot, almost in a polka-dot-like pattern, the whole face of the earth. People are running about desperately, fighting with what they've got. I don't know where Sam is, but somehow I know she's okay. Alive or dead, she's okay.

I look back at Alex. He's still working on Agatha's head along side Henry and Russell. Eugenia and Katie are busy tightening their grip on Legion. Dorian, too, is holding his ground right over Legion's head. Behind him I see two little fairy wings—Luz—who no doubt is holding another cord. I don't see where the rest of my family is, but I know they are fighting. A great sense of relief comes over me, and for the first time in…well…ever, I feel peace for them and peace for myself. It's a foreign thought, especially given the current situation, but I feel it. We are all okay. It's over….

Chapter 21

It's not over.

That blissful, peaceful moment doesn't last very long; it's abruptly snatched from me by a foreign, frantic feeling. Rage. A desperate frenzied kind of fury, like I've backed myself into a corner and I can't get out. I want an out, but I can't have it. It's too late!

In confusion I turn, and look all around me, *I need an out! I have to get out of here! I hate to be bound!* Bound. Agatha! Somehow I'm her—or in her mind, or she's in mine—I don't know. Turning my head sharply in her direction, we lock eyes. She's pleading with me, genuinely pleading for help. "This is new," I mutter. I've never seen sincerity in her eyes before so I'm taken aback.

"What do I do?" she implores. She knows her time of reckoning has finally come and now she wants leniency.

Anger wells up inside of me, and I'm about ready to tell her, *tough luck*, when another thought—a command—comes to mind.

"It's never too late." And I see a way out for her.

I float up to her and hover right in front of her nearly decapitated, huge face. A lazy ribbon of white fog crosses right in between us. There's something unnatural to this fog, at least unnatural to Earth. I've seen it before too. It's Cherub fog, or whatever they make that hides Heavenly things from mortal eyes.

"Turn yourself in," I tell Agatha, ignoring the circling fog. "Release the rest of the spirits who have given their wills to you, and tell them to go back to Prison. Then *you* go back yourself. Lead them there. Be their example."

She shakes her head. "But—but they'll see me as weak. I'll be done for. I'll be tortured for this for the rest of eternity," she pleads.

"You chose this."

"It's not fair. It's my nature, I couldn't change my nature."

"That was the whole point of life, to change our fallen natures. Lots of people have done it. Eugenia has done it, Henry, Alex, me…"

"Ha!" she sneers. "What has ever been fallen about you? When has it been hard for you to do the right thing?" she says with spite and jealousy.

"We've had the same life circumstances, we were both raised by the same foster parents, we've had the same weird gifts and abilities of communicating with the dead. The main difference between us has been in our attitudes and how we chose to use those gifts."

"I'm naturally morose," She states, in defense of her actions.

"I've never been particularly cheery," I counter, and Agatha looks away, angrily. However, I start to notice that she's deflating—quite literally. From her middle, spirits start to melt away, and those who were binding her, promptly catch the dark spirits.

As her now detached head shrinks, the dense fog increases, and it blurs her face temporarily from view. Alex, and all those who were trying to bring her down by force are now floating next to me, looking around, wondering what to do, until they see all the spirits oozing out of her like pus. For a split second, Alex and I lock eyes. He smiles brightly at me, and my heart leaps. We have a lot to discuss, but not now. I wonder when? There's so much going on right now, I don't know when it will ever be a good time to talk.

The impenetrable fog is making its way down toward the surface, and I can see that it is smothering several fires, but the whole surface of the planet seems to be ablaze and it will no doubt take some time for the mist to squelch all of it. I turn my head again towards Agatha, and she's normal size again. She looks as hideous as she did when I first found her in Spirit Prison, only worse, if that's possible. She not only still bears the scars, but she also looks haggard and used-up.

"What now?" She asks me, sounding mild and scared.

"You turn yourself in."

"What will happen to me?"

"I don't know." And I didn't. She destroyed the Earth. With the help of the Second One, she started wars and incited people to do horrible things. She's responsible now, not for just her own misdeeds, but for that of others as well.

"Will you take me back?" she asks, meekly. I agree, and we bring up the rear of the long procession of spirits who are being funneled into Prison. "I—I—I don't want to stay there for ever," she says with somber emotion.

"I'm sure that you'll be dealt with sooner, rather than later," I respond, seeing that the fog is blanketing the whole crust of the earth like a downy quilt, and an eerie hush has fallen over the surface.

The gates of Spirit Prison look very different from the Pearly Gates of Paradise. They are thick, gray, vault-like doors, which open from the center. It's made out of what looks to be a dark metal, with a simple pattern on them of a chain that wraps around the perimeter of each door panel. The handles are two large vault knobs, which have thorn-like spikes sticking out of the center.

Two angels are standing guard on both sides of the Prison doors, solemn and serious. They're Sentinels, no doubt, and they look like they were warriors in life, the kind that fought with handmade weapons, not guns. One of them looks Native American, the other Polynesian. Both are massive—football player sized.

At the vault doors, Agatha stops and looks at me. "What next?" She looks pleadingly, as if I could do anything for her now.

I shrug and shake my head. "You go wait for your judgment, I suppose."

"Would you...? Would you speak in my behalf?"

I choke on her words. "I have no idea what I would say that could possibly help you, Agatha."

"What happened to being different sides of the same coin? What happened to you understanding me and my motives?" She gets agitated and starts looking around, in a panic.

"I have nothing to do with what you've chosen to do with those similarities! I'm not responsible for your choices. You've made those all on your own!" I say, exasperated as well.

Quick as lightning, and filled with fury, Agatha rips a flaming sword from one of the Sentinels, and wields it dexterously in my direction. Caught off guard, the Sentinel tries to get it back from her, but she slices his outstretched hand clean through.

The other Sentinel is already holding out his sword in front of him, and out of nowhere several other points appear, effectively surrounding her by sharp flaming tips. I turn around, and see my entire family, plus Eugenia and Henry, each holding a sword, each looking like they mean business.

Agatha drops her sword and raises her hands. "Fine! Do it! I dare you all to erase me from existence! Do it! DO IT!" she yells with an eerie, arrogant, and taunting smile on her sinew and bone mouth. "I will not move until you spear me through!"

"You wish!" Eugenia says offhandedly, moving her sword down, and giving Agatha a vigorous shove into the darkness. The vault doors promptly shut behind her, and the Sentinels turn the thorny knobs into the locked position. The injured Sentinel performs this task one handedly, and once the Prison door is safely locked, he looks at what's left of his arm, then closing his eyes and pursing his lips with concentration, he grows a new limb as if he were blowing up a balloon.

"Believe it or not I've done this before, during training," he grins, and shrugs.

"I thought that once those things touched you, you were supposed to be a goner," Henry says, with marked disappointment in his voice.

"Nothing disappears for ever. But Flaming Swords have the unique ability to bind spiritual matter for a long time—unless you're in the know—and I only know because a Cherub had to teach me how to grow my toes back…and some fingers, and an ear, and a kneecap," he admits sheepishly.

"Ma`kaela here has terrible luck," the Sentinel with long, slick, black hair who looks like a Native American, says with a laugh. "If there's any way possible that a spirit might get hurt, he's sure to find it." The two Sentinels laugh jovially, and Russell joins in, patting Ma`kaela on the back with relief. Both Henry and Russell surround the two Sentinels and start bombarding them with questions, one about training as Sentinels, the other about the mechanics of the swords.

Suddenly more twirling rivulets of white fog start whirling all around us, making it harder and harder to see. Henry and Russell get totally obscured from view in a matter of seconds, and when I turn to look at the rest of my family, to thank them, they too disappear in the thick haze.

"Alex!" I cry with alarm. I still haven't talked with him. Things are not settled and I need to know where we stand. I think we're good, but…it's been so long, and there's been so much going on.

"Right here," his voice sounds like he's right behind me, and I turn to see his figure slowly emerge from the fog. "I'm right here," he soothes, stretching out a hand and gently stroking my hair. The relief that I feel at this simple gesture sweeps over me like a soft spring breeze. I look at him with trepidation, hoping to read his thoughts, but I'm too nervous to focus on them.

"I'm sorry," we both say in unison, then we both smile. He caresses my hair all the way down my back, and with his other hand, pulls me close to him. "You have nothing to be sorry about. I, however…" he sighs. "Could you ever forgive me, for the way I acted?"

He's back! Thank Heaven! Literally. The Alex I know and love is back from whatever inner darkness in which he was trapped. "I was never mad." I quickly admit. "And even if I was, I would forgive you every time." My response seems to sadden him.

"Yes, you would." He shakes his head and closes his eyes, pushing away the guilty memories of how harsh he had been. To veer him off those dangerous thoughts, I cup his face with my hands, and leaning in, I kiss him, linking with him, and only him, in the process.

It's like a dream, a very real dream, where we actually feel—physically feel—just as if we were living it in the flesh. But we're not. What we're experiencing are the memories of what it was like when we kissed. Our eyes open and we realize this, and we both feel a bit crestfallen. He didn't *really* feel my hands tangled in his hair, and I didn't actually feel his hands sliding up my back as he gently pressed his body closer to mine, nor did I feel his fingertips tracing my lips. Yet the memory is vivid enough to revive all those pent-up feelings. We are linked, and that means that we now know how the other felt when we experienced those feelings in mortality. It's both exhilarating and vexing as memories of intimate times we've spent together resurface. It's maddening! These recollections are so intense and so real, that I'm glad for the privacy that the fog has offered us.

Memories of my heart beating wildly against my chest by the mere sight of him reemerge, leaving me breathless. I'm ecstatic. All I can think of now is that Alex is back. The one who in life found me lost in the rain, the one who whisked me off to the lake on graduation day, the one who shared dreams with me, and read to me while sailing half way around the world, that Alex is back. I can hear his thoughts again! I can reach him again! We are one again!

Only the sound of a clarion cuts our blissful remembrances short. As we look away from each other's eyes, the fog parts, and we see an angel standing some distance away holding a sizeable key in his hand. The rest of our family is still surrounding us; they're all at arm's length actually, and have been all along. Good thing they can't read minds! They too are looking at the angel now, just like we are.

Behind the angel comes Legion, completely bound by a thick black chain, and at its chest there's a huge lock. The large key that the angel is holding seems to be the key that fits that lock. Legion's seething, but it seems that there's nothing that it can do about this as it thrashes about like a rabid dog. It looks perfectly bound, and completely unable to loosen the chains that imprison it. Just in case, though, it's also being escorted by several burly Sentinels, who look armed and ready.

"Where are they taking it?" I ask.

"I'm not sure," Alex replies, and we watch as Legion, the dragon, disappears from view, along with its security detail.

"Well, the Millennium will start now, won't it?" my father says casually, as he and my mother glide to our side. He looks carefree and has a mischievous sort of grin on his face, which seems vaguely familiar to me.

"You look good, Leo." Alex says frankly.

"So do you...for a dead guy."

"What have you guys been doing?" Alex asks with a smirk.

"The High Council offered us a chance to do what we wanted to do all along, which was to help undo some of the damage that I created by crossing over into the mortal realm the first time, and brought you along." He points to Alex. "Everything that happened since your death, Alex, has been my fault." He shakes his head vigorously as if trying to shake a bad memory loose. "Then you come in and...you did what you did to save me!"

"What do you mean?" Alex asks, not following Leo's words.

"Didn't you know?"

"Know what?"

"Tess opened the rift for Agatha, so I wouldn't have to. She took the fall for me, so that I wouldn't have more crimes against me. A foolish thing to do, of course, but I appreciate the gesture—daughter." He smiles and places the palm of his hand on my cheek.

It's odd to hear someone call me daughter. I like it. "You suffered enough for me, *Dad*." I try the word "Dad" and it sounds different on my lips. I don't think I'd ever really said it before. Not like this anyway, not filled with love.

"I—I didn't know that," Alex says, baffled. "I knew that you..." he sighs. "I've been such a jerk!"

"Yes, you have," both my parents say in unison. "And for that I—" My father purses his lips at us in mock anger as he tries to come up with some appropriate punishment. "You'll have to bring her home by ten o' clock every night from now on," he finally says, settling on that punishment as appropriate.

"When's ten, when is it night?" Alex asks, looking around the vastness of earth's skies for a clue.

"I don't know. You'll have to figure that out on your own." Leo says, with mock contempt.

We all burst out laughing. Once the laughter subsides, the issue of time actually starts to intrigue us. By now all of my family and Alex's family are gathered in one big clump. Celeste rushes to my side and pries me away from Alex to give me a full, hearty embrace. "We have so much to catch up on!" she says exuberantly.

"We do," I agree, and the moment we're back together like this, I realize how much I've missed her.

Time. We exist outside of time now. How long has this fog been coating the earth? Minutes, hours, days…years? How are the mortals below faring? As if on cue from my thoughts, all of us look down below. Only thick cottony white clouds can be seen.

"Should we go down below?" Leo suggests, obviously responding to my thoughts. I forgot that my parents could read my thoughts.

"Dang!" I say, embarrassed. Had they been listening to Alex and me earlier? A sudden, teenage-like fear of what my parents might think comes over me. I try to rationalize this by listing the facts: We're all grown-ups now, and in fact, we're dead—and I am married, after all. Yet that inexplicable, youthful, bashfulness still persists.

"What are you stressing about?" my father suddenly asks, bewildered and suspicious.

"Nothing, not a thing," I say. "Yes, we should go down," I quickly agree, lest they should probe my mind further.

What were puffy white clouds from above look like dark, ominous mists from the surface of the earth. This murky haze has extinguished all the fires, and there's absolutely no light at all. People are moaning and lamenting as they huddle together in the rubble, and in crevices. Some others rock back and forth, crouched in a fetal position, completely silent, too afraid, too stunned, or just too tired to weep. There are dead bodies that could not be buried, because there's no light at all. Mortal eyes could not see through the impenetrable darkness that the vapors caused. I worry for Samantha and wonder where she is, or if she's even still alive. Part of me wishes that she'd be dead, and spared from this particular Chapter in Earth's history. But another part of me wants her to still be alive, and unharmed, as well. I've always wanted a long life for her; I wanted her to experience more in her body before it was snatched from her. Yet she might have…. For all I know she could have lived a long time, and years could have elapsed while we fought Agatha and the dragon.

"Look!" Alex tugs at my arm and points toward the sky, from where we just came. A tiny dot, like a speck, of light, or a distant star appears in the darkness.

We all look up and watch fixedly as the tiny light grows in size. As it grows, we notice that some mortals around us see it as well. Some start pointing to it and gazing at it, in mystified muteness. Others look at it and soon lose interest in it, giving themselves back to their grief and their moans.

Soon though, the glow grows and grows, and turns into brilliant rays. They pierce the fog, and develop into sharp slanted beams. No mortal can now ignore these rays of light that are coming from this single source. All the mortals turn almost at once, and stare at the spot. They're barely breathing—waiting, as it were, for the other shoe to drop. Some feel agitated and fear for their safety; others seem to be mollified and soothed by the light. The beams of light cut through the fog like knives, and the whole world seems to be collectively holding its breath right now, waiting to see what will happen next.

The light slashes a tunnel through the fog, and we can now see something, or someone, right in the middle of that blinding light. It looks as if an avenue has been carved out, just for whatever it is that is heading straight down to Earth. I can hear several people murmuring, saying that a meteor is falling down on them. This rumor causes several to run about in confusion, trying to seek shelter, but most of the mortals are simply rooted to their spot. They shield their eyes and look up, both curious and petrified with fear.

As this object moves closer, the single dot turns into two, then three—the third being larger in size. After a moment I realize what that the two smaller dots are Seraphs, pulling a Roman chariot. Inside the chariot, *He* stands—the First One—majestic and glorious. Flying next to Him, several Cherubs are blowing their trumpets, and following the Cherubs trail the High Councilors, not in spirit form anymore, but resurrected and in the flesh!

From the surface of the earth, a few people get caught up, and ascend up to the chariot. "Is that...?" Leo says, squinting.

"John," I say. "And Mathoniaha and the rest of the Aeonians."

Once the light that surrounds them dissipates somewhat, they join the ranks with the rest of the High Council.

Awestruck, we all stare in silence. One thought seems to be prevalent among all of us present, living and dead. *"Wow!"*

Right when we think this is it, and nothing more amazing than this could happen, the clouds part and a thick column of light appears, like a tunnel made out of light. It streaks down, right in front of the chariot, and just like an elevator, it stops right on that spot, then shoots back up to where it came from, leaving behind, a beautiful sound and several small, golden forms.

The sound is that of a high-pitched, cathedral-like choir of children, singing in pure and soft tones, like crystals tinkling in the wind. It's hypnotic, and all of us, mortals and spirits alike, stare spellbound at the source of these tiny voices. The sound comes from thousands of small children, who are floating in mid-air, gleefully singing as if this were a well rehearsed recital.

Some of them are very small—babies even, who are being held by the older kids. They are not spirits; they're all immortal and perfect.

"The Eternals' court," Katie mutters in a soft whisper, not wanting to dispel the magic of the moment.

"What?" Irene asks, confused.

A vague pre-mortal memory of visiting a place where all the Earthly children that died in infancy went, comes to mind. All the children there were being taken care of by angels, and it was literally where the Eternals dwelt. I manage to explain this memory to my family, and Katie pipes in with some of the details that I've forgotten. Celeste says that she too recalls visiting such a place before she was born, but her explanations are cut short by the strangled croak of a mortal woman from the surface.

"Julia!" the woman exclaims, choked up with joy and fear. "Julia! Julia!" She starts jumping up as if wanting to take flight.

From the group of hovering children, a single girl of about five years turns her head and spots the woman. The child claps her hands and flies down toward her mother. Seeing this, other parents start to sift through the ranks of returned children who miraculously hover above them. In no time, a grand reunion starts to take place, not just from the mortal realm, but also from the spiritual realm. Spirits, who had long ago lost their children, fly straight to the little flock, as if guided by a magnet. In time, all the children are claimed and the first wave of true rejoicing is felt.

"So this is it!" Dorian exclaims. "The end!" The words seem oddly ironic. The most expected date since the world began, *the end*, and it is here, and we are watching it.

"So now what?" Henry asks, and we all look back at him with answerless, vacant stares.

Chapter 22

A thousand years of peace goes by quickly for the dead. That is…if you don't dwell on the nuisances of not having a body.

For Alex and me, these years have been laden with vexation. Every time I look into those piercing aqua colored eyes of his, my head goes into a spin cycle. The memory of that tingling sensation that I would always get around him, coupled with the infusion of adrenaline washing through me, just like it used to when I was alive, still grips me every time. But it's become, more and more, a fleeting memory. And just like a butterfly, try as I might to catch it, it's always just out of my reach.

Not until now do I realize how much my emotions and my physical reactions worked in unison to create that feeling of a spark that kindles dry, parched wood, that burns and crackles with delight. Or the rush of emotions in your torso that seem to wake up every single nerve ending in your body, making it dance with joy. The memories of these feelings have teased me now for a lot longer than the actual mortal experiences, yet they have tormented me with their intermittent presence, and have exasperated me to no end. I still feel all the emotions, but my mind knows that something is missing and it pines after its loss. I've never missed my body more.

Alex has felt it too. I haven't had to link with him to know. I can see that same frustration registered in his eyes every time we're around each other—like someone has ripped a particularly sweet and juicy fruit out of his hands just as he was about to take a bite.

We have had plenty of time to talk and set things straight. He told me about his turning point. "It was the Seer Stones," he explained.

"The what?" I asked, because I had never heard of those.

"The Seer Stones that are on display at the Museum of Heavenly Artifacts." he explains. "These stones were used by John the Revelator, Moses, Isaiah, and others to see the future. Henry, Eugenia and I were messing around, and we picked them up and took turns trying them on. Eugenia and Henry seemed to like what they saw, but I…it was different for me. It was awful! If I ever felt haunted before, this topped it all."

"What did you see?"

"Me. I saw myself, and my fate, if I didn't change. I was standing before the Eternals being judged, and feeling like I would rather be obliterated into dust than face them as I was. I didn't want *Them* to know me as I was, but in the vision, it was too late to change. They were pronouncing my fate and punishment. They were going to make me pay for my own sins *all by myself.* Just as they pronounced my verdict, I started to feel what that suffering entailed. It was excruciating, intolerable, and I knew that I couldn't endure it. I removed those seer stones like they were burning coals. I only had them on for a few seconds, and still, I couldn't endure the thought of that punishment. So right then, I resolved to do something about it.

"I left Henry and Eugenia, and went straight to find someone who could help me. I flew straight into some huge Cherub named Drymus. He asked me if I was now ready to set things straight. I thought he was a bit presumptuous, but then he told me that you asked him to help me."

"I did. You weren't listening to me—" I tried to explain, hoping that he wouldn't be upset.

"Don't apologize. I was an idiot."

"Did he have you Open the fast way?"

He nodded. "It was like jumping from the oven to the frying pan! I thought I made a mistake. But he showed me what you went through for me...he showed me *your* Opening. That gave me strength to continue."

As it turns out, those Seer Stones were also responsible for triggering a change in Eugenia and Henry. They later confided in us what they saw in the stones, and how that changed them—mostly Eugenia—who was at that time still confused about who she was.

"I saw myself as I am now," she told us. "I saw a happy, confident, selfless person, who had friends, lots and lots of friends. I also looked beautiful again, which helped," she added contentedly. "Henry was at my side, and we were in love. But it wasn't what I saw that changed my mind. It was *what* I felt and *how* I felt. I realized then that that's the feeling I've been searching for my whole entire existence. And I realized that it was within my grasp, if only I worked hard enough to get it.

"When I took those stones off my head, I didn't know how I was going to achieve that, but I knew I would. I started working on it as soon as I found my Spirit Guide. She told me to start small, by doing simple selfless acts here and there as I attended class. She told me to look for ways to serve others even in small ways—a smile, a listening ear, whatever.

"Before too long, I started to see a change in me. I was happier, freer, more confident…it was really a revolutionary idea for me!" And it was, we all agreed with her. Selflessness suited her well, and the interesting thing is that she is now one of the most selfless spirits I know.

Henry, however, admitted that the things he saw in his vision had not yet come true, but he suspected that they would come to pass soon enough. That was all he would ever say, and though we bug him about it to this day, yet he still won't budge. He says that he's afraid of jinxing the vision somehow if he tells.

The rest of us, who haven't had a chance to try the Seer Stones on, have had to settle for taking things as they come. Celeste, for instance, has had to deal with her whole melodrama without the benefit of knowing how it would all work out. I've told her that a movie would some day be made about her life. She said that the movie about my life would be better. I disagreed, so we put it to a vote among all our friends and family. It came back a tie.

The hardest thing she had to do was to tell her son, Leo, who his father really was. She had to admit with shame that she lied to her son, her second husband Ricardo, and stepson Eros.

"It was all for money," Celeste admitted to me while we strolled down an Earthly millennial sidewalk in Paris. We watched with a tinge of envy as mortal millennial children licked ice cream and splashed in a fountain.

"For what?" she questioned. "Money no longer exists. It all seems so…so…"

"Unimportant."

"Yes, precisely." She gestured with her hands. "I lied because I was scared. Max had died and I had just found out I was pregnant. I didn't know how I was going to take care of all these kids by myself. Then Ricardo shows up, cavalier and strapping as always, offering an out for me. He dangled my inheritance in front of me, the one that was revoked from me when I married Max."

"How did Max die, Celeste? Did he really fall in the well? Was it really an accident?"

"No," she said flatly. "Ricardo showed up and had a scuffle with Max. Max tripped, hit his head, and died. Ricardo panicked, so he threw him down the well, hoping to cover his tracks. Then he had the gall to come to me and offering his hand in marriage!"

"Wow…and you still think my life story will get the movie deal?"

Celeste laughed as she used to, before we were mortals. Memories of that pre-mortal time keep coming to my remembrance, little by little, and lately they have been coming back to me a lot more. I think it's in preparation for the judgment—*The* Judgment Day!

"How did Leo take the whole thing?" I asked her.

"He was stunned at first but, bless him, he's been through so much that he—of all people—knows the importance of forgiveness. He decided to look on the bright side—Max. He was thrilled to find out that Max was his father after all, and the two of them have been spending much time together."

"So what happened to Ricardo and Eros?"

"Ricardo just Opened not too long ago. Surprisingly enough, Max was the Spirit Guide who helped him through it."

"That man's a saint!"

"That he is," Celeste said dreamily. "Eros has been in Spirit Prison until recently. Richardo himself got him out and is helping him through the transition. He might be working on Opening, I'm not sure."

"I think he truly loved Agatha in life," I say. Eros, though much older, had married Agatha in mortal life, and I think that in her own way, she loved him too.

Miraculously, Samantha and Pete survived the last mortal war, and they were old when the end came. All those who were still alive when the First One came in his glory to take control over the Earth, were changed into Aeonian-like mortals. Sam and Pete were changed in the blink of an eye. One minute they were aged, and the next they were young again—a great reward for someone like them who saw nothing but war their whole life. For a change, they got to experience life in a paradisiacal world, where peace abounded and children grew up happy, fed, and free from sorrow. They had lots of children, and when they finally passed, they Opened straightaway.

When the dragon was released for the final time, those who lived during the Millennium were tested. For a short while, they were faced with the lies and the deceit that the dragon and its followers assailed them with. They were challenged, but not defeated, thanks to us—the host of Heaven—who came to their aid, and once more, defeated him. Some of the mortals who grew up in millennial earth, stumbled, but none were lost. Once and for all, we Earthlings proved ourselves capable of uniting and crushing the enemy of our souls.

Finally, Earth is ours. Forever!

Chapter 23

Nothing, absolutely nothing could have prepared me for this. I've heard it from Dayspring and Drymus a thousand times in the last thousand years, but it fails to compare to how it actually feels.

Feeling like an immortal being feels is an entirely new sensation. I know I've been without a body for a long time, and memories of physical feeling have dulled over time, but there are others who haven't been dead for as long as I have that agree with me—having an immortal body is awesome!

Smells, sounds, colors, textures, everything is enhanced and everything is heightened. Earth has been restored to its fully intended beauty and glory. Everything has an aura, not just people and animals, but everything! Soft waves of color surround every living thing—even rocks are alive now—or maybe they've always been, and we just didn't know it. Good chills run through me as I set my bare foot back on firm ground and link with the earth beneath. Ashes to ashes, dust to dust, my essence belongs here. We are one now. Everything is alive and interconnected; we understand the firm need to be part of each other. The earth wants *us* as much as we want *it*; we are as we were meant to be.

"Wow!" Alex marvels next to me. He's been getting better at linking with others, and is feeling the same thing I'm feeling—Earth calling us, welcoming us back.

"I know…"

"It wants us here!" he marvels.

"I never imagined that the earth would feel whole only with us inhabiting it."

"It wants us to plant it, to tend it, and grow it!"

"Make it bloom!" Katie, who is right behind us, bends down and digs her fingers into the dirt.

"Yes, it does," Alex echoes, awestruck.

Suddenly, Katie darts off and we see Jase zoom by us, hot on her tail. They are laughing about something. I smile. Our voices sound different too. They have a crisper, more accurate, and purer tenor. I bet I can sing now, and sing well.

"Look!" I exclaim, when I see a patch of flowers growing at the edge of a stream. I kneel on the luscious emerald grass, and bend over the blooms to catch a whiff of their scent. A soft, fresh, herby smell fills my nostrils and goes straight into my lungs. It's as if I've never smelled before! The grass is dewy, and smells of clean earth. Then I catch a whiff of another smell in the air, and follow that scent until I come to a grove of trees.

Alex follows close behind me. "Wait up!" he calls, pausing, like me, to smell everything.

Under the trees, it smells the best—woodsy—a mixture of bark, leaves, and rain. Inhaling deeply, I fill my lungs and exhale. "Hear that?"

Alex pauses, and listens. "What was that?"

"It happens when I exhale. Look!" I take in another deep breath, and then let it out. A rustle—soft, barely perceptible, but still there—as leaves and branches respond. "They're breathing!" I exclaim with awe.

Taking in another deep breath and letting it out again, Alex tries the experiment once more, and sure enough, as soon as his breath leaves his lips, the treetops take it in as if they were glad to have us back among them.

Placing the palm of my hand against the asperous, rough bark, I try to see what else I can feel from them. A full measure of contentment, that's what they radiate. It seems that immortal Earth is not only perfect, as it was meant to be, but also happy, joyous, as it was meant to feel.

Alex looks at me with an impish look, and in a flash is standing next to me, patting a lose strand of hair back behind my ear. He glides his hand all the way down the length of it, taking in the feel of each strand of my hair. He smells it. "It smells like you," he comments, then traces my features with the tips of his fingers. They feel like silk against my face. I close my eyes, and relish the sense of touch again—his touch. This sense is heightened too. My old memories of what it felt like to be caressed by him as a mortal seem feeble in comparison.

"And what do I smell like?" I ask amused.

"You. Just...you." He smiles, and leans in for our first kiss as immortal beings. I feel my new heart beginning to quicken at the prospect. I marvel at that simple automatic response, and I'm reminded of how a body used to work under these circumstances. My pulse accelerates, my palms get sweaty, my breath shallow, my cheeks heat up all the way up to my ears. I love it! I've missed it so much! My emotions and my body work in unison to create that feeling of having butterflies in my stomach—that quick flutter that starts in the middle and electrifies the whole body from head to toe. I close my eyes and take in the feel of his lips pressed against mine, moving slowly and deliberately. His fingers, sliding along my jaw line, then tangling themselves in my hair.

Right when I think I might explode from the inside out, I hear the familiar, booming sound of Russell's voice. "Who's hungry?" he asks, with a laugh in his voice.

"I'm going to kill him," Alex growls through gritted teeth, but doesn't let go of me.

"You can't. He's immortal," I remind him, not moving away from him either.

"Then I'll beat him up," he mumbles through another kiss.

"He might be stronger than you," I tease.

"Ha!" He opens his eyes and looks insulted. "I've always been faster, even if he's stronger. I bet I can still pin him before he can inflict any pain."

"Oh yeah? Wanna have a go at it?" Russell taunts, calling him out with one hand.

In a flash, Alex is at his side, and before Russell can even see what he is up to, Alex has him safely pinned to the ground.

"It's going to be a long eternity," Nancy sighs.

"I can see that," I say, looking at the two of them rolling around on the fresh turf, getting green smudges all over their white clothes.

"I wonder if there are Laundromats established yet?" Nancy says, and we both laugh.

Like bees flying back to the hive, the rest of the family finds us. Even Dorian shows up with Luz, and with her, my two aunts and my grandparents, Celeste and Max. My parents are nowhere to be found, but no one really worries, or asks too many questions. Heaven knows they never had much time to themselves in life.

Little by little, the group populates as if drawn by a magnet. Love, I suppose, is the draw. All present are loved ones, and what a huge group we are! My heart swells with pride at knowing that I have them all forever. Finally! All the fears I had before crossing the Veil—fears of losing them, of forgetting them, of living life alone—those fears have all been conquered. What I didn't realize then, was that our love for each other would form a tether that the Veil could never sever. That love made it possible for us to find each other, and to be connected in spite of distance, or forgetfulness. We were meant to be together—always!

"So where's this food you are speaking of?" Dorian asks Russell.

"I don't know. I just know that Heaven would not be Heaven without food. I've said so a hundred times," Russell says logically as he wipes some dirt from his chest.

"Just because you've said so it doesn't mean it's so." Valerie corrects.

"Well, we can't kill the animals," Katie cries in a whiny tone.

"I agree with Russell," my aunt, Amor, echoes as she steps forward. "I don't know what I'll do with my time if I can't cook something. Can you imagine?" she turns dreamily to her sisters. "We can finally eat all the pastries and cake we want to now, and we won't get fat!"

This comment prompts a furor of positive comments on the side of food and all the things that people wanted to eat now that we had our bodies back.

"Could we just think up food, like we used to think up things while we were spirits?" I suggest.

"I'm thinking of…bacon." Russell says, shutting his eyes tight, then opening them wide again. We all look around trying to find evidence of bacon anywhere, but find none.

"As always, I may have the solution!" Henry says sagely, as he strides in with a gorgeous looking Eugenia at his side. "We were just in another part of our new Earth, a part that is cleared for developing. We'll have to start all over, of course," he mumbles under his breath.

"What are you talking about?" Russell asks, exasperated already by Henry's roundaboutness.

"What he's trying to say is that there are Cherubs teaching people about our new diet," Eugenia chimes in. "There are tons of things that grow naturally that are good to eat. Nothing is poisonous any more, and a lot of the things that used to be inedible in mortality actually taste a lot like meat now. Like a substitute," Eugenia clarifies.

"So does cactus taste like bacon now?" Russell says with a sneer, and several people laugh.

"Do things need to be cooked?" My aunt Amor asks, suddenly worried that she'll have nothing to do for the rest of eternity.

"They said that we are free to experiment with plants, seeds, roots, nuts, fungi, herbs, fruits, algae, and anything that the Earth provides naturally for us, but animals are no longer food," Eugenia declares, as if she were laying down the law.

"Well that sucks!" Russell complains and folds his arms across his chest like a petulant child.

"It doesn't matter as long as it tastes like meat used to taste, right? If it tastes good, it tastes good!" Nancy looks around the group for support.

"We'll find you bacon, Dad, don't worry," Valerie says, with a roll of her eyes.

"Oh, look, Jase. Ostriches!" Katie says, and she's off again, chasing after them with glee. Jase smiles and with a glint of sheer joy in his eyes, takes off again after her. This might be a pattern for these two. The rest of us exchange glances, wondering what they could possibly find so interesting about a bunch of ostriches.

"Well...this is as good a time as any," Dorian states, stepping forward formally. "Luz and I are getting married." A hubbub of congratulatory comments rises from all of us. Alex and Dane pat him on the shoulder. Celeste, Valerie, and I take turns hugging Luz, and I throw myself into Dorian's arms, feeling a sudden surge of emotion come over me. My little, big brother! He's been bigger than me in size for a long time. Memories of him and me holding each other, just like this, on our bedroom floor—promising each other to be a real family, and not just foster siblings—come to mind.

"We don't want to steal Luz and Dorian's thunder, but we are renewing our vows and remarrying as well." Celeste says.

"What a great idea!" Valerie agrees, and turns to Dane with an expectant look.

"There's a long line of people who are doing this, now that we are back in our bodies," Celeste explains. "The ones that haven't been married go first, then those who want to renew their vows second. But the neat thing is who is officiating at all of these."

"The First One," Max finishes for her with great anticipation. "We can all be married or remarried by Him!"

Alex turns and winks at me. Then he comes to my side and entwines his fingers in mine. "How about it? Would you marry me—again?" he asks in a whisper, leaning into my ear. "This time, we could have a big wedding."

Right then, what sounds like a stampede cuts through the center of our little gathering. Jase and Katie are riding on the backs of those ostriches they saw. They're laughing hysterically, and the ostriches look just as happy and amused by this arrangement as they are. They rush by us in what looks to be a race. Behind them trail some other ostriches, which as they pass by us, are mounted by Dorian and Luz. Without question, Alex joins them as well, and it looks so fun that I do the same.

"May I please?" I ask the creature, who understands me perfectly. If a tree is aware of my presence, then an ostrich should be too.

The animal quickly bends down to let me get on, and as soon as I'm perched on its back, it takes off running after its mates.

Rediscovering Earth is fun and full of pleasant surprises, but the fun and games do not last long. Clarions are once again calling us to gather for the final Judgment. By now I've gotten all my memories back, from the beginning of my formation as an un-embodied spirit, to my entering into my mortal body, to my death, to after death, all the way to my present state as a resurrected being. Looking back, the journey looks a lot shorter than it seemed to me at the time.

For those of us who have dealt with all our issues and have Opened, the Judgment should be easier. In essence, we've dealt with all the glaring problems. We've asked for forgiveness and the First One has taken the stains away for us. We are clean. This gives us confidence and peace of mind. We have nothing to hide, nothing to be ashamed of. However, those who have not yet Opened look nervous and fidgety, and I feel badly for them.

A host of un-Opened spirits from Spirit Prison have been escorted to the place where the Judgment is going to take place. We're all outdoors on a pleasant meadow overlooking a large lake. It looks, in fact, like the place where I saw Him right before I Opened. I have this strange sense of déjà vu, and I feel like I just entered a time warp. Was that *my* judgment day? Or is this? Was I alone with him on that meadow, or were there others looking on, like now? I simply can't remember. I look at Alex, and he too has that same puzzled look, like he's been taken back in time.

The Eternals come in their full glory and oversee all those gathered with pleasant smiles. They look over the host and even though we're as numerous as the sands of the sea, they seem to look at each of us in the eye, and acknowledge everyone personally. Some shy away from their piercing eyes, but others gaze back joyously and confidently. The First One is with Them, He is one of Them. I've always envisioned that there would be some sort of courtroom that we'd have to enter. I envisioned a bar, and a mallet, or something that resembled an earthly court, but it's not like that at all. The Eternals simply hover in mid-air and survey us, pleased with what they see. And there's no delaying. Once the clarions stop, one of the High Councilors begins the proceedings and a gong is heard.

Reubium, the smallest Cherub ever, keeper of all records, glides ceremoniously in. He looks as if he enjoys this part of his job immensely. He carries a huge white leather bound book, a long white plume, and several thick scrolls. He hands the large white book to the First One, bowing his head reverently as he does so.

The First One opens the book and starts reading. This is the book of Earth Life, where the deeds of Earthlings are judged as a whole. Now and then He asks Reubium to recite from the scrolls he's holding. The scrolls contain the writings of the prophets, the warnings given, the laws, and the admonitions prophesied. These prophecies are judged against the general reception of them, and the outcome is shameful. It seems that every admonition from the prophets was met with a negative outcome. Time after time we had either killed the messengers, or treated them with disrespect and contempt. The prognosis doesn't look good, but somehow we still came together in the end and managed just barely to get things right.

Once we were judged as a whole, the individual judgment begins. Reubium brings out a scroll for each individual, containing our personal life as recorded by Angelic Scribes. My own short stint as one of those angels before the world was comes to mind, and now I hope I took good notes for that person's sake.

This public affair is only intimidating and shameful if you haven't Opened. As each individual steps forward, an image, like from a drive-in movie theatre shows up in front of that person. It's like a gigantic Probe—the Tattler—as I called it while Opening with Drymus. The well-edited version of each person's life, with all the reprehensible or evil deeds erased from the record and remembered no more, is displayed on the big screen, for everyone to see. The only mention or allusion to our less-than-perfect existence is when the First One has to vouch for us before the Eternals, saying that He knows us, and has paid the price for us to enter into Their rest.

As we watch, sometimes there's laughter, sometimes tears. Now we can relate to each other more fully; we see the sacrifices, the hardships, and the obstacles that each of us had to undergo. One thing becomes wholly evident as we watch—struggles made us stronger—leisure did not. As painful as it is for some, the Judgment is a great sociology lesson.

Those who are Open and have been vouched for by the First One as "His," stand at the right side of the Eternals. Those who He claimed to never know, to the left, and those who rejected Him entirely, even though they knew Him, are promptly cast out. These are those who in spite of many opportunities remain resolutely unmoving and unbending. They even come up to the invisible bar defiantly showing all their misdeeds, boastful, and prideful. This cocky attitude does not last long, though, because it's a façade. Their arrogance quickly melts before the Eternals and their all-knowing eyes.

Agatha is among these, and as her name is called, she straightens her head, relishing a deep breath with her brand new body—a gift that she takes for granted—and walks forward, head held high, pretending not to be scared to face the music.

"I don't know her," are His words, void of anger but short, cutting, and final. Agatha flinches at the sound of those words. Then her life starts to play before her and everyone else. It's an unedited version, complete with all her thoughts and secret deeds. She looks at her existence, from the time she was an intelligence, and tortured me and other, lesser intelligences just for fun. Then, as she was in spirit form, how she befriended the Second One, and obediently followed his lead. Her memories reveal her stint with the Fallen angels, and how she was responsible for delaying certain spirits their preparations for mortality. Eugenia's face is blurred from this replay. Only those of us who knew her then remember, but no longer care. Eugenia has changed, but Agatha hasn't.

In life, Agatha had not made many choices that were different from those she made in pre-mortal times. Over and over again, whenever she had a choice, she chose the wrong side. Then in death, her memories revealed how she managed to open a rift in Spirit Prison and unleash the most wicked spirits into the mortal realm. Here, too, my own face is blurred from that episode, so to those watching, it's clear to see that she coerced someone, and that someone has since repented—yet Agatha had not. Finally, it showed how she unified the escaped Prison spirits, and formed the great monstrosity called ROWE.

"How do you plead?" a High Councilor asks with great solemnity.

She looks at the Councilor with sheer hate. She doesn't want to condemn herself, but she has no choice. Repentance is now out of the question; it's finally too late. Panic starts to spread through her now, as she lets her response hover unsaid in mid-air.

"How do you plead?" he asks again.

The words seem to choke her, and stick in her throat. Then terror starts to set in, as she feels the cold, hard realities of her actions work their way through her. "No." she whispers in a futile attempt at denial. "No!" She presses one hand to the base of her forehead, as if trying to keep a migraine at bay.

"You must answer, Agatha. How do you plead?" The Councilor is void of any ill feeling as he repeats his question.

"Guilty!" she shouts in a deranged manner. "Guilty, okay! I plead guilty! There! Is that what you all want to hear?" she says in an accusatory manner, as if any of this was *our* fault. "*I* did it." Her voice sounds belligerent. "I brought about the end of the world! I! I! I!" Agatha shouts with ire, then her voice cracks. Right then, a distant, faint, disturbed laugh is heard, giving me the creeps. Two large Cherubs come to either side of her, and take her away, kicking, screeching, and practically foaming at the mouth.

"Where do you think they're taking her?" Eugenia leans over and asks.

"I'm not sure," I admit, hugging my torso and rubbing my goose bumps.

"There's a planet assigned for these souls. They won't interact with any other beings other than those who inherit that same world. They won't be allowed to leave that world either. They're stuck there from here on out." Dorian says wisely.

She wasn't the only one who was taken out kicking and screaming. There were several others, not a lot, but enough.

"I wonder what it will be like?" Eugenia mumbles.

"Much like Earth, I suppose, not at its best of course. I've heard that it will be an environment not unlike the environment that they helped create in life," Max pipes in. "Those who inhabit that planet will always be who they are and will never change. There will not be peace, because they never created peace while they could. There will be lying, cheating, stealing, all those things that they've always done and never repented of."

"The only difference is that they will have no hope of ever improving now." Dorian adds grimly. "They are stuck forever as they are, never learning or evolving, and in an imperfect world."

Chills run up my arms, and I can tell that Eugenia feels the same.

Once the Final Judgment is over, we are free to enjoy our inheritance. We are told to find or build our mansions, according to our wills.

"Live as you were always meant to live, in peace. Enjoy all that has been created and formed, and grow, improve, learn," was the admonition we got from the Eternals, who by the way, come and visit quite often. The First One took His place as ruler of Earth, and anyone can see Him any time they wish. The marriages are about to start, and I anticipate that they'll go on for a while. Alex and I put our names down on a large scroll that Reubium had started. He grunted a Hello when he saw me; he remembered me from pre-mortal life, when I had to help him with the filing of lives.

Henry is prompt to show us a part of Immortal Earth that has mansions already built, as the Eternals had said. "We can pick and choose whichever one we'd like!" He looks behind him, at a grand looking castle resting on a cliff.

"Oh we don't want that, Henry." Eugenia whines. "I told you where I wanted to live."

Henry shakes his head. "She's mad! Completely cuckoo." He circles his index finger around his right temple. "She wants to live in a Hobbit hole!"

"Tolkien lives there!" Eugenia cries with exasperation.

"You want Tolkien as a neighbor, is that it?"

"Yeah!" she says sarcastically, as if Henry was too dim to get it.

"That sounds like fun!" Luz chimes in. "Should we go see them?"

"Oh, we'd love neighbors!" Eugenia claps her hands and bounces up and down enthusiastically.

Dorian readily agrees, and the four of them leave to see about getting a hobbit hole somewhere in New Zealand.

"Alrighty then," Valerie looks around at the rest of us, turning her back on the departing party. "It'll take me a while to get used to the Henry-Eugenia thing," she says with a shake of her head. Russell too looks like he suffers from indigestion every time they are around, but he tries to get over it quickly. His father and his grandson's ex-girlfriend are now a couple, and he has to deal with it.

"We have found a castle in Ireland," Estelle says, as she cuddles up to the guy from the 1800's. "As soon as we get married, I want all of you to come over for a visit."

"Nancy and I will go back home, for those that want to find us," Russell says.

"I know it's not a mansion, but it's where we feel most comfortable," Nancy amends sweetly.

"Would you at least remodel the place, Mom? It needs some serious updating," Valerie implores.

"Our second home will be a houseboat, we still haven't decided where—Hawaii maybe," Russell says speculatively, while rubbing his chin as if deep in thought.

One by one, everyone shares their plans for their future residence. Dane announces that he and Valerie will also be moving back to their old house, if it's still there. If not, they'll rebuild. Katie and Jase say that they'll be going back to the Brazilian jungle to live in a tree house. That sounds like fun actually, now that snakes are no longer poisonous and mosquitoes no longer suck blood nor pester.

Celeste and Max state that they'll be going back home to Cielo Celeste, and my parents and aunts would live in islands nearby. "There are plenty of islands along that stretch of the river," Celeste says with a wink. I hesitate and shrug. That sounds like fun, too, but...for some reason it doesn't quite fit. "Well, you can always visit," she adds with a pouty look.

"Actually, I have a place in mind for Tess and me, but it's a surprise," Alex says mysteriously. We all wait for him to say more, but he shakes his head solemnly. "Not yet. It's a vow renewal gift. No clues until then."

Besides everyone's new place of residence, we take turns discussing what we'll do for the eternities. Some are going back to school so to speak. Henry and Eugenia have signed up to take classes from the masters at the Eternal's Academy. Some others have taken jobs as trainers for unborn spirits from other worlds that have yet to be created. Others have volunteered in their field of expertise to help our new society move forward. Alex and I have accepted a job as trainers for the Ixthys planet that Drymus had told me about. The aquatic creatures have captured my imagination, so after our honeymoon, we will take our posts. I will be a Gift of Discernment trainer and Alex a Gift of Wisdom trainer.

Everyone's wedding or vow renewal happens before ours. Alex purposely makes me wait until everyone else ties the knot. I don't mind; I'm busy designing wedding dresses anyway. My skills are in high demand now that we can actually wear clothes again instead of Heavenly robes. Silks, cottons, and other natural fibers have already been woven, dyed, and are being distributed in villages across the world.

The development of our new society moves along quite rapidly. Buildings, homes, stores, businesses, factories, crops, everything develops faster than ever before. In no time, I'm able to find fabrics, threads, buttons, and all kinds of sewing items needed for dressmaking. My hands move as quickly as my mind, Robyn's too, and together we crank out more fashion than ever. We're not the only ones of course. All of us designers, tailors, and seamstresses frequent the same haunts to get our materials. It's like a fashion farmer's market and Robyn and I have been able to meet some of our fashion heroes. Every time we get back from shopping we are as giggly as two schoolgirls.

While I've been sewing, Alex has been reading and attending philosophy and writing seminars with the best. He's getting writing tips from the likes of Milton and Dante, and discusses different philosophical issues with Socrates and Gandhi. I've never seen him this happy before, and every time our eyes meet, my heart leaps with joy at the fact that we are so insanely happy. It's such a foreign feeling to enjoy this level of peace that sometimes I fear I'm dreaming. But I'm not. It's real! Our immortal lives are very real.

In our spare time, we are learning to fly. Now that we have bodies again, the laws of physics bind us once more, but our brain capacity is limitless and we can learn as quickly as we want. Flying by thought alone is much like the Link—mind over matter—so a few of us are taking lessons from one of the High Councilors who has been resurrected longer than the rest of us. It's a good thing we heal quickly, because in the process of learning, we've broken several bones and dislocated many joints. A cut that Alex got by knocking his head on a tree revealed silver, not red blood. It was weird, but I guess that's what fuels our bodies now that we're immortal.

The minute Alex and I say: *"I do, for all eternity,"* we fly off together, partially blinded by the rice grains that our family and friends are throwing at us. No one has been able to get Alex to confess where he's taking me, or where we're going to live. I don't care. Not in the least. I'll live anywhere with him, as long as we're together.

We are not great at flying yet; we are more like frogs, taking huge leaps. Not beautiful to behold, but we've got time to get better. At our last long hop, he blindfolds me, and orders me not to peek. I assure him that I wouldn't dream of it. I would not spoil his surprise, because I have one of my own.

"Are you peeking?" Alex asks, after we take another huge leap. We're holding hands, and I have no idea in what direction we're going. I feel like I did while I was directionally challenged.

"No, I told you, I can't see a thing."

"Good," he says and pulls me up again into another huge leap. Then he makes me straddle what seems to be a motorcycle. "Sit and hold on to me," he orders.

"You're sure bossy nowadays," I grumble.

"We'll be there soon," he promises, then rubs the engine and we're off like a bullet. We snake our way through a series of turns and finally arrive somewhere.

"Okay! We're here." He helps me off the motorcycle, and as he pulls the blindfold off my face, my eyes quickly come into focus on a large mast and sail. "Tess, meet *Endless*. Our new home!"

"Endless..." I whisper, as I take in every angle of the beautiful sailboat. It's a huge fifty-foot sailboat with a cabin that looks more like a trendy apartment than a boat. It has three bedrooms and sleeps eight people. Our living room rests on a see through floor, so we can see the fishes below us as the boat moves.

"Wow!" I say with awe. It has everything we could ever need or want in it, the extra room inside the cabin being the most important part. "Plenty of room! It's perfect!" I exclaim.

"I know! We can have our families come visit us here any time."

"Or our own..." I suggest, gently patting my middle.

Alex's eyes grow in size and shock registers in his aura as he connects the dots. "Are—are—are you...?"

"Yes," I confirm triumphantly.

"But—but—" he looks around the boat and bites his lip. "You're going to get sick here, and this is not exactly the best place...not to mention...what if you miscarry—again?"

"I'm immortal, Alex. My body is perfect, the pregnancy will be perfect and so will this baby."

Relief washes through him like an ocean wave, removing all his worries and apprehensions with one swift swish. Then I get to watch as his mind starts to register the implications of what I'm saying, and his face lights up with excitement.

"Well, we can postpone this. Do you need a doctor? Do we need ultrasounds?"

"Nope. Nothing. When it's time, I'll push, you catch!"

"Just like that? How do I do it?"

"You'll learn."

"Yes, yes I will," he assures me, and starts pacing. "So what? Do we need to stock up on baby things?"

"I don't know." I shrug. I hadn't thought that far.

For the second time in our existence we sail off again, not into the sunset, but into a beautiful sunrise, the first of an endless supply of sunrises. We've lived, yet our lives seem to be just beginning, and our love story has no end.

In Memory of Byron.

Book Club Discussion Questions:

In your opinion, what does Heaven look like?

What is the fire and brimstone that the Bible speaks of?

The Bible talks about Cherubim and Seraphim. Who or what are they? What function do they serve?

When people die and their spirits move on, do they still suffer from the same mental and emotional ailments that they had in mortality?

What do spirits do all day?

Can spirits find love after death? How do they court?

www.ingramcontent.com/pod-product-compliance
Lightning Source LLC
Chambersburg PA
CBHW021030130626
46552CB00005B/1761